T0107562

THE *Abaya* CHRONICLES

TINA LESHER

iUniverse, Inc.
New York   Bloomington

The Abaya Chronicles

Copyright © 2010 by Tina Lesher

All rights reserved. No part of this book may be used or reproduced by any means, graphic, electronic, or mechanical, including photocopying, recording, taping or by any information storage retrieval system without the written permission of the publisher except in the case of brief quotations embodied in critical articles and reviews.

This is a work of fiction. All of the characters, names, incidents, organizations, and dialogue in this novel are either the products of the author's imagination or are used fictitiously.

iUniverse books may be ordered through booksellers or by contacting:

iUniverse
1663 Liberty Drive
Bloomington, IN 47403
www.iuniverse.com
1-800-Authors (1-800-288-4677)

Because of the dynamic nature of the Internet, any Web addresses or links contained in this book may have changed since publication and may no longer be valid. The views expressed in this work are solely those of the author and do not necessarily reflect the views of the publisher, and the publisher hereby disclaims any responsibility for them.

ISBN: 978-1-4502-6397-9 (sc)
ISBN: 978-1-4502-6398-6 (dj)
ISBN: 978-1-4502-6399-3 (ebook)

Printed in the United States of America

iUniverse rev. date: 11/24/10

To John
For all your support

INTRODUCTION

During a yearlong stint as a Fulbright Scholar in the United Arab Emirates, I interviewed many women about the changes in their lives in that oil-rich country.

Life has changed dramatically for women my age. They were born into poverty, and many lived in harsh desert climates in dwellings made of mud or palm wood, without electricity or plumbing. Most were married off as young teenagers and many women died in childbirth; others suffered the loss of infants and young children. Medical assistance was primitive at best.

After oil was discovered and first shipped out of the Abu Dhabi Emirate in the early 1960s, things changed in that part of the world. The emirate became part of the United Arab Emirates, a country formed in 1971 under the leadership of the beloved Sheik Zayed bin Sultan Al Nahayan.

Today, many Emirati women live with their families in government-provided or privately-purchased villas. Female high school graduates are flocking to universities—the numbers are the highest in the world. Women drive, own their own businesses and travel extensively. Arranged marriages still exist to some degree, and most women are expected to wed Emirati men. Since many national men are opting to choose foreign brides, the ranks of unmarried, educated women are rising every year in the UAE.

The number of residents of the country increases annually, to the point that UAE citizens are now a minority in their own nation, making up less than 20 percent of the overall population.

I twice taught in the UAE—first as a visiting scholar in 2001 and then again during my Fulbright year in 2006-07. Both times I served on the faculty at Zayed University in Abu Dhabi, and had the privilege of dealing with bright, young women from all levels of Emirati society, including members of the ruling family. Through them, and through the many women I interviewed,

I had a glimpse into the way females now live in the UAE, a country that borders the Arabian Gulf, or what most Americans call The Persian Gulf.

My initial goal centered on writing a non-fiction work about UAE women. Yet I was not intent on simply presenting statistics and overall descriptions of their lives; I wanted to personalize my work based on the interesting women I had met. I began to realize, though, that getting permission from those women for a non-fiction work would be nearly impossible because a few had expressed reluctance about being named publicly and because I had returned to America, far from the subjects of my interviews.

When a group of my former Zayed University students came to New York for an educational/cultural visit in 2009, I had a chance to spend some time with them. They inquired as to why I had not penned a book about the women in the UAE and I said that I felt it would be impossible to get the interviewees' permission for a non-fiction work. The girls suggested I write a novel with characters that represent women in their country.

So I proposed to my university that I be given a sabbatical to write my first novel, and the result is herein. It is my hope that this book will provide readers with an inside look at modern UAE women living in an oil-rich land dotted with extraordinary buildings and filled with amenities. In effect, I hope that this novel proves interesting and educational. And after talking to many American women who live and work in the UAE but seldom get to interact with national women, I tried to bridge the gap between the Emirates and America.

The characters and names herein are fictional.

Good dialogue and a bit of humor form an important link to readers for me, and I pray that those elements are evidenced in the book.

FYI: The "abaya" (a-by-a) in the title refers to the long black garment, often decorated with colorful trim, that UAE women wear over their regular clothes.

My thanks to my employer, William Paterson University, for granting me a paid sabbatical to pen this novel, and to Dairy Hollow Writers' Colony in Arkansas for allowing me to spend time immersed in the writing of the book.

Tina Rodgers Lesher
Westfield, N.J.

CHAPTER 1

Farah looked out from the second-floor windows of the modern and spacious Abu Dhabi villa. The 60-year-old woman watched as her grandchildren came out through the front door of the residence across the street and walked through the gates, the lone opening in the whitewashed wall surrounding the home. The three young boys got into a black Lincoln SUV with tinted windows, and off they went with one of the family's drivers to a private school less than a mile away.

That was life now for many Emirati women the age of Farah Abdullah al Matari.

Watching and waiting.

And being waited on.

Farah was sick of it.

*   *   *

Walking slowly to the oversized television set in the women's majlis, Farah signaled to one of the Filipino maids to turn on the 42-inch television set and play a taped version of Freej, a popular cartoon show about four old Dubai women who gossip about others in their neighborhood. The comedic offering provided such a delight for Farah because it reminded her of the times when she lived in a close-knit freej (neighborhood) in the area near the ruler's palace in the desert island town of Abu Dhabi.

As a child of the 1950s, Farah and her friends would spend hours playing in the sand-filled, would-be streets of Abu Dhabi. They would pass many of the older women, all wearing the traditional burqas, gold masks that partially covered their faces. Um Ahmed and Um Khalid were considered the friendliest and funniest of the bunch, and Farah and her friends loved to sit and listen to them as the pair described the comings and goings of everyone in the neighborhood of mud huts and barasti, dwellings made of palm wood and fronds.

"Um Hamdan wants to marry off that no-good son of hers to my lovely niece Khadija," complained Um Ahmed to a group of women sitting with her one day under a ghaf tree as Farah and a friend, Amna, listened nearby. "My brother and his wife should say 'No,' but they see gold in the air."

Um Khalid—so named because she was a mother (um) and her oldest son was named Khalid—kept nodding her head in agreement.

"That Hamdan boy has spent time in Dubai with some older woman and his mother knows that," said Um Khalid. "But now his family wants him to have a real bride and your niece Khadija is available, and your older brother really does like the smell of a gold dowry for her."

"It has always been that way with my brother," said Um Ahmed. "He'd sell his wife for a piece of gold."

"Which wife?" asked Um Khalid as the women and their friends started laughing, as did the youngsters Farah and Amna.

*　　*　　*

As a child, Farah always wondered how a woman felt if she were just one of the wives of a man. Under Islam, a man can have up to four wives but he is expected to treat them equally. Farah's mother, Reem, was the second of two wives of her father, Abdullah Issa al Matari, who made his living as a trader. He often would be away for months at a time, moving about the emirates by camel or boat. Abdullah would trade items made by Abu Dhabi women for other goods or foodstuffs that he would sell or barter with Bedouins or those he met along the way. When he was in Abu Dhabi, Abdullah spent hours sharing coffee with friends and sitting at the ruler's majlis, a meeting room where one could make requests or issue complaints to the ruler of the emirate. He also devoted hours to negotiating with those working in the souks, the outside markets, to buy hand-crafted wares for his trading work.

Both of Abdullah's wives lived in barasti literally just yards away from each other and he took turns staying at one or the other of these modest dwellings. Farah yearned for her father to give up his senior wife, who had never been too nice to the offspring of the second union. Farah was determined that, when she became of age to wed, she would be a first wife—and the only one forever.

She got her wish to be a first wife when, at age 15, she married Mansour Ali al Bader. She continued to be known as Farah Abdullah al Matari, as women in the Emirates use their maiden names.

As for the vow that she would be the only wife—well, that ended in the 1980s.

Farah often remarked that she could write a book about being the wife of a successful businessman who came home one night after more than 20 years

2

of marriage to announce he had taken a second wife, a 27-year-old Lebanese physician he met while on business in Beirut.

Farah still remembers the day soon thereafter when Mansour brought that bride, Esra, into their home in Abu Dhabi, the town that had become the capital of the United Arab Emirates after seven emirates had banded together to form a country in 1971. After a week of receiving the silent treatment from Farah and her four angry children, wife Number Two insisted that Mansour rent her an apartment overlooking the Gulf. That is where she still resides, with two twenty-something sons who wear Western clothing and spend a lot of time hanging out at malls. Esra works part-time on the staff of a medical center but spends most of her time at an art gallery in which she has an interest—not just in the art, but reportedly in the handsome Saudi owner.

Farah knows she has the makings of a good book, if only she could actually write it. But her early education was limited to learning to read parts of the Quran. In her late 40s, she took English classes at the Women's Institute and became quite proficient in speaking the language, although her writing was still quite limited in both English and her first language, Arabic. Perhaps, she thought, maybe one of her granddaughters could interview her and write a best seller.

Mansour had suffered a fatal heart attack when he was in his early 60s. Under societal norms, a widow, especially the senior one, usually moved into the household of her eldest son and his family. In the past, before the discovery of oil had made Abu Dhabians wealthy, the son then supported his mother or spinster sisters who would have had no source of income. Farah, though, had exhibited a bit of an entrepreneurial spirit in her younger days. When the town began to blossom into modernity after the oil discoveries and Mansour began buying small shops and other businesses, she insisted on becoming a "sleeping" partner in some of them. Until the city took over the taxi companies, she also owned a number of cabs operated by Pakistani drivers and she still derived monthly income from selling out to the new entity. Her investments in real estate, including several fancy high-rise apartment buildings on the Corniche, had put her into the millionaire ranks. The last thing she needed was an inheritance from Mansour, whom she officially had divorced shortly before his unexpected passing.

To satisfy the wishes of her children, though, she and her unmarried daughter, Hessa, agreed to move to a newly-constructed villa across the street from the home of Farah's older son, Khalid, and his wife, Ayesha, in the Mushrif section of the city. That would make her offspring happy and would still keep her out of the household of her daughter-in-law.

*   *   *

CHAPTER 2

Rowena Pagan looked down at the scruffy nails of her 10th client of the day.

"I want you to draw little hearts on the thumbs," stated the patron, an Emirati woman whose reputation for being demanding was well-known by employees and other customers at Your Nails, an Electra Street salon.

Rowena never expected that her art education degree from City College of Manila would yield her a job in an Arab Gulf country, far from her husband and two children. But unable to secure a teaching post or job in her field, she headed to Abu Dhabi where her aunt and several cousins already worked.

Your Nails featured an all-Filipino staff with the exception of the manager, a Lebanese national who represented the owners, two wealthy Beirut women who reportedly had nail salons in other major cities in the region.

Rowena looked up toward the manager, who nodded her head as if to say "Yes, you have to do what this woman wants."

Rowena knew this client only by her first name, Ayesha, and was cognizant that she was a person with "wasta." Everyone knew what that term meant: those with "wasta" were important Emiratis who could have an expatriate deported with a dial of a mobile phone. They had clout. Ayesha always let the nail salon staffers know that as, each time she came for an appointment, she found a need to get on her mobile phone and bark orders, in English, to someone at the other end. Usually it was one of her maids at home. After she finished the call, Ayesha loudly would comment with such words as "I cannot understand why these people cannot figure out how to clean my chandeliers. They are incompetent like most foreigners are."

Like her nail salon colleagues, including two of her cousins, Rowena would not respond in any way to such remarks. The possibility of entering into an argument could spell career doom for her, and feeding her family back in The Philippines was the most important consideration for the 32-year-old Rowena.

Ayesha would find it hard to say that Rowena was incompetent. Before heading to Abu Dhabi, Rowena had completed a six-month course to become a certified nail technician. The classes extended beyond the typical nail decorating work and included instruction about dermatology and physiology. Rowena landed the award for the top student; even then, she needed to exit the country to make a decent living.

So, after painting Ayesha's nails with a deep purple polish, Rowena removed some special glitter paint from her assigned drawer, and designed small hearts on the client's thumbs. The creative touch drew "Oohs" and "Ahs" from others in the salon, but it failed to yield even a five-dirham tip from the obnoxious Ayesha. She did have a request of Rowena, though.

"Take my mobile, press 2 and that will get my driver. Tell him I will be outside as soon as these nails dry."

As Rowena followed through with the phone call, she was quietly seething.

*   *   *

They referred to themselves as the "Coffee Klatch" group, a term picked up from their American professors. In fact, it was while studying at Women's University in Abu Dhabi that the four young women spent many of their lunch hours together, often at a mall just a few blocks from campus.

Many times they would laugh about the fact that they could sign out at Gate 2 and spend time away from the small campus.

When Women's University opened in September 2000 to educate the top national female high school graduates, students had to spend all day, five days a week, on campus. Going on a class field trip meant having a parent or brother sign special forms. Mobile phones were forbidden, and when a student's hidden phone went off one morning at an assembly with an important sheik in attendance, the girl was expelled from WU—and all other national universities in the country.

The girls often had listened to their older sisters and cousins lament the restrictions imposed on students in the early years of WU. But things changed every year at the school, where the instruction was in English. New professors and administrators kept coming and going from Australia or the U.S. or England, while students became more vocal about the need to lift restrictions.

By the time the Coffee Klatch girls began their collegiate studies, Women's University was starting its seventh year. No longer did enrollees have to spend all day at the university but only those hours when they had classes—in concert with the American system that the university was emulating. And while mobile phones were still technically forbidden, no one paid any attention to that rule since every student had one, or two, with her. The girls just made sure they turned them off during class periods.

Now, as they were a few months from the end of their studies, the quartet sat at a downtown café and "shot the bull" with their favorite professor, Dr. Teresa Wilson, an American who taught them that phrase and others.

"I wonder if our graduation ceremony will be in this century," remarked Iman al Bader as the others shrugged. "It is insane how we never know when it will happen."

Graduation at WU was the one thing that failed to mirror the U.S. system, where commencement ceremonies are held at the end of senior year. The Women's University graduation usually came months later at the convenience of Sheikha Hend, a member of the ruling family and the beloved main patron of the university. She reportedly funded many of the school's activities, including graduation.

Iman was the only one of the Coffee Klatch friends to have attended a graduation ceremony, and that was just a few weeks previously when her sister, Miriam, finally got her degree after finishing the year before.

"You were there, too, Dr. Teresa," said Iman. "Was it not crazy or what? Even my grandmother, Farah al Matari, thought it was bizarre and she was not happy that the sheikhas came in so late. She always has a fit about that."

The professor smiled broadly as she thought about that evening. Her niece, Abby Wilson, a 32-year-old Manhattan real estate lawyer, had been in Dubai on business and had traveled to Abu Dhabi for a few days before heading back to the States. Teresa wangled two tickets for them to sit in the VIP section at the Abu Dhabi Downtown Theatre for the ceremonies.

Abby was so stunned by the unusual event that she offered to write about it for the monthly email newsletter that her aunt sent to family and friends:

Aunt Teresa has agreed to let me hijack this "edition" of her newsletter so I can describe one of the more interesting evenings we spent together while I visited her in Abu Dhabi. We attended Women's University graduation at a beautiful theatre and sat in the VIP section.

The program (in English, thank God) said the graduation started at 8 p.m. and the theatre was packed at that time. All women. Not a man anywhere. Even the security guards were women. Aunt Teresa said she has been to several Emirati weddings with only women in attendance; the men celebrate together on another night.

Well, forget 8 o'clock. "Time means nothing in the Emirates." That is actually written in one of the pamphlets given out to expatriates when they arrive here.

My colleagues here show up at the law offices on time but our UAE clients often arrive late. Drives us crazy.

But this was a graduation! It did not start at 8—or even 9! About 9:20, from a side entrance in the front of the theatre, came a whole crew of women dressed in abayas, long black robes that cover their regular clothes, and shaylas, the veils that cover their hair. The faces of the young women were uncovered and you could see the tops of their hair. Not the older women, though. They had on these gold masks—Aunt Teresa called them burquas but they are not like those horrific face coverings in Afghanistan. These are odd masks that cover the wearer's nose and go over the mouth like a mustache.

Now every woman in the place—more than 1,000 were there—stood up as these important women sashayed in. Why? Because these ladies were all sheikhas, members of the ruling families of Abu Dhabi and Dubai. The older ones were escorted by female Army officers to fancy, high-backed seats lined up in front of the first row all across the theatre. Some of the younger sheikhas walked to seats in the VIP section where we were—the first 10 rows or so on one side of the theatre.

The ceremony started with a welcome address up on the screen by the university's president—a sheik who cannot attend the festivities because he is a male. (I thought the president would be a female since it is a women's university). Anyway, this talk was in Arabic with English subtitles. Then some student got up and read a speech in Arabic on behalf of Sheikha Hend. Apparently nothing starts until she shows up. She even determines when graduation is—and this one was 10 months after the girls finished college. Apparently she had been traveling overseas for awhile. But she does not speak—others do it for her. And we have no idea what was said. After almost two years here, all Aunt Teresa knows in Arabic are taxi directions.

As this speech was being read, and I am not exaggerating, a crew of maids came in. I guess they are from the palaces. They were carrying silver plates of food and some fancy coffee pots. They walked across the floor in front of the first row and served the important sheikhas. It was like a party right smack during the ceremony. And not only did they serve the royals, but they came up the aisles to our section and—seriously—handed silver trays with food to the person at the end of a row. We passed them along after we took pastry or whatever.

At this point, I started to chuckle quietly. When I finished college, some aged politician spoke and they gave an honorary degree to some man who invented a new type of bottle cap. Boring! (But it started on time and was over in an hour-and-a-half).

The speech was finished and then—boom. The lights went out. You could hear the women mumbling. Aunt Teresa always said the electricity grid is not great in a city that puts up buildings in three months' time. But alas—within 30 seconds—there was LIGHT. I emphasize that word because we had a Light

Show! It must have cost a bundle. It was spectacular. The theatre was filled with beams of light and all kinds of pizzazz. When it ended after about 10 minutes, everyone stood and cheered. Like a rock concert. I loved it.

Then they had some sort of a drama. Young Emirati girls on stage—different ages. Finally one dressed as a college student with her books. I guess they were depicting the life of a national girl as she goes from kindergarten to college graduation. But I have no idea since it was in Arabic. Remember, the university instruction is in English but graduation is not—apparently so the older women, many of whom who do not speak English too well, can understand it.

Now it was time to pass out the degrees. All of a sudden, a big hole emerged in the center of the stage; sometimes you see an orchestra come up that way at a concert or Broadway show. But no—this brought up a long table decorated with hundreds of flowers. Some of the sheikhas were escorted to that table from which they could present students with their sheepskins. Even Aunt Teresa was not sure which one was Sheikha Hend—she and most of the women in her family are never photographed so people do not know what they look like. And the older women look alike with those masks on.

Some graduates got more than degrees. Those who garnered Dean's List honors, for example, also got a box. Inside, according to our sources—meaning the women sitting near us—was a check for 20,000 dirhams, more than $5,000. (Aunt Teresa has a friend who teaches at a private girls' high school funded by the ruling family. At graduation, the girls got diamond watches as well as money. When I graduated from high school, I got a clock to take with me to college.)

The graduates wore caps and gowns that were open at the front. Thus, you could see their floor-length beautiful dresses underneath. They all had long, flowing, professionally coiffed hair. No short hair cuts to be seen. Maybe that is against the societal norm—who knows? But what caught the eyes of every attendee were the diamonds. Diamond necklaces. Diamond foot-long earrings. Diamond bracelets and rings. The front windows at Harry Winston look shabby compared to the gems worn by these graduates.

I kept uttering "this is a bit weird" as my aunt sheepishly nodded in agreement. Heck, she was not going to vocalize her opinion of the evening at that point because she wants to keep her teaching job, and every negative remark heard by others could get her a step closer to a one-way ticket home to New Jersey. There is no due process here, my fellow lawyers tell me. Anyway, I think Aunt Teresa was loving the graduation cerermony.

You could tell when a young sheikha was walking across the stage to get a degree; I think three of them finished this year. As a sheikha's name was called, ALL of the sheihkas in the audience stood up and walked down to the front to personally kiss the graduate (one kiss on the right cheek and then on the left, or vice versa). One of the sheikhas—Aunt Teresa taught her and said she is a terrific young woman —even walked behind the table on stage and hugged every woman sitting there, including the foreign administrators.

By the time this whole graduation was over close to midnight, I was exhausted from witnessing the spectacle. But there was more to come. We walked out of the theatre into the lobby. The place was filled with tables laden with filet mignon appetizers, and the usual hummus and other Middle Eastern fare. And the flowers on the tables were simply spectacular. We got to speak to lots of people, and even I got kissed by many of the graduates introduced to me by my aunt. They are lovely young women and they all love Aunt Teresa.

As things wound down and women started to leave, many of the older ones, probably relatives of the graduates, reached up and grabbed flowers from the giant arrangements. They were all walking out with flowers. I don't know if this is a cultural thing, or they just felt the flowers would be wasted if left in the vases. So off the women smilingly went with their long-stemmed red roses.

And off we went—to Aunt Teresa's apartment and a good bottle of red wine in long-stemmed glasses! It was a great evening.

*   *   *

Farah picked up her mobile phone and called her best friend, Amna. They had not spoken for two days, and that was a record for the pair, who were best friends from the time they were youngsters living in the neighborhood on the Gulf. As children they were inseparable except for the summer months when Amna and her family would go to Al Ain, an oasis town. Those trips, now made by car in less than two hours, often took 20 days or more through the desert by camel, and many travelers did not survive. That included Amna's mother, who died unexpectedly on one of the journeys when she was only 29.

It was because of these rough journeys that Farah's father, Abdullah, refused to take his two families to Al Ain and they weathered the hot summers in Abu Dhabi.

Amna, the petite widow of wealthy businessman-diplomat Hamid al Shari, lived in a villa next door to her son Nasser's residence just a few blocks from Farah, and the women frequently visited each other. They often traveled together to Dubai with their daughters and granddaughters for one-day spending sprees, especially during the annual shopping festival there.

"Hello, my dear friend," said Farah. "And what are you doing this lovely morning?"

"Waiting for your phone call," responded Amna. "Ready for a walk?"

"Yes. I'll meet you near the Atlas Building in an hour-and-a-half," said Farah. "And I am wearing my new tennis shoes."

She laughed as she put on some warm-up pants and a tee-shirt under her abaya and then stepped into the new white sneakers she had bought the day before at a small shop behind the gold souk.

Until of late, Farah would wear only long dresses made by a top tailor in the old souks. Nothing but dresses under her abaya. That was expected of older national women. But her granddaughters kept telling her that that she needed to exercise. And she knew they were not kidding as her weight was starting to balloon toward the 80-kg mark. After all, what kind of exercise does one get when she need not ever make a bed, clean the floor, cook dinner, plant flowers—or do anything that requires physical labor. Like many Emirati families, hers had the services of cooks, maids, nannies, drivers, and landscapers. Oil money had been good to the people of the United Arab Emirates.

Farah had started to cut back on the heavy foods that had become a staple of her diet, especially the pasta that had become popular fare in the Middle East. She was trying, often in vain, to give up her beloved desserts, including cake and ice cream.

Yet the art of exercise had eluded her.

Iman and Miriam Al Bader, daughters of Farah's other son, Tahnoun, had to plot to get their grandmother into an exercise mode. One day, about three months before when they were visiting from their home a mile away, they told Farah she should stop being a "couch potato." They giggled as they remembered their professor, Dr. Teresa, who told them many such American phrases.

"You are calling your grandmother a potato?" asked Farah.

"We mean you have to get off the couch and into the gym," said Mariam, who had been working in a marketing post since she graduated from Women's University. "Like I do every day. I work and then I work out!"

"You're 23, dear. I'm 60."

And then Farah threw in her usual mantra: "And I had all my kids by your age."

The girls' eyes rolled. When were their elders going to realize that young women now go to universities and work? Marriage will come later or perhaps never.

But, perhaps out of boredom, Farah agreed to go later to the Ladies Club with the girls, who realized their grandmother lacked any type of appropriate clothing for a workout.

So off went Mariam and Iman. They did not need a driver to take them to their destination because, like most young Emirati women, they drove their own cars these days. They headed to a sports store and bought a warm-up suit, shirt and sneakers for their grandmother and cheered as she later put them on. Then they all headed to the Ladies Club and onto the treadmill. Seeing one was nothing new for Farah—her son Khalid had a complete gym in his home across the street—but walking on one was a different story. Yet away she walked at about a three-miles-per-hour speed as her granddaughters, on either side of her, were literally running on their machines.

Not only did she enjoy the brief workout but she had a healthier feeling as a result. On the way home, in the back seat of Miriam's BMW, Farah texted Amna to tell her about her exercising experience. Farah was getting the hang of texting—another thing taught to her by Iman, who called her grandmother "really cool."

Amna could not stop laughing at the idea of her friend dressing in gym togs and undertaking the slightest bit of physical exercise. But when she related the gym experience tale to her own granddaughter, Mona al Shari, who happened to be Iman's close friend, Amna knew what was coming. Mona headed out to buy workout clothes for HER grandmother.

"If Auntie Farah can do it, you can do it," said Mona, using the familiar "auntie" that girls often called friends of their mothers or grandmothers.

So, several times a week, Amna and Farah began taking breaks from their lap-of-luxury existences at home and heading to the Ladies Club. Sometimes they worked on the elliptical machines or rode stationary bikes. They even signed up for a 55-and-older class that was filled primarily by expatriate women.

Farah's son, Khalid, was not amused when he found out his mother was hanging out at a gym.

"You want a personal trainer? Fine. We have one at my home, right across the street from your villa. I hired her to work out in the morning with Ayesha. We have a gym, for crying out loud."

Farah looked straight in her son's eyes but spoke gently: "Khalid, you actually think your wife gets up before noon to do anything?"

*   *   *

Teresa Wilson had earned a reputation as a topnotch public speaking instructor. Her doctorate was in communication and she had completed research on interpersonal skills in the banking industry, in which she had worked for nearly 20 years. But along with teaching some communication research classes at Women's University, she took on the public speaking course—and made it so popular that she had two sections every semester—with waiting lists.

It was not easy to instruct the young Emirati women on the art of getting up and speaking before an audience. Many had trouble with English, especially those who finished government high schools where the instruction had been in Arabic. Others had strong English skills as a result of previous education at schools based on a British or U.S. or Canadian curriculum. The main problem, though, was overcoming the shyness exhibited by many of the girls. For the most part they were quiet and polite, traits that had been taught to them by their nannies, tutors, and mothers.

Teresa often related the tale of the first month she taught at WU three semesters previously. She had taken her UAE driver's test that morning, and announced to the class that she had passed and could now drive her new car. The students all stood and clapped and high-fived each other.

She was surprised and told them so.

"They told us at orientation that you were all SHY," she said.

"Shy?" asked one of the students.

"Yes," said Teresa.

Then that student left class. Teresa had no idea why but said nothing and started her day's lecture.

About five minutes later, the student returned with a cup of tea for the professor.

Teresa was puzzled. She looked at the girl as if to say "Why?"

The student said: "You wanted CHAI, right?"

Experiences like that made Teresa smile, and also provided material for her monthly email newsletter.

*   *   *

CHAPTER 3

Sheikha Asma was a few months away from finishing Women's University. That would mean the end of a routine she had undertaken since grade school: wake up early, pray, get dressed, eat breakfast, exit the palace, get in the Mercedes limousine, and head to school.

Not alone. A maid or nanny would go along in the car with the slender, black-haired Asma. And when school was over, one of those household staffers would be waiting right outside to accompany Asma to the chauffeured automobile.

It mirrored the daily activities for other female relatives of The Ruler, as well as for the girls from other wealthy Abu Dhabi families. These were the elite—the young women who had never stepped foot in a government public school. Most of them stuck together—the "rich cliques," as other university students or professors quietly called them.

Life for Asma included spending much of the summer at a luxury apartment in Knightsbridge, the London area that was a second home for many wealthy Gulf families. It is well-known in Abu Dhabi circles that, if you go to Harrod's on any day in the summer, you will run into someone you know. The family also owned residences in Cairo and Switzerland, so Asma and her siblings often found themselves on private jets heading to those spots with their parents.

Asma knew no other life than that of a sheikha, but sometimes she wished she were just one of the ordinary students at the university. She always seemed conscious that she should stand erect and walk tall—she had learned the art of good posture as well as good manners from her parents and governesses.

Sheikha Asma hated the fact that she could not join her classmates on field trips to Dubai or to local radio stations. Family rules did not allow her to be part of those activities. She often felt out of place at the university because many of her classmates shied away from her, believing that sheikhas did not want to bother with them. So she spent her breaks at the university café or canteen with her cousins or with her two best friends from high school, Iman al Bader and Mona al Shari.

Sometimes being a sheikha, though, had its advantages. When a renowned actor or politician from abroad came to speak at the university, the sheikhas were ushered to a private room to have a photo taken with the guest. The hired photographer knew that the picture was not to be released to anyone but the royal family, as the shiekhas were not to be photographed for public viewing.

And when it came to grading, even Asma realized that sometimes the professors gave a boost to the sheikhas. After all, who would want a parent of a sheikha-student calling to complain about a grade? The prospect of a permanent flight back to New York or London did not sit well with these expat profs.

Asma was a good student, however. She had earned top honors in high school at the girls' section of Al Koba Academy and had been chosen to be the student speaker at graduation. Her command of English was on par with Americans, and she rarely spoke Arabic.

One day she was sitting with her female relatives at the palace.

"What are you going to do next year?" asked her aunt, Sheikha Mowza, as the two of them sat together on a couch.

"I have no idea," said Asma. "I can't stomach the idea of sitting around and doing nothing like some of our cousins. What do you think I should do?"

"Get out of here. Go to grad school overseas," said Mowza as Asma smiled in response.

Sheikha Mowza was the lone female member of the clan with a true free spirit. She was 29 and the youngest of 10 children, of whom Asma's mother, Sheikha Lubna, was the eldest. Asma and her cousins loved Mowza because she refused to adhere to every restriction that her family tried to put on her. From the time she was a young girl, Mowza knew that her family intended to marry her off to a second cousin with whom she attended school until the sexes were separated in the fourth grade. She remembers that he had a hard time learning to read and would pull the girls' hair when the teacher was facing the blackboard. Mowza refused to marry him after she finished high school and then again when she earned a degree in business management from a university in Al Ain. His mother was outraged; her mother was embarrassed. Mowza did not care; she wanted to keep going to school. So when the family was in England right after Mowza's college graduation, she took the liberty of having a driver transport her to London School of Economics to speak to the admission officials. She was quickly accepted (the dean recognized her last name, she said) and spent a few years there before earning her master's degree. Under pressure from the family, she then returned home and, with one of her brothers, Sheik Ahmed, set up a real estate investment firm on Hamdan Street. As often as she could, though, Sheikha Mowza traveled to London.

"Well, Mowza, you got to go to London for grad school—that was great," commented Asma. "Of course, all our relatives are all still upset that you are single."

"Maybe not for long, Asma," snickered Mowza. "And it is not going to be a cousin in the UAE."

Asma looked at her aunt.

"Oh my goodness. Some guy in London, huh?"

Sheikha Mowza just winked as she left the room. She was heading to the airport.

*   *   *

Farah arrived 30 minutes early at the Atlas Building where she was to meet up with her friend, Amna. Instead of waiting in the chauffeured car, Farah got out and hurried into a nearby tower that housed a number of law firms, as well as a score of government-run companies, including the PR/marketing group for which her granddaughter, Mariam, was a budding account executive. Farah had called ahead from the car and Mariam was waiting in the lobby for her. They kissed—both cheeks—and sat down at a table in the building's café where Mariam was taking a break.

"I am always happy to see my granddaughter," said Farah, who then complimented Mariam on the gold threading that decorated both her abaya and shayla.

"It was just a few years ago when all the abayas and shaylas were black—completely black," said Farah. "I love the decorative look."

"Well, I am happy to see you all ready for a Corniche trek," said Mariam to her grandmother. "You and Auntie Amna are getting famous."

"For what?" asked Farah.

"For being the top seniors in exercise among all locals in Abu Dhabi, maybe in the entire country. All our friends and relatives cannot believe it. I think some are jealous."

Farah contemplated that statement for a minute. It probably was true. Many women her age seldom ventured outside their well-appointed UAE residences, and she was enjoying every minute of her newfound love of keeping in shape and meeting new people along the way.

"Well, I do not go to an office every day like you do," said Farah to her granddaughter. "I have people to run my businesses. And how is your job, anyway?"

Mariam said she loved her work because she represented the new generation of young women who had finished college and had entered the workforce. Two generations ago, women lacked an education and married in their early teens as Farah had done. A generation ago, many women would marry right after they completed high school. Now, with more than 90 percent of UAE women opting to get a free, government-sponsored college education, women want to work and marry later.

As they chatted, a handsome Emirati man walked by and waved to Mariam.

"He is my coworker," said Mariam as she waved back. "Went to school in New York."

Farah pondered the scene. She never thought she'd see the day when an Emirati woman would be able to sit in a public place without a veil over her face and even look at men who were not relatives.

"Is he married?"

Mariam responded: "No. And don't start getting any ideas."

Just then, Farah noticed a black Mercedes pull up outside.

"Well, there is Amna. I have to go, Mariam. If you get a chance, remind the maintenance staff here to clean the chandelier in the lobby. It looks dusty."

"Oh, sure," laughed Mariam. "I am going to talk to the cleaning staff as if I have some say over their work?"

"Just tell them nicely that your grandmother, Farah Abdullah al Matari, was here and thought it should sparkle. They know my name because I collect all the rent."

"Is this one of YOUR buildings, Grandma?"

"Yes. And someday it might be yours."

With their abayas and shaylas blowing around in the soft wind, the hefty Farah and petite Amna walked quickly on the Corniche, the lovely promenade that extended practically the length of the Arabian Gulf coastline on one side of Abu Dhabi. American expats often described it as a marble and cement boardwalk minus the sleazy taffy stores and game kiosks.

The goal for Farah and Amna was to walk all the way to the end of the Corniche where their drivers would pick them up in the parking lot. About a half-mile into their trek, they saw four women, dressed in Capri pants and baseball caps, walking quickly in the opposite direction. They recognized one woman from their senior exercise class.

"Hello, Helen," Farah yelled as the quartet stopped for introductions.

Helen Walker was a regular at the Ladies Club gym; she had joined Farah and Amna for coffee a few times after they finished their exercise class.

Transplanted several months before from New York to Abu Dhabi when her spouse agreed to open a Middle East office for his Manhattan-based law firm, Helen was an attractive, athletic blonde in her late 50s. Farah and Amna loved hearing her talk about traveling to Bermuda to play golf with her friends and hosting her annual Christmas party at her Long Island residence. In return, Helen got to hear how the lives of Farah and Amna had changed so radically over the years because of the discovery of oil in Abu Dhabi. She learned about the neighborhood where the two Emirati women grew up and how Farah and Amna wore burquas up until about five years ago.

"We decided to show our faces to the world," smiled Farah one day as they were sitting in the gym's café.

"If my skin keeps getting wrinkled, I think I will go back to it," chimed in Amna.

Now, as they greeted Helen on the Corniche, she told them that she and her fellow walkers were part of a larger expat group.

"We call it the AA," said Helen as her three American friends laughed.

Farah and Amna had no idea that the letters were a play on words for Alcoholics Anonymous. That organization was not a part of life in a country of Muslims who do not drink alcohol.

The AA, Helen explained, stood informally for Americans in Abu Dhabi, a group of about 70 or so women who gathered for social events, book clubs, bridge games, etc.

"My daughter-in-law Judith should join," said Farah. "She is American. She and my son Tahnoun own a home in New Jersey. Near the beach."

"You mean the Jersey shore?" asked one of Helen's friends. "What town?"

"I forget," answered Farah. "I was there once and we had to go on a parkway to get there from the airport."

Amna then noted that "my two children were born in Washington, believe it or not. When my husband worked at the UAE Embassy. I love Washington. That is where I learned English. What a small world."

Helen and the others bid farewell to Farah and Amna who continued their walk as they conversed with each other.

"I so enjoy Helen," said Amna. "You know, we should get to know more Americans. Our sons went to college there and I once lived there. You have a daughter-in-law from the U.S. Maybe we should invite the AA group to our homes."

"Good idea," said Farah. "Years ago our families often hosted people from other countries. Remember the British lady who was so kind to us when we were little? I think her husband was here because we were a British protectorate then. She often sat with our mothers and aunts. But that was because everyone was together. The locals and the Westerners. We did not have massive homes with big walls around them. Those walls are barriers to friendships, you know that?"

They continued walking and chatting about the latest version of "Freej" and how that TV animated cartoon show made them chuckle and think about the early days of their lives in the very area where they were walking. Finally, Amna and Farah reached the parking lot where their drivers were standing and talking to each other. The two men were from the same town in northwest Pakistan and happy to have jobs to help support their families back home. Upon seeing the women, the drivers clapped in unison. They were applauding the new exercise regimen of their employers.

Tomorrow the women would be together again—at the Ladies Club gym.

*   *   *

Six days a week, Rowena Pagan and her fellow staffers at Your Nails worked from 10 a.m. to 10 p.m. The lone exception was on Friday, the start of the two-day weekend in the UAE and the religious day for Muslims, when the shop opened only from 5 to 10 p.m.

Instead of spending Fridays resting from a busy week, Rowena took a taxi to the only Catholic Church in the city. There she met her aunt and cousins, and often they would later go to the Filipino Social Club for lunch. Back in Manila, they would attend Mass on Sundays in the tradition of Catholicism. But since Sunday was the beginning of the work week in the UAE, thousands of expat Catholics would head to Mass on Fridays since it usually was a day off for them.

It was nice to see the young Filipino men dressed in shirts and dress slacks for the service, and the women attired in dresses and suits. Attending the weekly Mass meant so much to these people, most of whom worked in jobs where they were underpaid and overworked. They all had the same goal: to make enough money to send home to their families and eventually to return to the Philippines when the economy improved and good jobs were available.

What Rowena loved most about Fridays was seeing her aunt, Cecelia, a 61-year-old highly-regarded beautician at one of the city's top beachfront hotel salons. She was considered the matriarch of the relatives in Abu Dhabi and always had interesting stories to relate. The attractive, dark-haired Cecelia was a Gulf region veteran, having worked in Kuwait City and in Jeddah, Saudi Arabia, before coming to Abu Dhabi several years previously. She knew life was tough for her younger relatives and always tried to boost their self-esteem.

"How are things going, Rowena?" she asked.

"Six more months before I get home," answered her niece.

That was all Rowena could think about—flying back to Manila to spend a month with her husband and kids.

"I truly cannot stand living this way," continued Rowena. "We are like cattle jammed into a small space."

She was referring to the apartment rented by Yours Nail to house all 17 of its Filipino workers. The place had three bedrooms, with five women in each—four in bunk beds and one on a mattress. The other two women slept on a pullout couch in the living room. They took turns cooking, not that they ever got to share lunch or dinner. They would pack the food in containers and "heat and eat" in a side room at the nail salon.

Cecelia knew a lot about the way her fellow Filipinos lived in Abu Dhabi. She, too, had a shared living arrangement funded by the hotel beauty parlor where she worked. In her case, though, only five women resided in a three-bedroom flat in the Tourist section of the city. Her flatmates, all younger, insisted that they double up in two bedrooms while the largest bedroom, which included a small private bathroom, was exclusively hers. Sometimes Rowena would go over and stay overnight with her aunt.

Cecelia also had a privilege that some of her coworkers and relatives lacked—she had her passport. In most cases, the business entities that brought overseas workers to the UAE to work in the service and retail trades would keep the employees' passports. The reason for that, the workers were told, was to prevent them from exiting the country before the end of their two-year contracts. At that point, the nail technicians or beauticians or retail store clerks would reclaim their passports and get an employer-paid airplane ticket home for a paid month. A high percentage of these workers then would return to the UAE for another two-year pact because they could not find work in their homeland.

Rowena swore repeatedly that she would not return to Abu Dhabi once her contract was up.

"No way. I might be able to survive the living quarters, but if I have to deal with one more woman like that Ayesha person, I think I am going to commit suicide."

Cecelia looked worried as she hugged her niece and said: "Life is not fair, is it?"

*   *   *

Teresa Wilson loved teaching this particular public speaking class at

Women's University because all of the girls were kind and smart. When she celebrated her 57th birthday, for example, the class surprised her with not one, but three cakes, all lavishly decorated.

"Who made these?" she asked after the students sang "Happy Birthday" in English and Arabic to her.

"Two came from the new French bakery on Najda Street," said Iman al Bader. "And Asma brought one."

Sheikha Asma smiled: "My grandmother has a great baker from Syria, and she made it yesterday. I had her make this one with your school colors—purple and white."

Teresa recalled that one day she wore a white blouse with a purple scarf and commented to the students that she realized she was wearing the school colors from her alma mater, St. Martin's High in northern New Jersey. She even did a brief "Go Martin's" cheer from those days. So the WU students frequently would pass her in the hall and yell "Go Martin's" to her.

Sheikha Asma said she had searched for a St. Martin's High website to find a logo for the cake but could not find anything relevant to the school in the New Jersey area.

"Oh, the school bit the dust about 20 years ago," commented Teresa.

The class fell silent. Then Teresa realized she had uttered another colloquialism and her students had no idea what she meant.

"Aye, aye, aye," she said. "OK. Let me explain. Bit the dust means something died. St. Martin's School closed 20 years ago so, in effect, it died. It bit the dust."

Almost in concert, the girls blurted out: "You are full of baloney, Dr. Teresa."

That was another phrase she had taught them and they used it constantly.

As they all sat in a circle on the floor and ate the cake, Dr. Teresa said she wanted some input on something she had been considering.

"We need to have a public speaking competition, I think. With any WU student participating. It will show how good our students are at public speaking and it will be a great preparation for the real world. What do you all think?"

"Do we need a sponsor?" asked Mona al Shari. "Maybe my father's company."

Teresa smiled. She should have seen it coming. When a WU club sponsors a holiday festival or decides to make a video, the students go out and get sponsors. Translation: they get lots of dirhams to finance their work.

"Do you all think we need a sponsor?" asked Teresa.

"Yes," said Asma. "You want a fabulous final competition, don't you? With flowers on the stage and prizes and good food afterwards."

Teresa said that would be fine—but she would need some help getting this all together. They had to work fast; the end of the school term was nearing.

"I can help run it," said Sheikha Asma. "I am not allowed to compete publicly but I can organize the event. Like I did last year for National Day. The Student Council can run it. Did you forget? I am the president of it."

Thus began the start of plans for WU's first public speaking competition.

*   *   *

The prospect of seeing one of the mega-mansion palaces lining a road out past the breakwater may have been of interest to some beautician expats, but Rowena's Aunt Cecelia had been through this exercise before, and she was not enthused about it. Whereas a typical in-salon hair appointment might last an hour with a client, working with a sheikha might extend past two hours or more per person. Although the sheikhas tipped her, still the overall loss of more tips from more customers affected her income.

This time her mandate was to go to a new palace that was home to a young sheikha who had recently secured that title after marrying into the royal family. Cecelia had heard about the wedding from some of her regular clients for whom she had created fancy hairdos for the festivities. More than 1000 women flocked to the wedding—the men attended another party—and, with no males present, these ladies dressed in long designer gowns matched with the finest jeweled necklaces and earrings. When the groom showed up late into the festivities to meet his bride, many of the women put on their shaylas and abayas. Each guest went home with a small gold vase, a gift from the groom's family that footed the bill. The entertainers were flown in from Lebanon and Paris. Guests estimated the cost of the wedding at about $1 million.

Cecelia was greeted at the palace door by a Filipino maid and they exchanged a few words in Tagalog and English. Ushered upstairs to a massive master bedroom and sitting room, Cecelia met the young bride who seemed gracious and unassuming. She had long, flowing black hair and was wearing designer jeans.

"One of my classmates at the Women's University told me about you," said the sheikha. "In fact, she said I should have used you for my wedding. But I had to go along with my husband's family's wishes and use their beauticians. They were paying for the whole thing."

"You are at the university?" said a surprised Cecelia.

"My third year. Do you think I was too young to marry? Maybe. You

21

know, I am from a business family and this was an arranged marriage. Of course, my family was honored that the ruling family wanted me to marry Sheik Jassim. So I agreed on the condition that I could finish school. And my husband is really supportive of this."

"You seem happy," said Cecelia.

"I am. Jassim turned out to be a great guy. I never met him until the wedding! We went to America on our honeymoon—New York, Washington and Vegas. He loves America since he went to college in Washington. We had a great time. We even played golf. I loved it and I want to keep playing."

Cecelia was offered tea or coffee as she chatted with her sheikha-client, whose first name she did not even know and was too embarrassed to ask. On one hand, Cecelia was keyed into getting the palace assignment finished quickly so she could return to the salon. But the warm welcome exhibited by this young woman made her so at ease that they continued talking for awhile before discussing the reason for the visit.

The sheikha wanted her hair cut to shoulder-length, what she called a "new fad" among her age group. For the most part, Emirati women had long hair, often extending down their backs, that they would hold with a clip under their shaylas. With Western television showing models sporting shorter hair, the young Abu Dhabi women were opting for the same, although not to the extreme. Hair to the shoulders seemed like a happy medium.

Cecelia had brought along her traveling case filled with the varied implements she might use for the hair endeavor.

"So your husband will like you in shorter hair?" she asked.

"I think so. I've warned him to expect some changes."

They moved into the expansive bathroom and the client sat in front of the mirror as Cecelia deftly began her hair-shearing artistry. The pair laughed as the tresses fell onto the marble floor. Cecelia then took a curling iron and continued the shaping. In the end, the sheikha was so pleased that she took out her mobile phone and aimed the camera on it toward herself. She snapped a photo and said: "Well, I am going to send it to Jassim right now so we will know soon what he thinks."

Within minutes, the sheikha received a text message that she read aloud to Cecelia. It said: "My wife the trendsetter!"

As Cecelia departed, she was given an envelope marked with the name of the hotel salon. Inside was cash representing the agreed-upon price that the sheikha had arranged with the manager.

"And this is for you, Cecelia," she said as she handed the beautician a 100-dirham note, many times the usual tip. "I hope to see you the next time

I need a haircut. And I think you may be getting some more business from those who want to follow a trendsetter."

Cecelia hugged the young woman, and got into the palace car that would return her to work. She felt that things were looking up for her.

*   *   *

CHAPTER 4

Sheikha Asma was alone in her room and watching "Dr. Phil," one of her favorite American television shows, when her mobile phone rang. It was her younger sister calling from downstairs.

"I cannot believe you cannot just come up here and speak to me," she said to Sheikha Rahma, who was a year younger and a third-year art student at Women's University.

Rahma was down in the kitchen with Ingrid, a German woman who was known as "The Lady." Wealthy Abu Dhabi families often welcomed a "lady" into their homes. Often it was an expat educator at one of the schools in the city or a Western woman whose spouse worked in Abu Dhabi. These women would provide friendship to the stay-at-home Emirati women and sometimes handle administrative tasks or shop for the family. The "Lady" sometimes would bring her own children to the homes or palaces to play with the owners' children who often were not allowed to engage in the typical after-school activities of other youngsters.

"Ingrid is making arrangements for us and our cousins to go to the movies at the mall," said Rahma. "You want to go? How about your friends?"

"When?" asked Asma.

"Tomorrow afternoon. For the Meryl Streep film."

"Fine," said Asma.

An outing to the cinema was not a typical go-and-buy-a-ticket undertaking for most women of the ruling family. They could only see films in the "golden" theatre at the multiplex facility. The ticket price was several times higher than that for other theatres in the complex. Each seat was roomy and included a small table where waiters would bring food ordered by the moviegoers. Luxury was the key at the golden theatre that was open to anyone willing to pay the inflated price.

When the sheikhas went to the cinema, though, they bought up all of the tickets in the fancy theatre so that they and their friends could watch the film privately. They also made sure that waitresses, not waiters, would be working in their theatre. In a room with all women, the sheikhas could toss off their shaylas and abayas and enjoy the film without adhering to the restrictions placed on them because of their status.

Asma told Rahma that she would call her friends, Iman al Bader and Mona al Shari. Even though they were able to go to the regular cinema anytime, they usually joined Asma in one of the theatre forays because they knew it was important for her to spend time with friends. Besides, it was a free afternoon of fun and food.

"Oh," said Rahma. "Do you think Aunt Mowza would like to join us? She might want a break from her work."

Asma jumped up at the mention of her favorite aunt.

"Oh, Rahma, I forgot to tell you about Mowza. She left for London again. There is something VERY interesting she mentioned to me. We have to get the scoop."

A curious Sheikha Rahma put down the mobile and raced upstairs to her sister's room.

*   *   *

Helen Walker strolled into her villa near the British Embassy and let out a big "Hi" to the two young women cleaning her home. They came once a week from an Abu Dhabi maintenance firm. While her friends often hired maids from other families to come once or twice a week and clean their apartments or villas, Helen wanted no part of such an arrangement. It was against the law; the family sponsoring a domestic employee was not allowed to share the employee with other families. So Helen dealt with the maintenance company and was happy to pay above-the-average rates for the work. It still was cheap by American standards.

On this day the workers were cleaning the oven and some of the kitchen cabinets. Helen told them to throw out some of the food, but the pair seemed hesitant.

"Throw away?" one asked.

"I bought those cereal boxes when my relatives were here for the holidays. They never touched them and I have no need for them."

Then Helen realized what she said. These young Afghan women knew the value of food. It was not to be thrown half-heartedly into the trash.

"If you want the food, please take it," she said. "Whatever you need, just take."

Abu Dhabi was filled with taxi drivers, laborers, domestic workers and shop employees from Bangladesh, Afghanistan, Pakistan, the Philippines and other countries where jobs were at a premium. They worked long hours for little pay but their salaries still bettered what they could make at home. Many of the male laborers lived in camps outside the city, while the women were sheltered in cramped quarters in apartments throughout Abu Dhabi. Helen felt a sense of sympathy for their plight. They all had a dream of coming to America, and could not understand why they could not fulfill that objective while others simply crossed the Rio Grande and lived illegally in the United States.

In a sense, the two young women from the maintenance firm were lucky. They did not bear the burden of wearing the restrictive blue burquas that were familiar sights in their homeland, and they were away from the ravages of war. Helen often wondered how life had changed for them.

Upset or perhaps embarrassed about discarding food items, Helen told the pair to stop working.

"We should leave?" asked one.

"No, I want you to stay. Sit down and have lunch with me."

The two women were surprised at the invitation.

Helen began to prepare chicken salad sandwiches as the cleaning women sat and told her about their lives. In halting English, they described the restrictions put on them in a Taliban-run town and how they longed to go to school. Food was hard to come by, they said, and that is why they hated to see the cereal discarded. They said few Afghan women made it out of the country to work in the Gulf but they had fled at some point to Pakistan and an employment agency there got them the Abu Dhabi jobs. But it cost the young women plenty—a large fee to the agency. Part of their salaries were taken out each month to reimburse the agency and they said it would take years to cover the entire costs.

As Helen asked varied questions, she was reminded of the many interviews she conducted as a newspaperwoman and how she ended her career so abruptly almost a decade ago.

Maybe it was time for Helen to think about writing again.

*   *   *

The "Coffee Klatch" group agreed to meet on a Saturday morning at the Janis Café on the Corniche. They were on a "thinking jag," as Dr. Teresa would say. The girls had read in an Emirates newspaper about a group of Dubai college graduates who had borrowed money from their families to open an art gallery. With the end of their college days looming, the Klatch girls thought they might think of a niche business to start.

"I know we can get the money," said Iman al Bader when they were together the previous week. "If my father won't come up with some money, I think my grandmother will help out."

That made Mona al Shari laugh.

"Maybe mine, too, if we can get the two of them out of their exercise routines long enough."

Essa and Alia, the other Klatch girls, also had access to family money and all figured that the problem was not finding the funding but choosing a viable business. This Coffee Klatch session was called for the girls to bring in their ideas.

Essa suggested a new gym. She argued that lots of women were now going out to gyms, and a really great facility would be successful in Abu Dhabi.

"With everything," she said. "The top sports equipment, a spa, a café, and a natatorium."

"What the hell is that?" asked Alia, who, to the embarrassment of her friends, had picked up some raw English words for her vocabulary.

"A swimming pool," said Essa. "Oh, maybe you weren't in class that day, Alia."

Essa explained that one day, in a communications class taught by Dr. Teresa, the students had to read their essays aloud. One girl, from a town outside of Abu Dhabi City, was struggling with the English language even after spending more than a year in introductory courses before taking college-level classes. Her essay centered on a day she spent at an all-ladies club in her town. She noted that she and her friends all went into the natatorium together.

"Dr. Teresa wanted to know what that was," said Essa. "She thought it might be a fancy Arabic word. The girl said it was an English word for swimming pool. Dr. Teresa said she never heard of it. So the girl took out her thesaurus and showed Dr. Teresa that natatorium was a synonym for swimming pool. Dr. Teresa told her she should throw the thesaurus into the natatorium!"

The girls all chuckled as they continued their business-related talk. A gym was a possibility but they recognized that they would be competing with others that were flourishing in the city. Still it was something to consider.

Alia thought an upscale abaya shop might be a good business venture. She admitted, though, that the city probably had too many at this point.

Mona, whose creative mindset always amazed the Klatch friends, suggested a business called TOTE.

"As in a bag you carry? You want to make tote bags? "said Iman.

"No," said Mona. "The business would be called TOTE for Taste Of The Emirates."

Mona had spent her internship at the national tourist agency, where she often accompanied visiting groups on tours of the city. She was always complaining that there were few tourist-type places to visit compared to other cities the size of Abu Dhabi.

"Let's say you are here on a trip from America," said Mona.

"I love America," said Iman, reminding the others that her mother "is from good old Philadelphia" and that her family spends summers in New Jersey.

"Well," continued Mona, "tourists really want to buy some Emirati things, taste our food, learn about our history. Buy gold jewelry. Interview Emirati citizens. Have their photo taken with them and have it framed in minutes. Buy our art—and have it framed. I know you can do some of those things at the Cultural House or a gallery. But I want it all in one place. We could have the visitors filmed as they answer questions about their trip here. That would be a great resource for our history. We could have a great restaurant with national foods. We really don't have a restaurant like that for visitors and expats. We could have an interactive exhibit about the country. TOTE would be more than a historical venue. It would be a bit upscale but fun. We want it to be on the stop list for every tour in the city. See, everyone who came would be getting a Taste of the Emirates."

The girls were all enamored of the idea, but a few things bothered them. What would happen at this TOTE venue when tourist groups were not around? Would locals support it or would the place be empty of all but vendors and businesses there? And what about the city's future plans for Saadiyat Island where the Louvre and the Guggenheim would be built? Tourists might focus all of their attention there.

They all agreed that Mona had come up with a creative idea but they had some hesitation about it for the aforementioned reasons.

Iman had said nothing to this point and her friends wondered what her idea would be.

"Well, you might think I am crazy but I thought we should have a cake business."

"You think we should bake cakes?" asked Essa. "I never baked a thing in my life. We all have cooks at home."

"Well, I like to bake," said Iman. "But we would not do the baking because we could never do what I want."

"And that would be what?" asked Mona.

"Do you girls ever see those cake shows from America? Where these bakeries make the most elaborate cakes? People want to make a cake that looks like a fire truck for a fireman's retirement party or a cake that looks like a ship. They do it. They are bakers who are artists and creators."

"I watch those shows all the time," said Alia. "I am amazed."

Iman pointed out that UAE people love cakes.

"Every occasion in my family we get a big, fancy cake from Josie's on Fourth Street," she said. "They are regular birthday cakes with lots of roses and stuff but nothing spectacular like a yacht or a Ferrari. People here would pay anything for a unique cake. If we could hire a top cake person from America, we could start one of these bakeries. He, or she, could train locals to do this."

"Really? You think a national woman is going to work in a bakery all day to make cakes?" said Mona. "You can count on your fingers the number of UAE women—or men— who do any kind of manual labor."

"No," said Iman. "You are wrong. You can count them on your thumb. But times are changing. Okay, we can hire and train foreigners to do the cake work, but if I were going to own this business, I might learn to do it myself so I could manage the place."

"You know, this is a good idea," said Mona. "I am intrigued. And maybe I would go for training, too. Not that I want to spend my life baking, but owning the place—that would be interesting. I will scrap my TOTE idea and focus on this."

"No," said Iman. "We should keep your clever name. We can call our business TOTE Cakes or something like that. After all, we will be selling a Taste of the Emirates."

*　　*　　*

As they did on every Friday, after men came home from the mosques, Sheikha Asma's family members gathered for an elaborate buffet at one of the palaces. This time they were at the residence of her maternal grandmother, and young cousins were running all over the terrace that overlooked the Gulf.

Asma's mother, Sheikha Lubna, was looking around for her youngest sibling.

"Where is Mowza?" she asked those around her.

"London. As usual," said Ahmed, the brother who was in business with Mowza. "She is, as she says, telecommuting from one of our apartments there."

"She spends more time in London than here," said Lubna. "What does she do there when we are not in London?"

In a few months, after school ended, Shekha Lubna, her children and some members of the extended family would leave the oppressive Abu Dhabi heat and head to London where they spent most of every summer. Others, including some older relatives, would head to Al Ain, an oasis town a few hours from Abu Dhabi. Many families from Abu Dhabi City have second homes in Al Ain and spend weekends there throughout the year. Al Ain not only provides a cooler atmosphere but is a pretty place with low, white villas and buildings. Its roads are a bit unusual, with scores of roundabouts, but traffic is not as problemsome as it is often in the burgeoning Abu Dhabi City.

Sheikhas Asma and Rahma said nothing as they listened to their mother and others discuss Sheikha's Mowza's frequent travel schedule. The girls were not going to reveal what they knew about their aunt's London life.

After Asma had apprised Rahma about Mowza's remark that she might soon move out of the spinster world, the sisters made a phone call to their young aunt in London. They practically begged her to cough up information about her love life in the British capital. At first Mowza demurred, but after a half-hour of pleading from her nieces, Mowza admitted that she was "spending a lot of time" with a 36-year-old executive.

Rahma asked her if the "guy was a Muslim" and was relieved when her Aunt Mowza said: "Yes, of course. He is British-Arab." The idea that a sheikha might be involved with a Christian or a Jew would be too much for members of the older generation to fathom. A sheikha from this family was expected to tie the knot with a sheik, usually a cousin, or a member of the ruling family of another emirate. Anyone outside of the circle might not be welcome, although a Muslim man from a well-known family could have a chance. Mowza might be treading on shaky ground with her siblings and parents, but not with her nieces. They issued their verbal support.

"Go for it," Asma said in the phone conversation. "I think you deserve a love marriage."

"Well, the relationship has not reached the engagement stage yet," said Mowza. "But I am meeting his family this coming weekend."

Sheikha Mowza promised her nieces that she would fill them in after her visit with the man's family. The girls knew that meant Saturday and Sunday in London, as opposed to UAE weekends of Friday and Saturday.

Now, at the Friday family lunch, Asma and Rahma heard their mother's voice, aimed at no one in particular.

"And when will Mowza get married?" said Lubna. "And to whom at this point? All of the eligible cousins are married. She has passed up a lot of opportunities to wed. She might wind up as a second wife to someone."

At that point, Asma chimed in.

"Times have changed. We go to college now. We don't need to get married off to cousins who don't bother to work or get graduate degrees. Ones who live off the family money. Let us lead productive lives before we get married. And let Aunt Mowza go. And, by the way, we would rather be single our whole lives than pushed into some arranged marriage to some sheik cousin who already has a wife."

As Asma said that, she looked at one of her aunts who had been married off a decade before to some older sheik with a first wife. Their aunt had been miserable from day one, and, after five years and two children, she moved back into her parents' palace and insisted that the family allow her to divorce her spouse. The aunt was smiling and nodding her head in agreement.

*   *   *

Ayesha al Baloud arrived at Your Nails for her weekly manicure/pedicure. This time, she also booked a threading of her eyebrows. Like many Emirati women, she had deep, dark, well-shaped eyebrows. Some expats thought you could recognize a national woman by her lovely eyebrows.

Rowena took one look at Ayesha and sighed. While Yours Nails did not take appointments—it was so popular that clients had to show up and often wait quite a while for an appointment —Ayesha was among those who would arrive before the regular 10 a.m. opening. She would stand in the line outside the door and state almost vehemently to others waiting: "I want Rowena. No one else. Some of those other Filipino girls are no good. They shouldn't even be working here."

Helen Walker was among those who also waited outside the salon that day for its opening. She could not believe what she was hearing. As she looked around, she saw others, including two Emirati women, shaking their heads in disgust at Ayesha's remarks.

The managers accommodated Ayesha because of her "wasta" and always assigned Rowena to handle the services. Rowena hated every moment of it. Today was no exception.

As Rowena began the threading procedure with Ayesha in a private room, the manager knocked on the door to tell her staff member that she had received a phone call.

A phone call? Rowena knew that her mobile phone, the one she shared with a friend, was not allowed at the nail salon, so she was a bit taken aback by the idea of a call at work.

She excused herself and walked out to the main area of the salon and to the reception desk. The manager handed her the phone.

The caller was her Aunt Cecelia, phoning from the beauty parlor where she worked.

"Rowena, your mother just called me from Manila on my mobile. John Michael fell down some steps and is hurt pretty badly. He is going to need surgery."

Rowena broke into tears. Her fellow nail salon employees and the clients looked up at her.

"Oh, my God," she yelled into the phone. "I have to go home."

Her aunt was telling her they would get the money together for a flight home.

"Don't listen to what your manager or the owners say. You are going home," said Cecelia. "I am leaving work and getting a cab to get over to the nail salon."

Rowena had no details as to what happened to her 3-year-old son, but she knew that she had to get to Manila to be with him, his 7-year-old sister, and her husband, Adrian.

She sat and cried in a chair near the reception desk as word spread to fellow employees about the phone call. Clients also heard the news, and Helen Walker wanted to know how they might help.

"She doesn't have the money to fly to Manila. I am her cousin and we send our money home," said Joy, who was giving Helen a pedicure. "We might be able to pitch in 50 dirhams each if we are lucky."

Just then a voice rang out from a private room:

"Rowena. Where did you go? Come here and finish my threading."

Everyone in the salon looked in the direction of that room. One of the two Emirati women turned to the other and said: "It's Ayesha al Baloud. Khalid al Bader's wife. She never stops, does she?"

One of Rowena's colleagues opened the door of the private room and said: "I will finish the threading for you" to which Ayesha responded: "I am paying for Rowena, not you."

Then the manager headed toward the room, walked in, and closed the door. No one could hear the conversation but, in a few minutes, Ayesha walked out and angrily exited the salon.

The manager then told the crying Rowena: "You have six months left before we buy you a ticket home. The owners say you can go home now if you get your own ticket but you have to be back in two weeks. Let me get your passport from the safe."

Aunt Cecelia had just entered the nail salon and was hugging her niece.

"Rowena, let's find out when the next flight is and how much it costs."

One of the two Emirati women, ignoring the fact that her nails were not dry, took out her fancy mobile phone, looked up airline schedules on the Web and said: "There is a flight to Manila in three hours."

As others listened, the abaya-clad woman made a phone call to a travel agency. She spoke in Arabic so most employees and clients could not understand what she said.

Helen and the other expat clients looked at the other Emirati woman who was listening intently and shaking her head as if to say "Yes."

The woman explained: "That is my cousin on the phone. She booked Rowena on the next flight. First class. She even booked a car to take her to the airport. She put it on her charge account."

Everyone in the place applauded.

Cecelia and Rowena marveled at the generosity of the woman, and walked over to hug her.

"And if you need a good doctor over there," said the woman to Rowena, "I can get you some names. Here is my email address. Let me know how your son is doing."

Rowena looked at the name on the business card: Jalilla al Zabi, M.D. Medical Director at New Road Hospital.

"I will email you when I get there," Rowena said.

All the way to Manila, she kept thinking how her impression of Emirati women was way off base.

*   *   *

CHAPTER 5

Farah al Matari and her youngest daughter, Hessa al Bader, an account manager at a government-owned bank, were enjoying a leisurely Saturday morning breakfast on the terrace of the villa they shared. Hessa was detailing her latest exploits on the golf course and her mother was listening half-heartedly. For the past eight or nine years, 37-year-old Hessa had been almost mesmerized by the game. Farah initially told Hessa that she did not think her daughter should engage in a sport that mostly attracted men, but Hessa was insistent that golf was a good game for women because it taught them about teamwork and honesty in addition to providing good exercise.

Hessa was introduced to the game by Judith Shanley al Bader, her American sister-in-law. Judith was an active member of an Abu Dhabi golf club where she played in a women's group made up mostly of expatriate women. Only a few Emirati women had taken up the game as most families discouraged women from a sport where they would play on the same course as men.

Judith's daughters, Miriam and Iman, had no interest in golf. They were active in tennis, and played regularly at Abu Dhabi Tennis and Racquet Club.

One summer, when she was in her late 20s, Hessa joined Tahnoun, Judith and their children at their summer home in Avalon, N.J., an affluent shore town where Judith's family had vacationed since she was a child. Iman and Miriam, along with their younger brothers Mohammed and Diab, loved the Jersey beaches. It was almost ironic that young people from a desert island on the beautiful Arabian Gulf would prefer the Atlantic Ocean shoreline. What the boys craved were the regular beach volleyball or basketball games with their maternal cousins, the children of Judith's siblings who also owned homes in Avalon. For Iman and Miriam, the attraction was being free of the restrictions imposed in their Muslim homeland where, when they did go to a beach, it was at the Ladies Club where men were not allowed. In Avalon, they could lie on beach towels, with their head scarves and long, thin swimming pants on, and take in the scenery of people and the ocean, all the while conversing with their cousins and other relatives. In addition, they could put on bathing caps and body surf in crashing waves, something that Abu Dhabi had somewhat lost when it started to reclaim land for off-islands on which to build malls and hotels.

Hessa had little desire to lounge around on the beach. She was athletically inclined and had played on the volleyball team during her university days in Al Ain and later while she was attending graduate school in Cairo. She also had played basketball with her brothers in the family's backyard where a net had been placed after her brother Tahnoun came back from his first year at the University of Pennsylvania where he had become involved in intramural sports.

During that summer in Avalon, Judith convinced Hessa to come to a nearby club and take golf lessons. Hessa, it developed, had a natural stroke and within a few weeks was playing full rounds with Judith and her friends. When Hessa returned to Abu Dhabi, she joined a country club and became one of its most active female golfers.

When she first started to play in the UAE, Hessa wore the traditional Emirati head covering, the shayla, around her hair. As it flowed, though, it often interfered with her swing. So she switched to wearing the hijab, a covering that was tight around the neck but left the face uncovered. Over the hijab, she wore a golf visor to block the sun. Most times when she was on the course, she was the lone Emirati female so she stood out in the group.

Hessa's interest in sports led to her appointment as a member of Abu Dhabi Women's Sports Federation, where she had been instrumental in pushing for more participation for women in a variety of sporting activities. The group had been successful in setting up leagues in football (soccer) and tennis, but golf was just beginning to draw a bit of interest. Hessa herself was so enamored of the game that she had purchased one of those inexpensive artificial putting greens and placed it in her office so she could practice her stokes before the bank opened. Her co-workers often joined her early in the morning for five minutes of fun competition.

As Hessa enjoyed juices and toast with her mother, she said that she would be off shortly to play in a mixed event at the golf club.

"Well, who is your partner?" asked Hessa.

"Jon Chang from the Chinese Embassy. His wife does not play golf but she will be at the club restaurant when we finish. Oh, and Tahnoun and Judith also are playing in the event. But the good news, Umy, is that on Wednesday night in the women's Interclub league, my partner and I beat the best team from the Dubai Golf Club. Two women from Scotland and they usually win everything. I played well but my partner, a woman from America, was terrific. She is about 60 years old and can she play golf! She had two natural birdies."

"She is 60 and plays golf?"

"See, I told you, Umy. Women your age are into golf. They are active. That is why it is so good that you and Auntie Amna are into exercising. Not too many Emirati women your age are half as active. "

"We are pioneers," laughed Farah. "Your mother the pioneer. But I am not going to play golf. I still can't believe you go out and play that game with men."

For the umpteenth time, Hessa explained that, to play in most events at the club, she would have to compete with men since so few national women played the game. So she would sign up on her own and then, if a gentleman added his name as her partner, she would gladly play. Every one of the men with whom she had played golf was respectful of her—and happy, it seemed, to have her as a partner. Twice she had been in unofficial championship events with one or two other national women who played golf, and had come out on top in the scoring. So sometimes her male playing partners would call her "UAE Champ Hessa" just for fun.

The truth was that Farah was supportive of her daughter, especially after Hessa was featured in a piece on the Dubai television station about her being the most active and most skilled Emirati female golfer. Many friends and relatives saw the report and Farah was proud to receive their congratulatory phone calls about her daughter. Farah long before had stopped worrying as to whether Hessa would ever marry. Her daughter was happy at 37. She had friends, a good job, a master's degree and a true interest in golf and other sports. Plus she was a smart investor; she owned four apartments in Cairo and a few buildings with her mother in the UAE.

Farah recalled being the same age, and being so unhappy after her husband took on another wife.

"Oh, by the way," Hessa said to her mother. "This year there will be an official national championship just for women—at the new course in Dubai. I was invited to play. It is in two weeks. Wish me luck."

"Can I go see you play?" asked Farah.

"You really want to do that? I would be honored."

*   *   *

Dr. Teresa Wilson sat in a Women's University conference room with Sheikha Asma, Mona al Shari, Iman al Bader and a few other students. In planning for the public speaking competition, they had one major decision to make: what would be the topic for the student speakers?

"I was thinking it should be about women and the Emirates," said the professor. "A topic that everyone knows about and could address with ease."

"You mean perhaps a topic like How We See Our Future or something about careers?" asked Mona.

"I don't know," said Dr. Teresa. "I want you girls to make the decision."

One student, Maitha, whose abaya covered what would be considered a vastly overweight body, said she thought "good nutrition" would be a possible topic.

No one said a word.

Then Maitha, one of the best-liked students on campus, said: "Well, I could strut across the stage as an example of what NOT to eat. That would make it so real."

They all laughed, knowing that Maitha's humor often masked a sadness in her voice about her rotund figure.

"Actually, nutrition might not be a bad idea," said Iman. "We all seem to avoid the good food in favor of spaghetti and French fries."

That was true—the top sellers in the WU cafeteria were those two foods, not the hummus or babaganush or chicken tiki that were always available.

"Ok, nutrition is one idea," said Asma, who was happy to be overseeing the committee. "How about education and women? We are number one for the percentage of women in universities. That might be interesting."

"That is a possible topic," said Dr. Teresa. "But it might be too much repetition from the speakers. I was hoping we could pick a topic that was more debatable, so to speak. A topic that would get different ideas from speakers—and would cause everyone to listen. Without its being an official debate with all the rules of pros and cons."

Sheikha Asma thought for a moment and then said: "Well, I hear a lot of young women talk about their future marriages. Our country is changing with women getting married later or not at all."

"So what are you proposing?" asked a puzzled Iman.

"I am thinking about all those arranged marriages. Like in my family—and in some of yours, too. I mean, why do parents decide who their daughters should marry?"

Maitha, who came from one of Abu Dhabi's wealthiest families, was excited.

"Hey, you hit it, Asma. My older sister got married last year. The mothers set it up. It lasted about two months. He had a few girlfriends on the side. He was verbally abusive to my sister, too, I think, always putting her down. And because SHE wanted the divorce, my father had to pay back his father for the wedding costs. My sister blamed my parents for their lousy choice of a spouse and she has not spoken to them since. She took off for Geneva to work for the UN. My grandmother said years ago that divorce was common in tribal families and the woman would marry someone else, maybe become a second or third wife. Not these days. My sister just got the heck out of Dodge, as you would say, Dr. Teresa."

"Wait a minute," said Dr. Teresa. "Who here favors a topic like 'Choosing a Spouse?'"

They all did.

"What do you think the university's academic vice president will say?" asked Iman.

Asma sort of laughed in her sweet way.

"That woman freezes everytime one of us sheikhas asks her anything. She thinks she will get fired if she says 'No' to anything we ask for. It is a running joke with all the cousins. Remember when my cousin, Sheikha Sara, complained because she got a C in Spanish from that crazy guy who taught here last year? The academic VP talked to the guy and Sara wound up with a B plus. And she had failed just about every test and quiz. She did not even deserve a C. So don't worry about the academic vice president. I will tell her that the Student Council is running this competition. And that will be it."

Maitha was in her glory.

"Can I be one of the speakers? Please."

"The competition will be open to everyone," said Dr. Teresa. "But, Asma, we need to have preliminaries. We just can't stick 10 girls out there on the stage. They should have good material and be good speakers. I am sure the ones who already took public speaking will be the best of the lot. I will get other professors to help with the preliminaries. So check with the dean, make an announcement and we will start the preliminary rounds in two weeks."

As she walked back into the office she shared with two other professors, Teresa remarked: "I need your help with our public speaking contest. Believe me, you are going to enjoy this topic."

*   *   *

The Coffee Klatch group met again to take stock of their idea to get into the cake business.

"My father looked at me as if I was crazy when I told him about TOTE cakes," said Essa. "He thought this would stop me from going into the family real estate business."

"Wait a minute," said Iman. "One thing we all agree on. We can have our own careers. We will hire people to bake and to run the business. This is our sideline, our investment. But we all can get regular jobs or whatever."

"Yes, and I told him that," said Essa. "And then he offered me whatever I need to help get the cake business going. He said he could look for a space for us in one of his buildings on 32nd Street about a block from the Corniche. Lots of parking. A good location."

Iman said she had asked her grandmother, Farah, what she thought about a cake business.

"Turns out she loves those cake shows on the Food Channel and thinks our business will be a hit. She will give me whatever money I need, as long as I promise her I will also go to law school or get a MBA. And my mother used to work in a bakery so she is all for it."

"Your mother WORKED? She WORKED? In a bakery?" cried out Essa.

"Maybe your Emirati mothers did not work because they got married as teenagers and did not go to college," said Iman.

"Wait—so your mother went to college in America and then went to work in a bakery? That is a load of crap," said Alia, whose word choices made her friends shake their heads.

An irritated Iman explained that when her mother, Judith, was in high school and college, she worked during the summers at a bakery at the Jersey shore, where her family had a home.

"It wasn't that she was poor. My grandfather is a partner in one of Philadelphia's top law firms. But everyone in America gets summer jobs. That's the way it is. So my mother worked at Ann's Bakery in Avalon for about five summers. It is still operating and we go there almost every morning for donuts and bagels when we are in New Jersey in the summer."

"So your mother actually bakes cakes and pies?" asked Essa. "What does your cook do?"

Iman shook her head.

"My mother did not bake at the bakery. She worked at the counter. The cook does our baking. But my mother often does it with her because she enjoys it. We all do."

"Must be an American thing," laughed Mona, who put the session back on track by asking questions.

"Who will do the business plan? What about the staff? One of the most important things is to figure out how we get some top-notch American baker to come here and be the star of our shop. She will have to train people to do the baking with her."

"Does it have to be a woman?" asked Essa.

"No," said Iman, "but it might easier for us all around if it is a woman. That way, we can spend more time with her and not run into any problems in that respect."

They all agreed.

Alia took on the job of writing up the business plan. As colorful as she often was with her verbal language, Alia was a top business major who had won the department's writing award in her junior year.

"OK," she said. "Right away, I need to know this. Essa, Find out about the space on 32nd Street and how much rent we will have to pay."

"Rent? He better give it to us for free," said Essa. "My father can well afford to give us free rent."

Iman thought for a minute.

"I am not sure that it would be smart to take free rent. We should pay and expect the same response as regular tenants when we have problems or want to get more space."

After mulling that over for a minute, Alia said: "You are right. We have to do it right from the start. No free rent."

They all nodded their heads in agreement although Essa seemed a bit puzzled.

"We take money from our families but no free rent?"

"Yes," said Iman. "And as I told my grandmother, she can give me money but it will not make her a partner at all. We all will own this business outright. Her money is a loan to me and I will pay it off."

"Yep," said Alia. "Take it from the half-American here. She thinks she will REALLY pay back that money. Baloney."

They split up some other duties. Through the Internet and perhaps some phone calls with her cousins in the U.S., Iman would start researching the best cake shops in America with the hope she might find a baker to come to the Emirates. Mona would find out from her father how to file for setting up a new business in Abu Dhabi and how a website would be secured for TOTE cakes. Essa could have an early lesson in real estate development by discovering how they could hire architects and contractors to design and build space for the combination baking kitchen and retail shop.

With this meeting finished, Iman and Mona jumped in to Iman's car and headed north. Ninety minutes later, they were racing down the indoor ski slopes in Dubai.

Where else but in the Emirates could you ski in 90-degree weather?

*　　*　　*

Sheikha Mowza was calling from London. Asma turned on the speaker phone on her mobile so she and her sister Rahma could listen together to their aunt.

Mowza: "Hey, how was that movie you went to at the mall?"

Rahma: "The film was good but we wanted to go to a café in the mall afterwards with some of our friends, and, as usual, Ingrid and our darn nannies shot us down with the usual sheikha-not-being-seen-in-the-world stuff."

Mowza: "When will it end?"

Asma: "Who knows? Okay, let's hear about the guy and the visit to the family. What is his name, anyway?"

Mowza: "Hassan Hadad. His family came to England from Beirut in the early 1970s and he was born here. He goes back to Lebanon infrequently—maybe once every few years to visit relatives or for a wedding or something. That is about it. His family made sure he and his brothers and sister learned Arabic but they speak English most of the time. Hassan went to London School of Economics, too, but before I went there."

Rahma: "Where did you meet him?"

Mowza: "At the gym in our building. He lives on the 20th floor. We were working out at the same time and started talking about nothing—the equipment and exercise. He knew that I wore head scarves so he assumed I was Muslim. Then one day he asked me if I would go out to dinner with him and I said I would. I think he was shocked that I agreed to go. Heck, I was shocked that I said yes. But this guy is truly handsome."

Asma: "Maybe we have seen him when we are over there since our apartment is in the same building."

Rahma: "No way. I never saw any handsome Arab guys in the apartment building."

Mowza: "Well, he only moved in here about six months ago. He works for a British energy investment company and was living in New York until he was transferred back to London. I have been spending a lot of time with him when I am here and I am crazy about him."

Asma: "You are not living with him, are you, when you are there?"

Mowza: "Asma, knock it off. You know me better than that. Your good aunt, remember?"

Rahma: "What about this weekend? You met his family?"

Mowza: "Well, his family lives about an hour away from London. Turns out his cousin was visiting from Lebanon and all the relatives were getting together for dinner at Hassan's parents' home to see the guy. So Hassan invited me to go to the dinner and thus meet the whole family."

Asma: "And...so what happened?"

Mowza: "Well, for one thing he found out who our family is. He had no idea. He only knew I was from Abu Dhabi. So I get there—his family has a lovely home—and I am introduced to everyone and the cousin from Beirut hears my last name and immediately wants to know if I am from the UAE royal family, if I am a sheikha. I don't want to lie so I say 'Yes' and everyone sort of stares at me. Hassan looks shocked and says 'No Way.' The cousin says he knows Sheik Rashid from college in Cairo. That is how he recognized the name. I said I really don't know Sheik Rashid —he is one of our Al Ain distant cousins—but I say we have such a large family and we aren't too royal. Everyone laughs and nothing more is said about it until Hassan and I are driving back to London and I explain how we are part of the Ruler's family and yes, we live in palaces, and I hope it does not matter since I think he and his family are great."

Rahma: "His response?"

Mowza: "He said he felt bad that we go to McDonald's sometimes for lunch. He figured that sheikhas don't normally eat Big Macs. I said, to the contrary, they are our favorites, after French fries. That is why I always want to go there. So we just laughed about the royal thing."

Asma: "This is too funny. So when are you going to tell the family about Hassan?"

Mowza: "I don't know. But he is coming to Abu Dhabi for the Energy Conference next month. Maybe when I get back there in a few days and I am working with Ahmed in the office, I will tell my brother, see what he thinks about it and then ask him what to do."

Rahma: "Oh, our dear uncle Ahmed. Your brother and business partner. Word on the street—well, from my WU friend whose brother hangs out with him—is that he has a Jordanian girlfriend."

Mowza: "No. Really? He never mentioned that. Not to me. Why would he? And being a man, of course, he can get away with marrying a foreigner. The family would agree to that. But we have to marry Emirati men, we are told. Otherwise, they say we may lose our citizenship. It is simply unfair. And I am going to be the one in this family who takes up our cause."

*   *   *

Ayesha al Baloud looked at the clock. It was close to 11 a.m. and she was still in bed, watching a soap opera on an Arabic channel. She turned and pushed a button on the wall. That was the signal for the Filipino maid to report to the bedroom and, within minutes, Angela was standing next to the woman of the house.

"I will need coffee and some buttered toast and tell your sister to put some of that new jam on the toast, too," said Ayesha. "And then after I eat, you can get the bath ready for me."

Angela said "Yes, Madame," and exited the room. She walked downstairs to the kitchen to find her sister Lourdes, who worked for the family as its cook.

"The queen wants coffee, toast with butter and that new jam we got at the markets," said Angela. "And then, of course, I have to get the bath ready."

The pair rolled their eyes in unison. How many times had they felt like telling "the queen" to get off her throne and do something worthwhile. When she wasn't lounging in bed, Ayesha was walking around the house and ordering the staff to do one thing or another. Often she would head in her chauffeured car to small boutiques to buy more clothes or go to the nail salon or the beauty parlor. That was her life, and Angela and Lourdes could not understand how even a woman with money could be happy with such a lackluster existence. They felt sorry for Ayesha's three sons who seemed to get little attention from their mother. Their Filipino nanny was more concerned about their welfare than was their own mother.

But Angela and Lourdes stayed with the family because of Ayesha's husband, Khalid Mansour al Bader. He was kind and considerate. After Angela and Lourdes arrived to work for the family several years before, he hired their husbands to work as drivers and handymen around the house. Khalid, whom they always called "Sir," had built a series of bedrooms in the basement level of the home for members of the household staff. When Lourdes gave birth to a son, Khalid put on an addition to what was called the out-building, a structure that had a large extra kitchen and storage space. He had his contractors build a small apartment on the back and gave it to Lourdes and her husband and the new baby. The child, Joseph, now close to 5, attended a private Catholic preschool and spent much time playing with the Al Bader boys.

From the time of their arrival, Lourdes and Angela wondered how this exceptionally nice Khalid al Bader could have chosen Ayesha al Baloud for his bride. They got the answer from his mother, Farah al Matari, and his sister, Hessa al Bader, who came across the street to see the Al Bader boys one day when Ayesha was in Dubai to visit her relatives.

After spending time with their grandmother and aunt, the three boys went to the backyard to kick a soccer ball around with Joseph and with Angela's husband, who took a break from tending the gardens. Farah and Hessa sat in the kitchen of the villa and had some coffee. They asked Lourdes and Angela to join them.

"So what is it like working for my sister-in-law?" asked Hessa with a smirk on her face.

Lourdes and Angela looked at each other. They did not know if being candid would be the best choice in answering the question.

Hessa persisted.

"Really? What is it like? My mother wants to know, too. Don't you, Umy?"

43

Farah sighed and said: "It sure must be interesting."

Lourdes chose candor and said: "I just don't understand the woman. She is one demanding person. And she does nothing really but sleep and watch television and shop and go to the nails place or to get her hair done or whatever. I don't see any friends come here or anything."

Angela said that Ayesha spent her waking hours "ordering me around since I am her maid. I am happy that she spends so much time watching TV in bed. It gives me a break."

Farah mumbled something like "what was I thinking?"

Hessa looked at her mother and agreed: "What WERE you thinking? You were the one who set it up. The binocular brigade."

"The what?" asked Lourdes.

"Well, that is what my friends and I call it. The binocular brigade. UAE mothers of marriage-age sons go to women's weddings and they start looking around for girls who might be ideal brides for their sons. It's as if they take binoculars—I mean they don't really—and focus on beautiful young women who are all fancied up to attend these weddings. You know, there are hundreds of girls at these events. Well, my mother here was part of that binocular group and that is how we got Ayesha in the family. I was at that wedding."

"You were," said Farah, "and one of the women asked me if you were my daughter and that you would be an ideal wife for her son. You threatened me if I let her come to the house because you said you were not marrying into her family!"

"Forget me," said Hessa. "Tell about Ayesha."

Farah provided the details. She was sitting with some of her friends at that wedding and they were all eyeing the beautiful young women who had shed their abayas and shaylas and appeared in designer gowns with lots of jewelry. Girls spend hours in getting their hair done and makeup applied for these weddings. After all, the young unmarried women know that prospective mothers-in-law will be out looking for wives for their sons. Where else would one find a wife in a country where unmarried men and women seldom socialize together?

"Khalid was in his early 30s," said Farah, "and still not married and he said maybe it was time. I had been telling him that for a few years but a mother waits until her son says it is time to look for a wife for him. So at this wedding I was geared to looking for a lovely woman. As my friends and I sat there, Ayesha passed by with her mother. One of my friends knew the mother from Dubai—Ayesha is from Dubai. So they stopped and chatted with us. Ayesha's mother, Nama, by the way, is really a nice person."

Lourdes and Angela agreed. They had met her many times and even been with Ayesha to her mother's Dubai home, and could not figure out how Ayesha could be the daughter of that lovely woman.

"We spoke for a few minutes and you, Hessa, came over from a table where you were with your friends and talked to Ayesha. Correct?" asked Farah.

"Yes," said Hessa, "and Ayesha smiled and asked what business my family was in. I remember that. Sort of odd. She probably wanted to know if we had money or something."

Farah recalled speaking to Ayesha's mother and asking if her daughter were married. The mother had replied "not yet" and Farah got the impression that her son might be a likely candidate for this girl's hand in marriage. All of the women at Farah's table knew the story of the Al Baloud family in Dubai. They had been in the forefront of the building boom and owned many properties and businesses in that emirate. The women encouraged Farah to consider Ayesha as Khalid's bride.

When she told Khalid about the young woman, he encouraged his mother to go ahead and see if a match could be made. Khalid, too, was familiar with the Al Balouds and had done some business with Ayesha's brothers and cousin. Khalid, as with most Emirati young men, trusted his mother for choosing his wife. And Mansour—Farah's ex-husband, was alive then— knew some of the Al Balouds and was happy for his son Khalid.

So, as Farah told Lourdes and Angela, she called ahead to Ayesha's mother and asked if she and some of her female relatives could visit the Al Baloud home, In effect, she was telling Ayesha's mother that they would be coming to ask about a possible match between her daughter and Khalid.

"And so we went to Dubai and we met Ayesha and her mother and her aunts and everyone was thrilled. Seems as if they had checked out the family to make sure we had enough money to make Ayesha happy because she was used to having good things.

"So, Khalid never met Ayesha until the wedding. He did call her once because he wanted to know where she would like to go on a honeymoon and to tell her that they would be living in an apartment I was adding onto the house I had then. Khalid's father was living in an apartment with his second family so going there was out of the question. Well, Khalid got the impression that Ayesha was not delighted about moving into my home, but I felt the same way when I got married. It is tradition, or it used to be anyway, that a couple move in with the groom's family. In this case, Khalid and Ayesha were going to have their own apartment in my home. And eventually they would get their own home. Anyway, Khalid spoke to Ayesha for about a half-hour and he seemed fine with the whole thing. And he had heard that she was a beautiful young lady—and that is true."

"And Umy, the wedding cost what?" asked Hessa.

"Don't ask. Your father and I argued over that. The groom's family pays, and I know your father was having some difficult times as Esra, his other wife, was spending like crazy. So I had started to make quite a bit of money in my own businesses and I agreed to pay for the women's wedding and he paid for the men's wedding. Let me tell you—he got the better deal. The women's wedding—well, we had hundreds, maybe a thousand women there and I hired singers from Jordan and Qatar and invited people from other countries and paid for them. That is what we try to do if someone is coming from out of the UAE. I think I went overboard because my other son, Tahnoun, got married when he was young in America. Her family paid for it."

"And I hosted a women's henna party for Ayesha," said Hessa. "We brought in an artist to paint brown henna art on our hands. These days we read that synthetic henna art can lead to medical problems. Anyway, we had a pleasant evening with lots of dancing and I enjoyed being with her friends and aunts."

"Was your son Khalid happy after he got married?" asked Lourdes.

Farah just shrugged.

Hessa started to laugh.

"When they moved into the apartment in our home, Ayesha seemed fine. Then Issa was born, nine months to the day they were married. The first nanny lasted two weeks. Another one lasted about a day. Same with the maids. My mother was going crazy. Right, Umy? We started calling Ayesha the princess behind her back."

Angela and Lourdes chuckled together.

"We promoted her," said Angela. "We call her the queen."

Farah said she had never seen anyone act like her daughter-in-law did after she had children.

"I thought she would get over whatever it was. But it did not change. And she kept demanding a house and Khalid was waiting for the city to distribute more homes. But finally he just bought a villa on his own. Well, with my help. Believe me, I was willing to help!"

The phone rang and Lourdes answered it.

"Yes, Madame. Yes, Madame. Yes."

When she hung up the phone, she turned to Farah and Hessa: "The princess, as you call her, wants dinner precisely at 8, after she returns from Dubai. Hammour. Pistachio-crusted. Said the recipe is in today's newspaper. And, as usual, she probably won't even eat it. She will want something else for herself."

"Lourdes," said Farah. "Did she ask about her boys?"

"No, she did not."

Just then, they heard the front door open and in came Khalid. He was happy to see his mother and sister in the kitchen with Lourdes and Angela.

"We came to see the boys. They are outside now," said Farah as her son greeted her.

"I came home to see them," said Khalid. "Thought I would take them and Joseph out for ice cream. Oh, did Ayesha call?"

"Yes, just now, sir," said Lourdes. "She wants dinner at 8. Pistachio-crusted hammour. We have plenty of the fish but we will need to go out and get pistachios and today's paper that has the recipe."

Khalid al Bader shook his head in amazement as if to say he could not believe his wife would expect the domestic help to find a recipe in the day's paper and then whip it up.

"OK. You don't have to go to the markets. I will get you the newspaper and some pistachios when I am out with the boys."

After he left, Lourdes turned to Farah and said: ""As we Catholics would say, your son is a saint."

*　　*　　*

CHAPTER 6

In a brief announcement sent to the faculty, the provost of Women's University announced that classes were canceled for the upcoming Sunday upon the mandate of the Ruler of the Emirate to give workers a free day in appreciation for their dedication to projects in Abu Dhabi. Since Friday and Saturday were the regular weekend days in the UAE, Dr. Teresa Wilson welcomed a three-day break to take off on a brief trip. She picked up the phone and called her travel agent.

"Can you book me into a hotel with a spa in Muscat?" she said.

Within a half hour, the agent returned the call with all arrangements made, including bookings for daily massages.

So late Thursday afternoon, after her last class of the day, Teresa flew out of Abu Dhabi Airport to the capital of Oman, an adjoining country. After checking into the luxury hotel, she called Betty Watson, an ex-WU colleague who had taken a dean's post this year at a major Omani college. Betty had offered to host Teresa who said she preferred to be at the hotel for the spa treatments and the pool. So Betty planned to join Teresa for dinner the next night and then on Saturday afternoon for a tour around the city.

The weekend jaunt provided Teresa with a report for the popular monthly email newsletter that she sent to family and friends:

The flight provided a scary moment for me. I was sitting next to a woman who told me she was from the Sudan and headed to a visit with friends in Oman. She wore a colorful long dress and a matching headdress that is often worn by African women. Anyway, I was reading a Maeve Binchy book as we approached Muscat, and I noticed something extending over the woman's lap. It looked like a long, repeat LONG, nail file. At least three times the length of a regular nail file. It was pointing right at me. I almost gasped when I saw it. What in the name of God is it, I thought, and how did she get that on a plane in this era of security? I waited a minute and said: "What is that?" and she said, "It is for my nails." THEN she started using this thing to file her nails; she had not been doing that before I asked her what the darn thing was.

I noticed that a blonde woman on the other side of the aisle was watching this scene unfold. Believe me, I was happy that we were just about starting our descent into Muscat at this point. When I went to the baggage area to claim my luggage, the blonde woman came up to me and said: "I was a bit worried when I saw what looked like a weapon." I agreed. Turned out this woman is from the States and was on her way to visit her husband who works for an oil company in Oman. We both agreed that, had we seen this type of whatever-it-was on a plane going into an American airport, we probably would have had to report it. As it was, all I wanted to do was get to my hotel room and hot tub.

Talk about luxury. My room was gorgeous and overlooked the Gulf of Oman. The hotel has three outdoor pools and I was in a lounge chair at one of them by 9 on Friday morning. I went down to the beach a bit later and walked into the clear blue/green water. The colors of the Arabian Gulf are similar—you know I spend a lot of time at a beach club in Abu Dhabi when I am not teaching or playing golf—but this water had an interesting feature. It was calm and I started to walk out and I must have been a city block or more out from the beach and the water was only up to my knees. I did not go farther but I saw some others out another block or so. I looked at the horizon and saw a few ships and wondered if we could walk out that far!!!

Also on the beach: people riding horses. You can sign up at the pool reception desk to go horseback riding but I had no desire to do that. I must say the horses looked healthy and well-groomed—made me think of the Central Park horses that don't get that kind of treatment. So I just sat around (yes, I had an umbrella over me as I do all the time in Abu Dhabi and I wore my skin-protective jacket over my bathing suit when I went in the pool!) and I read more of my book. Then it was time to head into the spa—entrance is right off the pool area—for a glorious massage. How I love my massages. In the early afternoon, I had lunch at the pool bar before heading back to my room for a nap.

Betty joined me at the hotel for dinner about 7 and we had a delightful meal in an Italian restaurant. Why is it, that no matter where I go in the world, I find Italian restaurants? Betty loves Muscat, and says she has become active in an American expat group that has bridge groups and a book club. But she has not found as interested a Scrabble partner as she had back at our club pool in Abu Dhabi. For those of you new to my monthly communiqués (I know some of my friends send this one to others, why I do not know), I reported last year about a Scrabble game with Betty at our beach club in Abu Dhabi. She had been playing there at poolside every Saturday with another WU faculty member who was away one weekend so Betty asked me if I wanted to play. I expected my word creation *talents to be as strong as they had been when I played Scrabble with family members, but was I wrong. I swore she was making up things, especially when she put down a word spelled **ai**. She said **ai** was a three-headed sloth or something like that. That was the last time I played Scrabble with her or anyone at WU. Despite her pleas, I refused to play the game with her in Muscat!*

On Saturday, I mulled what type of treatment I should get at the hotel spa and decided I might try reflexology because it seemed to be a special type of foot massage. Suffice it to say that I have had my lone reflexology treatment in life. It felt as if pins were being inserted into my feet; I even asked the lady if I was getting acupuncture by mistake. She said "No—just using my hands." And her darn long nails, I think. I could not wait to return to poolside. Later, Betty came to the hotel and we took off in her car for a tour of Muscat. Not much to see—a lovely university campus, lots of low buildings, the embassy area, and, of course, the souks. Love those markets. Abu Dhabi's famous old souks burned down a few years ago and are being replaced with modern shops. I love these old souks with kiosks and lots of bartering. I bought a handmade wall hanging after a round of negotiating with a tradesman.

We ended up at the Grand Mosque. Every tourist stops there to see the beautiful structure and the extraordinary massive rug. We had our hair covered with scarves and in we walked. Then a guard came up to me and said I had to leave. The blouse I was wearing has sleeves that don't quite reach my wrists and no woman is allowed in the place unless her arms are covered all the way. So I was escorted out of the mosque. Yes, I was ejected from a mosque. Another first for ol' Teresa. Add it to my resume!

It was a fun break from work to visit an interesting country. Some day I might just teach in Oman. I am getting to love this part of the world, and educating my American friends and relatives about it. Hope you learn something from these missives!

*   *   *

Judith Shanley al Bader walked into the board of trustees meeting at Al Koba Academy. She was in her eighth year on the board, and every meeting proved to be an education for her.

One time, a few years back, the sheik arrived—the one who actually started the school in the early 1990s and still was its primary patron—to declare that he wanted the boys' section of the school to be closed for a week so he could take his sons falcon-hunting in Pakistan with some other important friends and their Al Koba student-sons. The headmaster, an Egyptian man who studied in America, nicely tried to suggest that losing a week in school might put the academy in jeopardy for its certification.

"How?" asked the sheik. "The Ministry of Education reports to us."

Judith surmised that he did not mean the ministry reported to the academy's board, but rather to the sheik's family. It probably was true. The family technically owned the emirate and its natural resources, although it had been generous in providing homes and businesses and farms and high salaries and health care to fellow nationals.

The headmaster shrugged his shoulders and that drew the ire of the sheik.

"What is your problem?" he said to the headmaster. "It is just a week."

Judith could not sit silently.

"What about our girls' section? Would that be closed, too?" she asked.

"Oh, that could remain open," said the sheik. "No girls on these trips."

Judith sat here thinking about her own upbringing in Ardmore, an upscale suburb of Philadelphia. At least once a year, her father would take a week off from his law practice to go camping with his son—and his daughters.

She had been asked to join the board when she had all four children at Al Koba—Mariam and Iman at the girls' school and Mohammed and Diab at the boys' school across the street. Now only Diab was left at Al Koba; he was a high school junior and the star of the school's basketball team. Throughout the years, Judith had muddled through board discussions about curriculum; the school followed a British model until changing to an American-style one in 2004. She led the fight to allow the girls' school to have intramural sports. Judith also headed personnel committees, including the one that had hired the Egyptian headmaster after his predecessor, a Canadian, became a "runner," a term used to describe a foreigner who takes out a loan from a local bank, goes home for the summer and never returns nor repays the monies.

She thought about all of these past issues as she entered the board meeting and greeted Nasser al Shari, the father of Iman's friend, Mona, and son of Amna, the longtime friend of Judith's mother-in-law, Farah. Nasser was a successful businessman and close friend of Judith's husband, Tahnoun.

"So I guess you heard about the girls' cake business," said Nasser. "Talk about creative young ladies."

"And what about your mom and my mother-in-law at the gym all the time," said Judith. "The world is changing, Nasser. And I think it is great."

The main item on the agenda was the budget. From the time of its inception, Al Koba had relied on the largesse of the ruling family to pay for most of the costs of operating the school. Tuition was free and all students were Emiratis. To get that designation, a student's father had to be a national even if his/her mother was of another nationality, so Judith's offspring fit the bill. Instruction was in English although students took one class in Arabic after parents complained that the children's national identities were being compromised as many seldom spoke in their native language.

The operating budget had increased dramatically in the past few years, as foreign instructors demanded higher salaries and better housing arrangements. In addition, the cost of maintaining the physical plant continued to increase, mostly because many Abu Dhabi buildings are constructed in record time with cheap labor and often, within five to 10 years, require extensive reworking to remain intact. With the opening of other good private schools in the city, Al Koba—once considered the premier educational institution for young nationals—was facing a decrease in enrollment because of the competition.

The headmaster stood to address the board.

"As our costs rise and our enrollment dips, we need to make some decisions. The sheik has told us that his support will remain at the current level but we will not be able to sustain our operations without additional revenue. It seems to me that now is the time to consider admitting expatriate students and charging them a fair tuition. We could start with 50 new non-national students next fall and maybe another 50 a year later."

He did not have to convince Judith that this was a good idea. She said she had a number of expat friends who were sending their children to other private schools and wishing they could get them into Al Koba.

Nasser agreed with the headmaster, too.

"Our children should go to schools with those from other backgrounds. This is a global society, especially here in the UAE where we nationals are less than 20 percent of the population. I know Emiratis who have decided against sending their children to Al Koba simply because it is restricted to locals. They prefer schools with an international student population."

The headmaster said he had asked the sheik, who seldom attended board meetings unless he wanted something special like vacation time for falcon hunting, what he thought about the expatriate student idea.

"He sort of shrugged…did not really answer the question," said the headmaster.

That was par for the course for this particular sheik. He had inherited many millions in dirhams and spread his wealth not only to schools but to a host of sporting endeavors including sponsorship of cigarette boat races and ownership of an Irish rugby team. His two wives did not get along at all, nor did their children who attended Al Koba. This sheik apparently had no specific job in life; he was not even a government official as were many hard-working male members of his family. A bright British accountant served as the sheik's assistant and handled most of his employer's business activities.

Judith made a motion that the academy move to accept non-nationals into its student body. Nasser seconded the motion.

"I am glad you are doing it this way," said the board chairman, a polite Emirati man. "We have learned that from you, Judith."

52

What he meant was that Judith had fought for the first few years she was on the board to have the meetings run under standard rules for such sessions. Previously, no motions were made or votes taken and Judith kept insisting that everything be on record. Her fellow board members would disagree, reminding her that this was not America and not a democracy. Judith did not care what they said. She kept badgering them until they decided to go along with her wishes. Now the meetings were run with specific rules that included voting for various actions of the board.

When the chairman called for discussion, Nasser again outlined his support for admitting children who were not UAE citizens. Others talked about the need to keep the school in operation and the desire to have UAE students mix with those from other backgrounds. When the vote was called for, it was unanimous.

"I will inform the sheik," said the headmaster.

"Don't bother, "said Nasser. "Call that British guy and tell him. Let him convince the sheik that we are right in doing this."

*   *   *

Hessa al Bader's face lit up as she read the English language daily at her desk. An article in the sports section described the recent hiring of a Swedish woman to teach golf at a major course located halfway between Dubai and Abu Dhabi. A few members of the department were taking turns at her in-office putting green before work started, and they listened as Hessa emitted a cheerleading-type yell.

"Yesiree," she said loudly. "This is good news. We have a woman golf instructor in the UAE. Now that is progress. And I want to meet this woman and take a few lessons from her."

A male colleague could not contain himself.

"You could give HER lessons," remarked Tariq Al Shamhi, noting for the others that Hessa shortly would be taking to the links to vie for the national championship for women.

Hessa made light of the upcoming one-round event that was limited to Emirati women.

"The truth is, we don't have many national women playing golf," said Hessa. "So I should come in the Top Ten just by entering. I thought it would be a two-day tournament but heard they decided to make it one round this first time."

"Not the point," said Tariq, a superb golfer in his own right. "There has been a big national championship for men for years now, and a few unofficial women's events, and it is time to have an official all-women's national competition. I think it will encourage other local women to play. I want my

14-year-old daughter, Latifa, to learn golf. I think she is a good athlete and would enjoy golf. And it would get her mind off losing her mom."

"I agree," said Hessa, who was glad to see the affable Tariq in such a good mood for the first time since his wife had passed away eight months before from cancer.

Tariq told his co-workers that they did not need tickets to see Hessa play in the tournament. They just had to show up.

"They play nine holes in the morning and, after lunch, play the other nine. Only one day."

"Oh," said Hessa. "Playing in front of people could make me nervous. Or maybe it will give me some encouragement. Who knows?"

Hessa's administrative staffers became enthusiastic at the idea of seeing their supervisor in a golf setting outside of the office putting game.

"I will be there," said Shamsa, the newest hire who starred on the basketball team at the women's college she attended in Jordan. "Maybe golf is something I would like to try."

Hessa's mobile phone rang. It was her niece, Miriam al Bader.

"Did you see the article about the woman golf coach?" asked Mariam.

"Just read it," said Hessa. "I hope I get to meet her. Maybe at the golf championship."

"Me, too," replied Mariam.

"Are you coming to it?" asked Hessa.

"Yes, along with my sister, my parents, Diab, Grandma Farah and others like Mona Al Shari and her parents and her grandmother, Amna. And Gram Farah said her friend, Helen, from the gym class, wants to come. You will have a rooting section. Maybe I will take up golf after seeing the tournament."

When Hessa ended the call and began her day's work, she found it hard to concentrate. She had defended her love of golf for several years as national women often criticized her for taking up a sport where she played on courses with men. She had repeatedly argued that golf provides a welcome relief from the stresses of working. She would explain how she wished other local women would catch the golf "bug" as she had after her sister-in-law introduced her to the game.

Now she was stepping into a new arena—becoming a role model for potential female Emirati golfers.

* * *

Cecelia got into her bed to curl up with a book. Not a book she owned—it was too expensive to buy books at the mall store on her salary and tips from the beauty salon. She sent money back to her children and grandchildren in

Manila, and kept enough to be able to buy necessities. Books were not in that category.

Cecelia's love of books was well-known to her family and flatmates. She truly had become self-educated through decades of reading.

For the past two years, she had received much of her reading fare from an American client who came to the salon every few weeks for a hair color or cut. The customer, Dr. Teresa Wilson, was a professor at Women's University. She loved to read books, too, and not only bought many but also borrowed paperbacks from hundreds available under a swap arrangement at the university. So just about every time she walked into the salon, Teresa brought Cecelia a few books to read, and the beautician would return them the next time the professor came to the shop. Often the pair discussed the books, and discovered that their reading choices were similar; they liked novels that told a story and also educated people. Teresa said that she had avoided reading novels for years—she liked nonfiction works— until she was flying somewhere with a friend and had nothing to read. So she reluctantly accepted the friend's offer of a Danielle Steele book to pass the time. Turned out the book was set in the era of the Russian Revolution and was packed with information about that period, so Teresa enjoyed the story—and the history lesson. She began reading Maeve Binchy books that gave her a glimpse of Irish families, and the Dick Francis works that taught her about horse racing. Cecelia became enamored of those books, too, after being furnished with them by Teresa.

This particular night, Cecelia was reading one of the Francis books when the phone rang in her bedroom residence.

"Cecelia," said the voice. "This is Jalilla al Zabi, the doctor who made arrangements for your niece to go to Manila. I met you when you came to the nail salon that day and got your mobile number, remember?"

Cecelia indeed had spoken to the physician to thank her for her generosity and also had furnished Jalilla with her phone number.

"Yes," said Cecelia. "How are you?"

"I am fine," said Jalilla. "I want to know about your niece Rowena's son."

Cecelia said that she had received a text message the day before from Rowena's mother. John Michael had undergone surgery for a badly broken leg and was coming along nicely.

"I heard that you selected the doctor," said Cecelia.

"Well, I received an email from Rowena right after she got to Manila and she needed the name of an orthopedic surgeon. I went to medical school in Ireland with several people from India and one is a good orthopedic guy in Manila. So I called him and he went right to the hospital where your nephew was a patient. He did the surgery—and at no cost. I was in Qatar the past few days at a medical seminar and did not have a chance to check on the outcome. Glad to hear the boy is fine. And how is Rowena holding up?"

"OK, I understand. Our relatives who work at Your Nails said Rowena called the manager and said she was coming back next week. I thought for sure she would not return as she cannot stand her job or her living conditions. But things are bad in the job market at home and Rowena is the type who finishes things and she probably wants to complete her contract."

"Amazing," said Jalilla. "I am amazed at the resilience of the Filipino women I have met."

Cecelia thanked her profusely for all of her help.

"And, by the way, how are you doing?" the doctor asked Cecelia.

"Oh, I am always fine but my hands are beginning to hurt me a bit. That worries me as I surely need them for my type of work."

"Did you see a doctor?" asked Jalilla.

"I am thinking about it."

"Don't think," said the doctor. "Just do it. You need to use those hands in your work."

"Well, we try to avoid doctors," said Cecelia. "All of us here. We have no insurance. I often wonder how we can have jobs and no health insurance."

"Look, I will talk to you about it when I see you."

"See me?" said Cecelia.

"I heard you are the best hair cutter in town so I booked an appointment for Tuesday."

Cecelia was puzzled.

"And who told you that?"

"Sheikha Zainab. Her mother is a friend of the family."

"Who is Sheikha Zainab?" asked Cecelia.

"You know her. Sheik Jassim's wife. They just got married. Unbelievable wedding. She said you came over to her palace and cut her hair. Now she is a trendsetter, it seems. So I want to get with the trend. You can cut my hair. See you Tuesday."

*   *   *

Senior exercise class at the Ladies Club took place in a long room with a wood floor and a mirror extending the length of one wall. The instructor, a lean British woman who probably was in her late 50s, used a microphone attached to a head set to bark out the orders for participants to march in place or move their limbs a certain way or lift small weights for strength training. She spoke in English, what she told the women was the "universal" language because "it is the only one I know."

As Helen Walker followed orders to take big steps to the left or right and then march ahead while pumping her arms, she thought how interesting it is that people from all over Europe and the Middle East speak English as well as their native languages, while most Americans she knew spoke only English. If she were back in the newspaper game, Helen might write about that disparity.

The exercise class was filled with interesting women—at least five were ambassadors' wives, mostly from Europe, and several were executives' wives from other Gulf countries like Qatar and Bahrain. A few were natives of India, including one who, according to Farah and Amna, was a doctor who owned a number of clinics and pharmacies in Abu Dhabi.

Like Helen, most of those in the class designed for women 55 and over were actually in their late 50s. In the U.S., a senior class of this type might be filled with women in their 70s and even 80s, but in Abu Dhabi, if you were 50, you often were considered old. Farah, for example, was a mother at 16 and a grandmother before she was 40. By age 50, she had put in the "old" ranks by her grandchildren. But things were changing as she and Amna and others their age moved to a healthier lifestyle.

Helen Walker also had noticed that she never saw truly elderly expatriates in the Emirates. She learned through her husband that foreigners need to be sponsored by employers and when workers hit a certain age, 60 or 65, they would be forced to retire. They thus would lose their sponsorships and be forced to exit the UAE and return to their respective countries. As she thought about these things while she was in the exercise class, Helen failed to follow the instructor's directions and went left instead of right and bumped into Farah. The two started laughing as Farah said: "Don't you speak English, Helen?"

Later, at the gym's coffee shop, Helen said she wondered why one sees so few truly elderly people in the UAE.

"Well," said Farah, "as you mentioned, expats cannot really retire here because they lose their visas. As for our people, many did not survive the harsh desert climate so we don't have many people in their late 80s and 90s like you see in the West.

"In days past, women did not live that long here; the lifespan of a woman in the 1960s was something like 45, I understand. Amna and I had friends who died giving birth. They were having babies every year and they were teenagers, as we were, too. It was awful. And many babies did not survive."

"Including ours," said Amna as she shook her head. "Farah and I both lost children. One of my babies lived for a few hours and Farah, one of your babies lived how long?"

"Six months. Maytha. One of my twin girls. The other one, Fatima, lives in Canada. Her husband is with our embassy there."

Helen hesitated before saying: "You both lost children?"

Amna said it was common, "that just about every woman our age lost children. Some at birth and some later in accidents or because of illnesses or whatever. Not like in America."

Helen bit her lip but said nothing.

*   *   *

Dr. Teresa sat down with Sheikha Asma to see how plans were going for the public speaking contest.

"The academic vice president said hardly anything when I told her the topic," said Asma. "She looked at me with a blank stare and asked me whose idea it was. I said the Student Council—we are running the competition. I said that you, Dr. Teresa, would help us only if we need it. So she said OK."

Asma had scheduled the finals in two weeks and sent out emails to all students about how they could enter.

"They have to sign up at the Student Council office for the preliminaries. The best 10 make it to the finals. We had several students come in this morning and sign up. I heard one say that her family wanted her to quit college and marry a cousin from Ruwais. She said she would win this contest because she was not going to marry the 'stupid' guy and was going to say just that in her speech. I doubt she will win anything because she is just angry and that is not good for a speech."

"You must have learned something in my class," said Teresa, acknowledging that Asma had given one of the most memorable and powerful talks in her speech class when she spoke about dealing with one of the family's cooks who had lost her family in a tsunami.

Another entrant, according to Asma, is a student who wears the niqab so only her eyes are visible and the rest of her face is covered.

"I don't know how we will even be able to hear her, but you never know," said Asma.

Dr. Teresa learned that Mona al Shari's father had given 20,000 dirhams to sponsor the contest and half would go to prizes for the best three speakers. Other monies would be used for flowers for the stage, videotaping of the event, food to be served buffet-style after the contest, and incidentals.

"I arranged for flyers to be printed about the competition and they should be ready tomorrow," said Asma. "The deadline is Thursday to sign up for the preliminaries and I expect maybe 20 to do so."

Dr. Teresa wondered what Sheikha Asma would say about choosing a spouse if her family allowed her to compete.

"In your family, you are expected to marry a cousin or the son of a ruler of one of the other emirates, correct?' asked Teresa.

"Yes, that is what is expected for me, it seems. But my brothers can marry anyone. My grandfather had several wives including a cousin, a woman from a Dubai business family, and a Lebanese woman. I heard he had a wife in Pakistan, too. But publicly they would never name the foreign wives. Their children would be known as the ones from the Pakistani mother or the Lebanese mother. My grandfather had all of his sons living with him after they got to about age 12. His daughters stayed with their mothers. I am happy to say my father has one wife—my mother."

"And your uncles?"

"Oh, a couple of them have two wives. You know I have several sheikha cousins at WU. Well, two of them are sisters. Both first-year students. But they are not twins. They were born six months apart. They have different mothers. They really are half-sisters but we don't really use that term. If you have the same father as another girl, she is your sister."

Dr. Teresa pressed the point: "Well, do you think you will be told to marry a cousin?"

"Frankly," said Asma, "I think I would rather be single than marry one of my cousins and maybe have kids with genetic disorders like many people have, including a few of my relatives. Or I would like to live overseas and maybe meet a nice Muslim man there. Not someone from a royal family but just a great guy."

"Oh," said Dr. Teresa, "and what would your family say if a sheikha went to another country and met a future husband there?"

"That is an interesting question, Dr. Teresa. That is something my family may be dealing with real soon."

*   *   *

CHAPTER 7

Judith Shanley al Bader walked into the Al Koba Academy gymnasium. From the bleachers on the other side, she saw a group of Emirati women, dressed in their shaylas and abayas, waving her over to them.

"Any cookies today?" asked one of the women.

"Yes," said Judith. "I got all your emails threatening to ostracize me if I failed to bring some cookies."

"Ostra-what?" asked one woman. "I don't even know what that means. Never learned that in my English class at the Women's Center. I said you better bring cookies or we would not let you in the gym."

The previous week, before another high school basketball game, Judith had brought large chocolate-chip cookies that were devoured in minutes by the players' mothers. Judith had baked them herself, and that astounded some of these Emirati women whose time in the kitchen extended mostly to discussing the day's menus with their household staffers.

"And I brought copies of the recipe," said Judith as she handed them out with cookies to the ladies.

"I love Judith's cookies," said Sabeen Gerami al Shari as she arrived to join the group. "I have been eating them for years, ever since I baked them with Judith in America."

"You have been to America together?" asked one of the Emirati mothers.

As they all munched on the delicious offerings while awaiting the start of the game, the women listened to Sabeen's story:

"I am Syrian, as you know, and I do not wear the abaya and shayla. I could but I really never have worn a head covering. Same as my mother and sisters. I grew up in Damascus but many of my relatives moved to America—mostly to New Jersey. When I was 20, we went to my aunt's home there for the holidays. Well, my cousin came home for a big dinner one night that week, and he brought his friend from the University of Pennsylvania. The friend was Nasser al Shari from Abu Dhabi. He was so polite and handsome and I wished he were Syrian. I remember he said he was one of a number of Abu Dhabi guys at UPenn and mentioned that one of them had just married a Catholic girl who also went there. I said: 'What did his family think about that?' and he said that the guy's mother and a sister came to Philadelphia for the wedding and they did not seem upset.

"Well, the next day my cousin called my aunt and said Nasser wanted to marry me. Just like that. I was shocked and laughed about it. We left the next day for Syria and I started to get calls a few times a week from him in the U.S. He went back to Abu Dhabi to work in his family's businesses after he graduated, and kept calling me. Then one day, he showed up in Damascus with an engagement ring.

"It's a long story but we got married in Abu Dhabi. His mother, Amna, had a big wedding for me. We flew to the U.S. for a month on our honeymoon. We went to Florida and then New York City. Nasser said he then wanted to visit Tahnoun al Bader, his Abu Dhabi friend who married the Catholic. Tahnoun had stayed in the U. S. for graduate school and he and Judith were living in a home in—where was it, Judith?"

"Devon, a suburb of Philadelphia."

"Yes," said Sabeen. "So we went and visited and stayed for about five or six days. We had so much fun together. Judith was pregnant and all she wanted to do was make big chocolate chip cookies and eat them. So one day, while our husbands were playing golf, that is all we did. We baked and ate and had a good time. Judith's mother stopped by and said she thought we were going a bit overboard as we had baked 25 dozen gigantic cookies that day. Of course, Judith's mom was eating them, too—she was such a great person. I loved your mom, Judith."

The game was about to start and Diab al Bader waved to his mother as he ran onto the court. Sabeen's son, Sultan, a sophomore, also was starting the game in place of an injured senior.

"My goodness," said Sabeen. "I hope he can handle it."

Basketball was a fairly new endeavor in a country where most people had an interest in boats and horses. Over time, though, with an influx of expats, the game became an important part of athletics at private high schools.

Judith and Tahnoun had moved to Abu Dhabi after their daughters, Miriam and Iman, were born a year apart and after Tahnoun had completed his MBA at Penn's prestigious Wharton School. Judith maintained her American style of dress, although she did don an abaya and shayla for a post-funeral visit or other occasion that might merit it. Using the education she acquired at Penn's Annenberg School, she handled public relations work part-time for the Al Bader businesses and became active in some expat reading groups and the golf club. Often she and Tahnoun attended athletic events, including the popular football (soccer) games in the UAE league.

But she never thought she would enter the coaching ranks of any sport until years after her arrival, when she happened upon a bunch of Al Koba seventh and eighth grade boys playing in the gym. They were trying—at least she thought—to play basketball but only the presence of a ball could indicate that they had any knowledge of the game. Her son Mohammed, who was among the group, kept telling the others that they had to pass the ball. But his words were left unheeded, as was his call for them to "dribble." Instead, a boy would grab the basketball and then just run with it down the court and throw it up toward the net. If another player got in his way, he would push him.

Judith could see the frustration on Mohammed's face. He had started to play basketball as a young child in Avalon, and the previous summer had spent two or three hours every evening at the town courts there with his cousins and other friends. He also played pickup ball with his father, Tahnoun, at the basket they had put up behind their Abu Dhabi villa. Mohammed understood how to play the game and what rules to follow.

One of the Al Koba math teachers—an Egyptian who doubled as a physical education instructor— came into the gym to monitor the activity that day. He knew Judith from her role as a board member, and came over to say hello. She said she was stunned at the way they were playing, and he said he had no idea about the rules of the game.

"Your son brought a basketball to school and he is trying to get the others interested," said the teacher. "But it does not seem to be working out."

"Can I help?" asked Judith. "I have played the game—well, the rules were a bit different for girls then—but I am a big Philadelphia 76ers fan and I know a lot about the game."

Thus, Judith became an informal coach for the Al Koba boys. For weeks, she would go to the gym and teach them the fine points of passing and dribbling and blocking shots. She would divide them into teams and let them play until a mistake was made. Then she would blow the whistle, explain the infraction, and get the game going again. Through a friend, she invited an American school in Dubai to send its team to Abu Dhabi and scrimmage against the young Al Koba students. While Al Koba was not victorious, the players learned a lot about the game through the experience.

All was well until the sheik called the headmaster to ask if it were true that the "American Judith" was coaching the Al Koba boys. It turned out that some conservative parent had complained to the school's patron that boys should not be coached by a woman.

The headmaster explained to the sheik that Judith was just helping out since the gym teacher did not know the intricacies of the game and that the boys really loved the sport. But when Judith heard about the inquiries and comments, she decided to forego her informal coaching duties, despite pleas from Nasser Al Shari and a few other fellow board members for her to ignore the sheik. When she insisted that her brief informal coaching career was over, the board voted at one of its meetings to hire a fulltime physical education teacher-coach for the boys' school.

Judith objected, to the surprise of her colleagues.

"No— we should not hire one phys ed teacher. We need two. One for the boys' school and one for the girls' school."

They hired a husband-and-wife team from North Carolina and sports interest zoomed at Al Koba.

Now, as she watched Diab handle the playmaking duties of his team and toss in his fourth three-pointer of the game, she recalled those early days when the boys struggled to learn how to bank a ball off the board or shoot foul shots. They had become seasoned high school players who could initiate good plays and handle defensive moves.

She thought about her older son, Mohammed, and his achievements as a high school basketball star. And that made her think about her late mother.

*   *   *

When Mona arrived on crutches at the university, her friends were curious as to what happened to her.

"Don't ask," said Mona as the young women sat in the cafeteria before classes. "Think big, fat Australian guy."

The puzzled girls turned to Iman al Bader, who had accompanied her friend into the room and was carrying Mona's laptop as well as her own.

"We could use some big, fat guy now to carry these," she said.

Then Iman enlightened the group about the cause of Mona's wrapped left ankle.

"Well, as we do often, Mona and I went to the indoor ski slopes at the mall in Dubai. You all know that Mona here is a true skier, unlike yours truly who goes slowly down the slope. Mona won the ski race in Zermatt when we were there with our families last year. Anyway, there we were enjoying the day and we had gone down about seven or eight times. Then we stopped for coffee and a snack at the café and got back on the chairlift to start again. So I am going down in my usual deliberate way and Mona has taken off at full speed. Then I see this big guy go by me—he must be 110 kg or more."

"Way more," said Mona. "He should be on the Biggest Losers on American TV."

"Anyway," continued Iman, "he is flying down past me and heading toward Mona and it seems as if he has no idea what he is doing."

"True," interrupted Mona. "He had never skied before."

"Then, I watch him stumble and fall, and then crash into Mona," said Iman. "I mean crash. He could have killed her, I swear. Everyone near us stopped as I did and we helped Mona up. She was shaking and crying because of the pain. The fat guy was not hurt and trying to help her but he could not even stand up without skis let alone with them on. The ski patrol brought up the thing they carry people in—I forget what they call it—and took Mona down to First Aid. You could tell it was her ankle and we prayed it was not broken."

Iman said she then called Mona's mother, Sabeen, who insisted that her daughter go to the U.S. Hospital in Dubai, not a public clinic where treatment was free. She wanted the best treatment possible for Mona. So Iman drove her friend there.

"Funny part was—sorry, Mona, but I thought it was funny—the fat guy offered right from the time he crashed into her to pay the medical costs," said Iman. "We said it was not necessary but he gave us his business card. He really seemed to be a decent person. He and his friend, a handsome lean guy by the way, offered to carry Mona to my car. Well, that would land us a few problems, having some foreign men carry the national girl through the mall to the parking lot. So we got a wheelchair and these two guys pushed her to my car. When they saw it was a BMW with a special license plate, they looked at each other. And the fat one said he could see why it was not necessary to pay the bills."

Mona said her mother arrived at the hospital two hours later with Judith, Iman's mother. By that time the X-rays had shown no break in the ankle, but it was severely sprained.

"Sometimes," said Mona, "that is worse, Auntie Judith said. But my mother was happy that it was not broken so they bandaged me up, gave me a prescription and here I am. And this is one sore puppy."

That was another phrase the girls heard from Dr. Teresa. She had slammed her finger accidentally in the car door after arriving one day at school, and when she got to class she showed her reddening finger to the class and said it "was one sore puppy." One of the students got out the thesaurus to check the word and said: "Why do you call your finger a dog?"

Just then, into the cafeteria came Dr. Teresa. She looked at Mona's crutches and said: "Don't tell me it is from skiing. That awful sport."

"Haven't you skied?" asked Sheikha Asma, one of the girls sitting with Mona.

"Yes, my husband loved to ski and I went along for the ride, as they say.

That means I skied but was not too interested but did it because he liked it. I think every time you go down a slope there is a message at the bottom."

"What would that be?" asked Iman.

"It is a sign that says First Aid Station. What other sport has a First Aid Station right there? Heck, they expect you to get hurt. You don't find that on the good old golf course. That is why I like golf."

"Oh, speaking of golf," said Iman. "My aunt is in the first official women's championship on Saturday. Want to go with us to Dubai to see it? My grandmother is renting a big bus and we are all going."

"I would love to go with you, Iman," said Dr. Teresa. "Right now, though, I want to know who is entering the speaking contest."

"I am," said Iman.

"I signed up," said Maitha, the happy, oversized student.

Asma reported that about 18 students had registered in the Student Council office or online by the deadline.

"I have sent them all out emails and said to prepare for the preliminaries next week, so please give me those times, Dr. Teresa."

The professor left to check with her colleagues about their availability to judge the preliminaries.

"Girls, did Dr. Teresa just say something about her husband?" asked Maitha. "I thought she was a single woman."

"She is a widow," said Iman. "My mother told me that. That is all she knows."

*   *   *

Sheikha Mowza was sipping a white mocha latte as she turned on her computer at the offices of CASPER, Inc. in Abu Dhabi. She and her brother, Sheik Ahmed, had named their firm after the friendly ghost who was a popular cartoon figure.

"We want to be understated, like a ghost of a company," said Ahmed, who eschewed the flamboyance of some competing firms.

He and Mowza never mentioned the ghost connection to anyone but a few friends. If someone did ask about the derivation of the name, Ahmed would rattle off words starting with the letters of the company name: Consulting, Acquisitions, Stocks, Promotion, Education and Research. In actuality, CASPER did undertake some of those types of activities as it handled real estate deals, conducted classes on real estate acquisitions, and published research about investing in developments. The firm handled promotion of some of its real estate holdings—apartment complexes, for example—more by personal contact with an elite clientele rather than through splashy newspaper ads or TV commercials.

The staff had grown in a few years from Ahmed, Mowza and two assistants to a team of 20 including specialists in varied areas. The brother and sister owners, both holders of graduate degrees from the London School of Economics, tried to be selective with their hiring and mostly chose top students out of highly-regarded business schools.

Sheikha Mowza's emails on this, her first day back from London, included two informal invitations—one to attend the first meeting of a group of women who wanted to form an association for businesswomen, and another from her niece, Sheikha Asma, who thought her aunt might be interested in attending an upcoming public speaking conference at Women's University. Mowza thought that was a bit odd, since she figured Asma would not be allowed to compete, but when she saw the title of the competition topic—"Choosing a Spouse"—she replied in seconds that she would surely be there to hear what the WU girls had to say.

Sheik Ahmed walked in, wearing the traditional national dress for men— the long white robe over his casual clothes and a checkered head covering called the gutra that was secured by a black rope referred to as an agal. At 34, he was one of the most eligible royals, as well as one of the most handsome in the country. He said he would not get married until he was at least 35, and so his mother and aunts were gearing up to find him a bride as he approached that magic age. Cousins were being mentioned all of the time to him, but he would just ignore the suggestions.

"And how was London this time?" he asked his sister.

"You got my messages, right?" she answered.

While staying in England, Mowza had made contact with a London-based development group seeking monies to build a hotel/office complex in New York. The group had an option to buy prime property near Central Park and needed investors to join in the endeavor. Mowza took along a British consultant who had done previous work for CASPER to a meeting with the key executives of the interested firm. They asked many questions, including what construction company might handle the work, how varied New York permits would be secured, and what expectation the London firm had as to the rental or sale of the apartments and/or the office space in the building. She and the consultant liked the preliminary drawings furnished by a top architectural firm. Moving into the New York real estate development arena had been something that she and Ahmed had discussed, especially as the market there began to decline a bit and purchase prices for land or buildings had become attractive. After nearly five hours of meetings, Mowza assured the attendees that she would return to Abu Dhabi and discuss the potential investment with her brother. One of the gentlemen asked if she and her brother would be able to get the approval for investing from other members of the ruling family.

"Why would we need that?" she answered. "We have our own company."

"Well," said the gentleman, "we assumed that women need to get permission from the men to make decisions."

Mowza tried to be calm as she addressed the group of men.

"You apparently know little about the women of the UAE. We have the highest percentage of women in college in any nation. We have women in our nation's cabinet and others serving as ambassadors. We sheikhas are very much involved in the business sector. My female cousins own schools and film companies and travel agencies and hotels and even race horses. Believe me, we don't need the okay from the males in our families to run our businesses."

Now back in Abu Dhabi, she and Ahmed pondered the viability of joining with the London group in the New York venture. Their consultant had assured them that the British firm was one of the most respected in its field, and Ahmed had called to confirm that with an American investment banker with whom the sheik had roomed in college in Washington. If CASPER did provide upfront investment funds, the firm would be the lead investor in the New York project and Ahmed and Mowza agreed that they would have to open a Manhattan office with a few staffers to be on hand as the project moved forward.

"Let me call my buddy Rob again and see if anyone he knows could open an office there for us," said Ahmed. "We better do that before we make a decision on this big investment. It is too early to call New York now so I will do so this afternoon."

"Hassan lived in New York. Maybe he can help with a name," muttered Mowza to her brother.

"What? Who is Hassan?"

"Oops. He is someone I know in London."

Ahmed was puzzled for all of a minute.

"You mean a guy you KNOW in London. I hope you don't mean in a Biblical sense as the Christians say."

"No, Ahmed. You sound like our nieces Asma and Rahma wanting to know if I am living with this guy."

"So our nieces know that you have a boyfriend in London?"

"Yes," I told them. "But they are good young women and will not tell their mother, our dear older sister Lubna, or our parents."

Ahmed wanted to know about "the guy."

Mowza explained how she had met Hassan and how she had visited his "great" family and how much she truly liked him.

"He is a good Muslim, Ahmed, and he went to London School of Economics, too. He has a great job in energy investment. He worked in New York and that is why I mentioned his name about finding someone over there to start an office. Maybe he knows some good investment people."

"Are you planning to marry this Hassan?" asked Ahmed.

"Maybe. If he asks me."

"Our family might get upset, don't you think?" her brother continued.

Mowza restrained herself from yelling. She was so frustrated by limitations set on the sheikhas when it came to marriage.

"This is the 21ˢᵗ century. We are no longer a desert tribe whose women were married off as kids so they would have men to take care of them when their parents died or whatever. And we should not be told to marry our relatives. That is ridiculous. Some of them never finished college or went to some lamebrain school. And what about those blood disorders some kids get because their parents are relatives? No, we need to marry respectable, educated Muslim guys with ambition, not necessarily with millions in the bank. We have our own money."

Ahmed was smiling at his tall, lean sister as she carried on while waving her arms.

"Okay. I agree. Marry whomever you want. You have my permission, although it might not count in this family."

"Well, Hassan is coming over from London for the Energy Conference next week. He is staying at the new hotel off 30ᵗʰ Street. Will you meet him?"

"Sure," said Ahmed, "and then you can meet my new Jordanian girlfriend who works in Dubai."

"I heard about that from Rahma and Asma," said Mowza.

"Our nieces must have a pipeline to news," said Ahmed.

"It is called Women's University. Their friends have brothers who know everything in Abu Dhabi, including your romance."

One of the office secretaries knocked on the door and walked in with an arrangement of roses.

"For you," she said to Mowza. "Must be from a secret admirer."

Not a secret for long, she thought.

*   *   *

Dr. Jalilla al Zabi was early for her appointment at the hotel hair salon. She checked in with the receptionist and then picked up a copy of an American women's magazine and started to read it. Five pages into the publication, she came upon an ad for bras. It had been blacked out with a marking pen, no doubt the work of censors who did not want photos of half-undressed women ruining the minds of young Muslims.

Jalilla was surprised as she thought that the "censor police," as she and others called them, had more or less proved ineffective. With wealthy Emiratis having TV connections that spanned 200 channels or more, people of all ages could see just about anything they wanted on television. One area where the censors did remain powerful was in determining what books could be banned in the UAE. If a book about the Emirates put the nation in a bad light, that work usually was not allowed to be sold in the country. Announcement of such a ban usually helped book sales, though, as Emiratis would buy those books when they traveled overseas in the summer. Dr. Jalilla even had a national friend who owned an e-reader that she bought in the U.S. and on which she downloaded every book she could not get in Dubai. As for the newspapers in the UAE—it was against the law for them to criticize the government or the ruling family. Jalilla often had been asked to defend that law in arguments with her friends and classmates overseas, and she never had a logical way to defend the rule.

As she perused the American magazine in the hair salon, Dr. Jalilla read a piece by an author who detailed her 10-month odyssey of travelling to meet women who made a difference in their home countries. One woman, who lived in a country near the equator, instituted a program to inform people about the dangers of sitting in the sun. The woman's bout with melanoma, the worst kind of skin cancer and one that can spread easily, had forced her to learn about the disease. She wanted to teach others, and she established a foundation to do that. Another woman focused on helping abused women who had no place to go in her country; she set up shelters where the women and their children could stay. A third set up a foundation to fund start-up craft businesses in an African country.

Jalilla pondered these undertakings until she heard Cecelia say: "Hi. I am ready for you now."

They hugged and proceeded to Cecelia's work area. Cecelia said her niece, Rowena, was due back in Abu Dhabi in a few days and that John Michael was doing fine. She thanked Dr. Jalilla profusely for all of the help.

"Glad to assist," said Jalilla. "I was just thinking that I should be doing more for people, anyway."

"And what is it you want me to do today?" asked Cecelia.

"The new trend cut, like Sheikha Zainab got. I saw her at her mom's house the other day and we all marveled at the great new haircut. The shoulder-length style is so becoming and a lot easier to manage than this long hair down my back. So I want to give it a try."

Cecelia asked again as she wanted to make sure that was what Jalilla wanted. The beautician was not about to cut hair that had been growing for years and then discover that the client did not like it. Jalilla insisted that it was time for the long locks to be shed.

As the veteran haircutter artistically handled the work, others on the staff came over to scrutinize the technique. Jalilla could see how the young staffers looked up to Cecelia and how professional she was in her dealings with them and with her clients. When the cut and shaping were finished, Jalilla became the hit of the salon. Other patrons came over to survey the haircut and all made complimentary remarks about it. As Cecelia walked out to the receptionist's area with the doctor, she ran into the next client, Teresa Wilson.

"Dr. Jalilla, meet Dr. Teresa from Women's University," said Cecelia. "She is my walking library."

Teresa explained that she always brought books from the university for Cecelia to read.

"She is one of the best-read people I know," said Teresa to the physician.

Jalilla called Cecelia a "genius" at new-trend hairdos, too. The doctor paid the bill and then handed Cecelia a large tip.

"Oh, and I have not forgotten about the pain in your hands. I want you to come over to the medical center on Sunday morning. I will be there by 8 and I will take you to a specialist."

"But I don't have insurance," said Cecelia.

"You won't need it. I have just decided to set up a fund to cover the costs of medical appointments for foreign women who need them. You will be number one."

Cecelia thanked her and then walked back to her station with Dr. Teresa in tow.

"You know, I used to be so nervous when an Emirati woman with wasta would make an appointment with me. Now I am really at ease with them. They seem to be more conscious of our situation. Times are changing."

"Yes, they are," agreed Teresa as she thought about the upcoming speaking contest.

*   *   *

Hessa al Bader took off the week before the big golf tourney. She wanted to have a few practice rounds on the course where she would be competing. Judith accompanied her there one day and they found the course to be quite challenging. Hessa was ready to pull out of the championship after having trouble on just about every hole. Judith calmed her down, reminding Hessa that she and the other UAE women competitors were not professionals and no doubt were lucky to score in the 80s on the 72-par course.

Tahnoun volunteered to play a round with Hessa the next day on the course located 100 kilometers away on the road to Dubai. As they drove there, the brother and sister talked about the family.

"If anyone told me a year ago that our mother would be out walking on the Corniche and going to a gym, I would have thought they were crazy," said Tahnoun. "She really is an amazing person. She went to classes to learn English. She even became a better business person than our father."

"Baba was not much of a father, Tahnoun," said Hessa. "He was out every night with his friends. He took on that second wife whom I cannot stand. And look at the trouble he gave you because you wanted to marry Judith."

"He threatened to stop sending me money at Penn," said Tahnoun. "Actually, he did stop. But Umy gave me everything I needed. And I was so happy that she and you came over to Philadelphia for the wedding. Judith's mother was thrilled."

"She was such a nice woman. You had a good mother-in-law. I have memories of the many visits she made to Abu Dhabi over the years."

"And my father-in-law is great. He still beats me in golf."

The talk turned to their brother, Khalid. Tahnoun said he was worried about him.

"Every time I see him, he seems overwhelmed. Not by work at our company but everything he does with the boys. He seems to be the mother and the father."

"Well, the princess—oops, Ayesha is the queen now as that is what the cook and maid call her behind her back—is the epitome of laziness and nastiness rolled into one. I feel so sorry for Khalid and the boys."

"I told him to divorce Ayesha," said Tahnoun.

"You did not," said Hessa.

"Hessa, the guy is going crazy. You think he loves her? No way. He is there for the boys. And he can fight to keep them if a divorce comes."

"Not with her family's money and power," said Hessa. "He'd have to wait until the boys were older to get them and raise them."

"Then maybe a second wife would be good for him," said her brother.

"Sure, let him take after our father and his two wives. That would affect the boys more than it would upset Ayesha."

They turned into the golf club and parked next to a green BMW.

"Ugly color," laughed Hessa. "It looks like the one Tariq from my office owns."

Just then Tariq got out of the car.

"What are you doing here?" she said. "Aren't you also on vacation this week?"

"Exactly, so I came to play golf with you."

A minute later, Jon Chang showed up.

Tahnoun explained that he had played in a men's group with Tariq and Jon the previous Saturday and told them he was planning to play a practice round with his sister before the tournament.

"They wanted to come, too, so here we all are. See, little sis, everyone is pulling for you."

Hessa began to think that her participation in the championship tournament was more important to her family and friends than it was for her. She realized that many people in the UAE were pushing for women to move forward in sports—and in life.

* * *

Mona limped out of the elevator to the second floor of the mall near the university, and walked slowly to the nearby café.

"Over here," said Alia. "And where are your crutches?"

"I sent them back."

"Back where?" asked Essa.

"I sent them back to the hospital in Dubai. I didn't really need them so I had to return them. They were rented. I am not kidding you. After they treated me, they gave me crutches. My mother assumed I would have to buy them. So when she was paying the bill, she asked about the price for the crutches. The nurse said we could not purchase them; they were only for rent. For something like 50 dirhams a day. So my mom paid the fee for 10 days, I think, and off I went. And today we had to send a driver all the way to Dubai to return the darn crutches. I swear, these private hospitals have weird rules."

"Anyway, how is the ankle?" asked Essa.

"Well, it was the size of a basketball but it is down to a tennis ball now. It hurts a bit but who cares. My problem is I cannot ski for awhile. That is like a death sentence for me."

Just then Iman arrived to join the Coffee Klatch group for its latest business proposition meeting. She was excited after talking at length to people in America.

"So I called my aunt last week to ask if she had any ideas about top cake bakers, and she said to call her daughter who just happens to be interning at the public station in Boston. And that is home to several food shows. So I call my cousin, who is our age and just finishing Boston University, and she says that she will speak to the people on the food shows. She calls me back two days later and says that one of the men who has a cooking show said there is a cake-baking show, like those on the Food Channel, out of the public TV station in Philadelphia, of all places. That is where I was born. Anyway, this guy told my cousin that the reality show is based on a cake shop run by two women with a staff of several other bakers. He said it is great show. Then I called my younger brother, Mohammed, a freshman at UPenn in Philadelphia, and asked him if he ever saw the cake show. He said no way did he watch any food show but he would ask his girlfriend about it. Yep, same girl he went to the prom with last year at St. Clement's Prep."

"Whoa. Your brother went to a dance with a girl at a Catholic school?" asked Alia.

"Yes. He graduated from there."

Iman did not want to explain the circumstances of Mohammed's two-year Catholic schooling, but said "it turned out that this girl's mother watches the show all the time and that, when one of their relatives got married, the cake, from that shop on the TV show, was in the form of a hockey rink because the groom plays for the Philadelphia Flyers. Guess it was unbelievable."

"So," asked Mona, "did you get in contact with the cake shop?"

"I called and explained that I was looking for someone to run a cake shop here in Abu Dhabi, but I might as well have used Arabic to speak to the woman who answered the phone—one of the owners, I think. She had never heard of our country or our city and I think she has never been out of South Philadelphia where the cake shop is. South Philly. Home of cheesesteaks."

"You mean they put cheese on your steak?" inquired Essa.

"No…yes…too hard to explain," said Iman. "But my dear aunt, who used to be a nun, believe it or not…"

Alia interrupted her.

"Like Whoopi Goldberg in Nunsense? Your aunt was a nun? She wore that outfit?"

"Yes, like a shayla and abaya for Catholics, but that was ages ago and she has been married for more than 20 years. Anyway, she offered to go down to South Philly—she lives out in the suburbs—and talk to the cake shop people.

"So she drove down there. She explained everything. She knows all about Abu Dhabi because she has been here to visit us several times. My aunt told the two owners that we would pay the airfare and expenses for one or both of them to come over here and speak to us about starting this business. These two women said they are not interested in working here themselves because they are happy with their business and their TV show in America, but they know a number of bakers, including ones on their staff, who might want to work here. So the two women could be consultants. They said they would come here to meet with us. They offered to leave South Philly and let their staff handle the work for several days. Amazing. Oh, and some videos of their TV show are on the Internet. One show features a cake they did for the Fourth of July. That is like our National Day. The cake had fireworks coming out it. Now that was over the top."

Essa said she would make the arrangements for the cake bakers to come to Abu Dhabi.

"Since my family owns a travel agency and a hotel, I can handle it. What about paying for it? I know you all want to do it the right way and not just have my father or someone pay."

Alia pulled out her business plan. Her friends were impressed by the document even before they read their copies.

"I spent a lot of time on this damn thing," said Alia. "Thank goodness, my mother showed me some business plans for her boutiques. I even showed this to my dean in the Business College at WU and he wants to use it for some paper he is writing. I put that off but I was grateful for his kind remarks. He thinks we are on to something. Oh, and he said his wife loves the cake shows on TV back in America."

Her plan explained the proposed project in detail, taking into consideration such things as rent, construction of the space in the building, and varied upfront costs, including marketing.

"Turn to page four," she said. "That should give you the answer as to how the trip for the American bakers will be covered. I put in funds for consultants and these women should fall into that category."

Mona wanted to know how much each of the four girls had to contribute in start-up money.

"Well, I am proposing that we start with 100,000 dirhams each. We should get that money as quickly as possible."

They all agreed that their families would give them enough for the seed money and then further cash when it was needed.

"My grandmother gave me money a few days ago," said Mona. "She and Auntie Farah are excited about this."

"Believe me, that is true," said Iman. "Our grandmothers are excited about everything these days. What a pair."

Mona next reported on her assignment from the last meeting. She indeed had inquired as to the requisite licenses needed for the business venture, and said her father suggested they hire a lawyer to handle all of that. He gave her the name of a female lawyer who had just returned to Abu Dhabi after being educated overseas and who had joined the firm that his companies used on legal matters.

"I phoned her," said Mona. "Her name is Fatima or something like that."

They all laughed. So many UAE girls are named Fatima that Dr. Teresa usually started the first day of the semester with one mandate: "All Fatimas please stand up." At least three girls would rise.

"Well," said Mona, "this lawyer said she would be pleased to help us to make sure that we get all of the licenses we might need."

"What will be the official name of our company?" asked Essa. "TOTE Cakes?"

Mona said the "lawyer thought the papers to start the business should be filed as Taste Of The Emirates but then we could market our products as TOTE Cakes."

Essa's job included finding out about architects and construction needs for the shop and kitchen. She said she had spoken to her father and a few of his associates. They zeroed into the name of an American architectural firm with an office in Dubai. The company specializes in interior architectural work rather than the design of large buildings.

"My father had an architect call me from that firm and he said this sounded like a job for one of the young women in the office. He said she is not only an architect but she loves to bake. He said she is always making desserts and bringing them into the office. Then he connected me to her. Her name is Eileen and she was delighted to hear about our project. Her husband also works for that company and she said they laugh about their wedding cake. They were married in America last year and he wanted a cake that looked like an office building because they are architects. Well, they talked some little bakery shop into giving it a try and the cake sort of fell over a bit. She said everyone was taking pictures of the cake that looked like the leaning Tower of Pisa. She sent me a photo of it the next day." Essa showed the picture to the others and they were amazed, not only at the lopsided cake but by the bride and groom.

"She is beautiful," said Mona.

Essa continued: "I asked Eileen to come down from Dubai and look at the space in my father's building. She is available when we are. And as for construction of the place—her firm has a few companies it deals with in Abu Dhabi but Eileen said we should wait until she looks over the site and gets some preliminary plans."

The Coffee Klatch group, now also calling themselves the TOTE Girls, decided to bring the American bakers over within a week or so, and to set up a meeting with the architect at that time. Mona would continue to work with the lawyer to secure the proper documentation for starting the business.

"And what do we do with the money we need to put in now?" asked Essa. "Where should it be? Alia, can you handle this?"

"I think we have to set up an account at the Corniche West Bank but only one person should have access to it. Otherwise, it might be a problem."

"I vote for you," said Mona.

The others agreed.

Alia gave them two days to give her their initial investment money.

Taste Of The Emirates was on its way to fruition.

*   *   *

CHAPTER 8

Mohammed al Bader called his home in Abu Dhabi from the freshmen dorms at Penn. His mother greeted him with a big "How are things in good old Philly?"

"I just wanted to tell you that I spent the weekend at Grandpop Shanley's house, and he said he is having surgery next week. I asked him what for and he said, 'Oh, nothing much.' He did say that Uncle Joe was going to take him to South Pennsylvania Hospital and he would be in there overnight. Anyway, Mom, I am on my way to class—biology and I love it—and I thought you would want to know about your father. Bye."

Judith Shanley al Bader certainly did want to know, but she prayed this situation did not mirror the one she faced two years before. That was when she was in Avalon and nearing the end of the family's summer vacation there before returning to the UAE. Her parents, whose summer home was a block away from hers in the shore town, had driven back to their main home in Ardmore, outside Philadelphia, because Judith's mom, Anne Shanley, had an appointment for a MRI at South Pennsylvania Hospital. She had not been feeling well and the doctors were mystified so they had booked this short procedure.

The results were back within a day or two, and Judith's father, Jack, called his daughter in Avalon to give the report. It was not good news.

"She has cancer. Liver. God knows how or why. You'd think I would be the one to get it from all that booze."

Jack Shanley did not mean he was an alcoholic. But he and his fellow Irish-American cronies enjoyed lifting a few brews after their twice-a-week golf games at their country club. He also had an extensive cache of costly wines in a climate-controlled room in the Ardmore house basement.

Judith was stunned by the news about her mother.

"Mom? The active golfer and tennis player? The health nut? How would she get something like this?"

The doctors had told her father that they always were baffled when health-conscious people were hit with such diseases.

"Where is Mom now?" asked Judith.

"At the club, having lunch with some friends. I doubt if she will mention it to them. She is taking it all better than I am."

"Did the doctors say they will operate or something?" asked Judith.

"No. The word they used was inoperable. They told me privately that it was advanced and I got the impression, although they would never say it, that this would be hard to beat. So I called my golf buddy, Charlie Warren. He is on the staff at South Penn Hospital as a general practitioner. He spoke to her doctors and got to check the records and he as much as told me—he was upfront about it because I wanted to know— that people with this stage of liver cancer might make it six months or so. He said I could check it out on the Internet because there is so much information."

Judith started to cry and said: "I'm coming to Ardmore, and I am staying there."

Judith drove to her hometown and sat down with her 66-year-old attractive, red-haired mother and discussed the situation. Anne Shanley was well aware of the battle she would be raging against the insidious disease in the months ahead, and yet she seemed resigned to the outcome. Judith gave credit for that to her mother's extraordinary faith; she went to Mass every morning and regularly distributed Communion as a Eucharistic minister at St. Michael's Church.

Judith made it clear that she wanted to stay in the U.S. to help her parents as they dealt with the situation. She did not want to be half a world away on the Arabian Peninsula while her siblings and father took on all of the responsibility. Tahnoun agreed with her and said he would take the children back to Abu Dhabi. Judith acknowledged that the girls, Miriam and Iman, had to return to Women's University, but wondered if she might keep the boys and they could all stay in the Shanleys' large home. Anne Shanley herself promoted the idea as she wanted a family atmosphere during the trying times ahead.

That meant that Judith had to find a private school in a week for Mohammed, who would be entering his junior year of high school, and Diab, who would be a freshman. Most private schools either were over-enrolled already or had required entrance tests administered the previous spring. But Judith's sister, Mary, the ex-nun, phoned the principal of St. Clement's Prep, a coed private Catholic school, and convinced the priest that the Al Bader boys were well-versed in English and had been educated all their lives at a private academy. Mary also mentioned that the school's lackluster varsity basketball team might use Mohammed's talents, noting that he held the one-year scoring record at Al Koba Academy in Abu Dhabi. She did not reveal that Al Koba only had a varsity team for two years.

So Judith and the boys stayed in America.

Anne Shanley exhibited a tireless spirit in her battle as she underwent a regimen of treatments and took a score of medicines. She continued to be as active as possible, playing bridge with her close friends and going to an occasional movie with her daughters. Mohammed and Diab spent hours playing Monopoly and Scrabble with their maternal grandmother and relating their experiences as the first Muslims to take the required religion classes at the Catholic prep school.

Anne was thrilled when Mohammed announced he would be starting for the varsity basketball team and she persuaded Judith and Jack to take her to her grandson's first game. She literally led the cheers as the tall, lanky boy, called Mo by his teammates, scored 30 points as St. Clem's Tigers outdueled a team picked to win the league title. Though her body was weakening, Anne continued to go to as many games as she could, even arriving in a wheelchair as the Tigers took to the floor in the finals of the city private schools' championship. The team lost but Mo was applauded loudly as it was announced halfway through the final period that he had broken the one-year scoring record for St. Clement's.

A month later, after several days in hospice care, Anne lost her battle. Tahnoun brought Miriam and Iman from Abu Dhabi for the funeral; they had also visited a few months before at Christmas so the entire Shanley clan could be together. Farah also came for the funeral. She said that, if anyone had ever told her back in the desert days that she would wind up sharing grandchildren with an Irish-American woman, she would have thought the person was mentally unsound. Yet she grew to love Anne and enjoyed being with her whenever Judith's mother came to Abu Dhabi or when Farah took a trip one year to Avalon. At the funeral Mass, Farah and her son, Tahnoun, joined in reciting an Arabic poem in honor of Anne, and the pastor noted that "this is the first time we have been honored to have Muslims participate in our Mass and we thank you."

Mohammed and Diab finished the year at St. Clement's Prep and then headed to Avalon for the usual summer vacation with the family. The plan was for them to go back to Al Koba Academy in the fall. But the St. Clement's coach and a number of parents of basketball team players begged Judith and Tahnoun to let Mohammed return for senior year as the team captain. They wanted Diab to stay, too, as he had emerged as a potential varsity star after leading the freshman team to a winning season. In the end, the Al Baders decided to allow Mohammed to live with his grandfather for a year and finish high school at St. Clem's, but Diab returned to Abu Dhabi and Al Koba.

Mohammed had a stellar senior season on the court for St. Clement's until he broke his wrist when he fell into the bleachers while trying to retrieve an errant pass. Still, he received several offers to play collegiate basketball but decided to follow his parents to UPenn and an Ivy League education. Watching his grandmother die and seeing how doctors worked hard in trying to save her, Mohammed had decided that he wanted to become a physician and thus would limit his competitive sports participation to intramurals.

Now, after learning from Mohammed's phone call about her father's pending surgery, Judith dialed her sister Mary's home.

"Mohammed said Dad is having surgery. What is going on? Do I need to come to Ardmore again?"

"Not unless you are into listening to a 69-year-old man describe his hemorrhoid operation," said Mary.

"Oh, my God, he has been talking about those for years. He drove Mom nuts. Thank goodness I do not have to fly over for this one. I never thought I would smile at the thought of hemorrhoids. I will make sure Mohammed knows so he won't be worried. I will tell him to visit—of course, after listening to Dad and his blathering about hemorrhoids, Mohammed may bag his plans to be a doctor."

*   *   *

Farah walked outside her villa to speak to the driver of the bus she had rented to take friends and relatives to the golf tournament.

"I want to bring some food and drinks," she said, "and wondered where I should put them."

"Ever seen a bus like this?" asked the driver, a well-dressed Pakistani, as she walked into the vehicle.

"Frankly, the only time I ever go on a bus is when we take tours, like in Istanbul and Athens," said Farah. "We always have drivers or my children or grandchildren drive me in their cars."

The interior of the lengthy bus was akin to what one might consider a party bus in America. Plush seats lined the sides of the bus so passengers faced each other. Each seat had a small tray, attached to the side that could be pulled up in front of the passenger. In the back of was a bathroom; Farah had insisted on this feature as she knew it was important for her guests to wash their hands before they ate. The bus also had a small round table and refrigerator behind the area where the bus driver sat.

"Looks great," said Farah. "I will send the cook and maid out with some food."

Just then a car pulled up and an American woman, dressed in a colorful golf outfit, got out. Farah did not recognize her and walked over to meet her.

"I am Dr. Teresa Wilson from Women's University. Iman al Bader invited me to go to the golf tournament. Am I at the right place?"

"Oh, yes, I am her grandmother, Farah al Matari. Iman talks about you all the time. She says you are the best professor and the most fun of all. She is going to be in the speaking contest, right? Everyone is into competition in my family these days. Iman will be here with her family any minute now."

'Well," said Teresa, "Iman and her friend Mona are always telling us about their grandmothers."

"Oh, Amna and me. We are having so much fun these days. We spent years just being at home and being waited on. It was so different from our childhood days. Now we are going to the gym and walking all over and meeting new people. And even going to a golf course today."

Then Farah heard a voice cry out: "We are here right on time, Grandma. Seven o'clock in the morning. And we could use some coffee."

It was Mariam, driving through the villa's gates. With her in the car were her mom, Judith; sister, Iman, and brother, Diab. Her father, Tahnoun, had left an hour earlier with Hessa so his younger sister would have time to practice before the tournament round. They had a driver take them to the golf course so they could return with the others on the bus.

Judith opened the trunk of her daughter's car and took out a number of light folding chairs.

"We might need these to carry around the course unless they let us follow in carts," she said as she handed them to the driver to put in the extensive luggage space at the bottom of the bus.

Farah's maids started to bring out trays of rolls and breads, as well as juices and carafes of coffee. They even had a large tray of chocolates and other candies.

Helen Walker walked through the villa's gates.

"We parked on the street," she said as she introduced her husband, Kirk Walker, to Farah. "Kirk and I are excited to see this. We read today in the paper that nine national women will compete."

Mona's BMW pulled into the circular driveway. Out got her grandmother, Amna, and her parents, Sabeen and Nasser al Shari.

Nasser greeted Farah by remarking: "It's a new day in the UAE. Tahnoun is so excited about this. And so am I. And who knows? Maybe Al Koba will have a girls' golf team someday."

"After they start a boys' team," said Diab as they all laughed.

A rather colorful car was next onto the property. Two men got out and the driver walked over to the assembled group.

"I am Hessa's colleague, Tariq al Shamhi, and this is Jon Chang. We play golf with Hessa at the club. In fact, we played a practice round with her and Tahnoun last week."

Farah greeted them: "I was expecting you. I have a list of everyone from Hessa. Thanks for coming."

Tariq went back to his car and brought out a large bag.

"The bank sent these. Golf visors and baseball caps with the name of Najda Bank. Like in the pro tournaments. Hessa can have a sponsor."

Diab grabbed a baseball cap and put it on.

"I love baseball hats," he said. "When I lived in America, I always wore a Phillies cap."

"Well, I am a diehard Yankees fan," said Teresa. "I have a Yankees hat in my car."

Kirk Walker laughed and said: "Helen and I love the Yankees, too. You must be a New Yorker."

"Well, New York City for years after growing up in North Jersey. I no longer have a place in the city. I kept our home down at Spring Lake on the Jersey shore after my husband died. That is where I live when I go back to the States."

Everyone took a hat or visor and put them on, even the national women who placed them over their shaylas.

Farah looked at her watch and said it was time to go.

"But where is Khalid?"

"Oh, Uncle Khalid just sent me a text," said Mariam. "They are coming now. They were waiting for Aunt Ayesha to get ready."

"Ayesha is coming? Did he really say that?" asked Farah.

At that moment, Khalid's Land Rover entered through the gates. Out got his three sons—and their mother. Ayesha was dressed in her abaya and shayla, like the others, but instead of slacks or jeans underneath, you could see her long, colorful dress as she walked. And she wore sandals while the others had on sneakers or tennis shoes or golf shoes to navigate the golf course terrain.

"So glad to see you, Ayesha," said her surprised mother-in-law.

"Me, too," said Amna, knowing full well that her friend, Farah, must be in a bit of shock after her regular descriptions of Ayesha being one to avoid family functions.

They were all about to board the fancy bus when Farah said: "Oh, we have one more person. A surprise."

Out of the villa came a lovely black-haired woman who said, "I have not worn an abaya in awhile. I just stole this from Hessa's closet."

It was Farah's daughter, Fatima, who had flown in the night before from Toronto. She had stayed overnight at a hotel so as to avoid seeing Hessa, and had arrived at her mother's villa after Hessa and Tahnoun had left for the golf course.

All the relatives hugged her and she said: "I hope my surprise does not affect Hessa's golf. But now all three of her siblings will be there to see her compete."

Farah looked at the small entourage and said: "Look, we just hope Hessa does well. She will be thrilled to see all of her supporters."

The day proved to be fun and enlightening for Dr. Teresa, who described it in another of her popular email newsletters:

What an interesting experience for me. I was invited by Iman al Bader, one of my students, to see the first major championship for Emirati women golfers. Iman's aunt, Hessa al Bader, who is in her late 30s, played in the one-day tournament that was at a beautiful golf club on the way to Dubai. Now golf is not popular with national women because they have to keep just about everything but their faces covered, and because it is known as a men's game. Seems that Hessa took up the game because Iman's mother, Judith, an American, took her sister-in-law to a course in Avalon one summer and Hessa loved the game. Yes, Iman's parents and a lot of her American relatives have homes in Avalon, about an hour south of my beloved Spring Lake.

A whole crowd of us boarded a fancy bus rented by Iman's grandmother, Farah. This looked like a bus for a rock star with velvet seats and individual trays. There were two or three TVs and Iman's young cousins were watching American cartoons. Iman said that her grandmother usually would have brought a maid or two along as they do to just about everything but her grandmother said she is capable of serving the food herself—and that is what she did. She came around to all of us and offered us food and coffee and juice. Her friend, Amna, whose granddaughter Mona also is my student, helped out. I sat next to Kirk Walker from Long Island. He is here with a law firm or oil company; I cannot remember. His wife, Helen, was sitting in the front with Farah and Amna. Helen, he said, takes an exercise class with them and now they have become friends. He mentioned that Helen plays golf, but has not gotten into it here since they arrived several months ago, and that she was a columnist at one time and he hoped she would go back to writing, maybe penning articles about the UAE.

Only nine women were in the one-day tournament and Iman said her aunt was surprised that there were even that many national women who played golf and were willing to play in a tournament. Hessa knew four or five others from Abu Dhabi and Dubai but that was all. Turned out that her competitors included two recent college grads—Dubai sisters who went to Arizona State, I think, and learned to play there.

Then there was a woman, maybe in her late 40s, from Sharjah, one of the seven emirates that make up the UAE. From what Farah said when she heard the woman's last name, this golfer is from an important family. Apparently this woman, whose name or nickname is Lori, has lived in London practically her whole life since her mother, a Brit, is one of several wives of a wealthy businessman. Lori is a UAE citizen by virtue of her father's nationality so she was eligible for this tournament.

I was introduced to Hessa before the tournament. She could not believe that all of us were wearing hats monogrammed with the words Najda Bank—that is where she works and her colleague, Tariq, supplied us with them. It is funny to see the Emirati women and girls wearing hats over their shaylas.

Besides those of us who came on the bus, a few other Najda employees showed up, all wearing the bank hats. Hessa was amazed at the number of supporters, but she got a real shock when she saw her sister, Fatima, a diplomat's wife who flew in from Toronto. Hessa looked a bit surprised, too, when she saw one of her sisters-in-law, not Iman's American mother, Judith, but her brother Khalid's wife, Ayesha. From what I could gather, all of them were surprised that this Ayesha had come along to the tourney.

The golfers went off in three threesomes, with Hessa in the middle group. I was impressed when she launched her first drive about 200 yards straight down the middle. I never hit that far in my life (except that one time in a Husband and Wife event when I hit the ball into a big oak tree and it took off another 100 yards down the course. Ray said it must have been blessed by the Pope. That is what I get for marrying a Catholic).

I have never played on this particular course, but it seems pretty difficult. Many of us were able to take carts to follow the golfers around as the rest of the course was closed for this small but important tournament. Those who could not get carts after they all were taken just stayed put on a hole and watched the groups come through, and then moved with their folding chairs to another spot under a palm tree. Remember this is a HOT country, and everyone takes carts. Hessa was driving one and Tariq, a coworker of hers, was riding along as a passenger and serving as her caddie.

Hessa made par on the first three holes but then, on the fourth hole, she hit her second shot into a small lake. She wound up with a triple bogey and she seemed down and out about it. The good news was that the other two playing in her group also hit into the water. One player—she is one of the sisters who went to school in Arizona— started issuing some curse words. I was in the cart with Farah, and she said that if "my daughter starts saying things like that, I will pull her right off this course." I like Farah; she is only a few years older than I am and she has been through a lot, I assume, because she was born when people lived in tents and palm huts and now she is really wealthy. Yeah for the oil money!

Hessa got back in the swing of things on the par-3 seventh hole. She was going to use a hybrid to tee off and Tariq switched her to the four-iron. Her shot landed about 12 feet from the hole and she putted in for a birdie. That brought cheers from the Najda hat group. By the way, Hessa was wearing long pants and a shirt, as well as a hijab—a tightly-fitted head covering with her face fully exposed. And on top of her head? One of the bank hats she got from her colleagues. I assumed all of the players would be dressed like Hessa, but Lori was wearing Capri pants and no head covering at all. The Arizona-educated sisters sported lightweight trousers and ASU baseball caps.

Iman's brother, Diab, a high schooler, was driving back and forth between the three golf groups and checking on his aunt's competitors. She was holding her own with most, but Lori, the Brit-Emirati woman, was three strokes ahead of everyone at one point. Hessa finished out the front nine with a par and wound up with a 41—five over par. She was in second place, two behind Lori, who bogeyed the ninth after missing a short putt, according to Diab.

The next nine holes would be played starting at 1 p.m., so we all headed to the clubhouse for lunch. Ayesha was using her mobile phone (they are banned on the course itself) and Iman said her aunt probably wanted to call the maid and demand she do something "like clean the backs of the artwork on the walls. She dreams up stuff just to order the maids and cooks around. But they love my uncle so they just go along with whatever she says."

Hessa's two brothers, who run Al Bader Enterprises, had arranged for a private room for their sister's support group, and we had a sumptuous buffet. Tahnoun told Hessa that she now had two sponsors—the bank and the family company.

Everyone looked a bit amazed when Ayesha said she had just spoken to her mother, Nama, who lives in Jumeriah, an upscale Dubai neighborhood less than 15 minutes from the course.

"She should be here any minute. The driver is a bit lost, but she wants to see the rest of the tournament."

The Al Bader boys were happy to hear their other grandmother was arriving, as was Farah, who said she always liked Ayesha's mother, Nama. Not 10 minutes later, Nama was eating lunch with her daughter and grandsons, and listening to everyone describe Hessa's every shot. Diab told Hessa and the others that the "British lady," as he called Lori, "is vulnerable."

Hessa reminded her nephew that Lori was competing because she is a legitimate Emirati.

"Only half," he said.

"Yeah, like you," said his father, Tahnoun, as they all burst into laughter.

"She is still vulnerable. Remember that, Aunt Hessa."

Iman told her aunt to "go for broke." When she said that, Iman looked over at me. I had taught her that phrase—and many others that the girls use constantly to baffle their friends and families.

I must say that I was having a great time in this group. You know, Americans seldom get to mix with Emiratis here. I have met Americans who have been here for four or five years and never once have spoken to a UAE citizen. It is a bit ridiculous, when you think about it. Heck, Iman and her family have a home in Avalon. Diab told me he lived in Pennsylvania for an entire year because his mom, Judith, wanted to be with her dying mother. He went to a Catholic high school there. It really is a small world.

I know you all cannot wait to hear about the rest of the day. Sorry about the lengthy newsletter but when I send a brief one, I get complaints from people who want to know more about my experiences. I should charge subscription rates. And if you are bored, hit Delete.

OK—so the threesomes took off again in the afternoon—and it was REALLY hot at this point of the day. Tahnoun, Khalid and their friend Jon Chang stayed close by Hessa's group and seemed to be enjoying their unofficial cheerleading duties. Kirk Walker went along with them; it turns out that he was a club champ for years in Long Island. I rode this time in a cart with Helen Walker, and we would try to figure out what club Hessa would take for each shot. Helen seems to know her golf; I told her that her spouse had told me she had been a columnist and wondered if she had covered sports.

"Gosh, no," she said. "I wrote about anything and everything, but not sports."

"For what paper," I asked.

"Many papers," she said but did not elaborate.

Diab was continuing his updates on the other groups as he went back and forth in a cart; his aunt Ayesha was with him for the back nine. She was writing down the scores of each competitor for him and seemed to be actually enjoying her role. They reported that, after the 14th hole, Hessa was still in second place by two strokes to Lori, who was playing in the final threesome. One or two of the players were getting double and triple bogeys on every hole, according to Diab.

"We think Aunt Hessa has one person to worry about," Diab told Helen and me. "And she is the one who is not pure."

Helen and I were startled.

"How can you say she is not pure? You know something about her private life?" asked Helen.

Diab and Ayesha both smiled.

"You are not pure in this society unless both of your parents are Emirati," said Ayesha.

So I was getting an education while enjoying this golf tournament. The 15th hole was another par 3. This time Tariq shook his head at Hessa with her club selection. He handed her a nine-wood. (I love my nine-wood). She put the ball right on the green and, with two good putts, recorded a par on what looked to be one of the toughest par-3s I ever saw. The Al Bader followers once again applauded her good play.

Diab and Ayesha came over to our group as Hessa waited to tee off on the 17th after making another par on the previous hole.

"That Lori missed the green on 15 and got a bogey. Hessa is only one behind," said Diab.

Hessa bogeyed the 17th and got par on the 18th to wind up with 82, 10 over par on the course and a respectable score in this historic amateur event.

The report from the 17th was that Lori bogeyed that hole so the Brit-Emirati approached the 18th still with a one-shot lead over Hessa, who was finished and watching the action with all of us. Lori's drive was fine but her second shot fell 20 yards short of the green. She hit a chip shot beyond the hole and missed the putt coming back, and wound up with a bogey.

So Lori and Hessa were tied at the end of the round.

Everyone was quiet as the officials announced the next step. Hessa al Bader and Lori al Mulli would be in a sudden-death playoff starting on the 18th and then going to the 1st hole if necessary.

I heard Farah ask her grandson, Diab, why they would be playing "death." He explained to his grandmother what that meant and she said: "OK, she will win after one hole."

Diab kept muttering his mantra about Hessa's opponent: "She is vulnerable."

The two women went back to the tee at the 18th and hit their drives as we spectators waited up at the green. Neither player could manage to hit her second shot onto the green, with Lori about 20 yards short in front and Hessa's ball off the green in short rough. Lori chipped to within six or seven feet of the pin and marked her ball. She seemed to be in great shape to make a par although Diab whispered again that "she is vulnerable." He surely is a funny young man!

Hessa looked at her ball and took out what appeared to be a pitching wedge to use to chip on. Then she looked at Tariq and he was removing a five-iron from her bag. Hessa looked baffled. She took a few practice strokes just as if she were holding her putter. Then she got into position, and with the five-iron, putted the ball over the bit of rough, and onto the green. It landed two inches from the cup. We cheered as Hessa went over and knocked it in for par. She knew that, at worst, she had done well enough to continue on in the sudden-death play.

Everything got quiet as Lori took two practice strokes and hit the putt to get a par herself and continue the playoff. The ball looked good but then veered to the left and just a bit past the hole. She had failed to match Hessa's par.

You would have thought we were at the finals of the U.S. Open, where I have been three times. We were tossing our bank hats in the air and everyone was hugging the UAE women's champion.

Hessa walked over to Tariq and gave him a hug.

"I know, Mom," she said to Farah, "that you might not like me to hug a man who is not related to us but Tariq al Shamhi won this for me today. Not only did he help me along the way but I never would have used a five-iron to chip out of the rough on the extra hole."

Tariq moved his arms back and forth as if he were putting.

"Use a five-iron like a putter because it goes up in air a bit and lands on the green. And then goes straight where you aim. Always a five-iron now, Hessa."

Then they had a ceremony and presented Hessa with a gigantic crystal bowl. Photographers were all over the place. Hessa asked the one from the largest English-language daily if he would take a photo of her and her family members and friends. Everyone lined up and the guy snapped a few photos.

That explains why today's front page has a color picture of all of us with the national champ. Right in front is Farah, dressed in her abaya and a shayla that covered part of her hair. Just several years ago, she said, she would have been wearing the gold burqua on her face and would never be photographed in public.

"It's a new day in our country," she said. "I am getting my picture taken—see my face—and I have a champion daughter."

We had a lot of fun on the bus on the way back, making Hessa give a speech and having her brothers and Mona's dad, Nasser al Shari, sing some funny Arabic songs—well, I guess they were funny because there was a lot of laughing and clapping. Even Ayesha seemed to be enjoying herself. I heard Farah quietly tell her that "I spoke to your mother and am glad you are going to that doctor person." I have no idea what that meant.

We were back at Farah's by 6 and found the walls around the house decorated with lots of balloons and UAE flags.

"Who did that?" asked Farah. "Not me."

It turned out that, as soon as Hessa won, her niece Iman texted her friend Asma—she is a sheikha from the royal family and is not allowed to go to these public events—and Asma arranged (she can do that) to have balloons delivered within an hour to Farah's. Asma and her sister Rahma came over and put them all over the walls along with many UAE flags. They were just leaving when we arrived. I teach them at WU and they are great girls.

We were heading to our cars when Farah waved us all into her home. Courtesy of her household staff, a bountiful feast awaited us. More people arrived—Tariq's teenage daughter and Jon Chang's wife came to join us—and a bunch of other bank employees showed up as well as Essa and Alia, who are two of my WU seniors and close friends of Farah's granddaughter, Iman, and Mona al Shari.

The party went on for hours. I like the fact that they have such fun without alcohol. At one point some deliverymen showed up with a three-layer cake with a real golf ball on top and the words: "Hessa the Champ" on the cake. The card said it was from Sheikha Lubna, who is the mother of the two sheikhas who put up the balloons. Farah said "it is a lovely cake" and then her granddaughter, Iman, and her friends, started crying out things like: "Wait until we start our business. You will see a REALLY outstanding cake." Farah laughed and said she had forgotten where her investment money was going. Apparently, Iman and the other girls are going into the cake business. I have no idea what that is all about but I am sure they will fill me in.

Hessa said at the party that she heard I played golf and that Helen does, too. Her sister-in-law, Judith, the one who got Hessa into golf, suggested we all get together and we agreed we would love to do that. I have been playing at the small golf club in the city but Judith and Hessa belong to the Dhabi Club about five miles away and they said we could join there. Iman and Mariam said they may take up the game that their mother and aunt love; I think this tournament psyched them up. Sabeen, Mona's mother, who is Syrian and, like Judith, does not wear the national garb, revealed that she is already taking lessons. So Hessa said that she just might have her own annual golf tournament for friends and relatives.

It was a great day and another step forward in the lives of Emirati women.

Sorry about the lengthy report. Now I am going to have a glass of Chablis and hit the sack.

*   *   *

CHAPTER 9

Cecelia got up early and took a taxi to New Road Hospital, a tall white structure off Khaleej Al Arabi Street. She inquired at the reception desk as to the offices of Dr. Jalilla al Zabi.

"She is the medical director and does not see patients here," said the receptionist.

"She asked to see me at 8," said Cecelia.

Just then Dr. Jalilla walked through the entrance.

"You beat me here, Cecelia. Come with me."

As they took the elevator to the fourth floor, Jalilla said her new hairdo had generated a lot of comments.

"Compliments, compliments. I got so many compliments the other night at a party at my cousin's house. Thank you, Cecelia."

As they walked into the doctor's impressive office, Jallilla noticed that Cecelia was carrying a book with her.

"Like that professor I met at the salon said, you really are a reader, huh?"

"Always have been," said Cecelia. "I enjoy books and learn from them. This novel is set in West Africa and it is educational as well as interesting. I will finish it tonight. Books take me places I will never get to see. I have three more books to read and then return to Dr. Teresa. She is a great woman. Like you are. I am always telling her about Rowena and my other relatives here. You know what she did for us on Christmas Eve? I only worked for about four hours that day; my bosses are a bit more generous than the ladies who own Your Nails. Rowena normally works seven nights a week and just gets daytime hours off on Fridays. Well, Dr. Teresa gave me a gift certificate for 1500 dirhams at the fancy Italian restaurant, La Spago. The nails place let the girls out at 6 that night—a Christmas gift, I guess—and I took Rowena and a few relatives to the restaurant. We felt really blessed."

"I want to get in touch with Dr. Teresa," said Jalilla. "She might be a good contact to give me ideas about this new foundation I am starting. Can you get me her contact information?"

"I will send it by email," said Cecelia. "I can use the computer at the salon after work today."

"What time do you have to be at the salon this morning?" asked Jalilla.

"In an hour-and-a-half. I have my first client then."

"Well, the coffee is on here—we have a great guy, from Manila by the way, who handles the maintenance on this floor. His name is Frank and he comes in at about 7 and first thing he brews a pot of superb coffee for us in our little coffee room, as we call it. Let's head down there before we see Dr. McAvoy."

They passed Frank in the hallway and Cecelia recognized him from the Filipino Social Club. They spoke for a minute and Cecelia said she was about to drink a cup of his "superb coffee."

"You know," she said to Dr. Jalilla as they began to sip the coffee, "Frank was a teacher in Manila. The private school where he taught burned down and was never reopened. He needed a job and came here. He loves to read, too. We are always talking about books when we see each other on Friday mornings at the Filipino Social Club. But he does not have access to books as I do and he is more into history and science stuff."

Jalilla thought for a moment and said: "I have to do something about this."

The pair then took the elevator up to the sixth floor and walked to a sign announcing "Plastic Surgery." Cecelia wondered what that had to do with her hand as they walked into an office and Jalilla introduced her to Dr. Ben McAvoy.

"Ben, here is Cecelia, the woman I was talking to you about. The best hair stylist in Abu Dhabi."

"Well, I better let Mary know about you," he said, explaining that he and his wife were new to the country and she had asked him to check with Dr. Jalilla about a hair salon.

"Cecelia just cut my hair," Jalilla said, throwing off her shayla. "See. I love it."

She explained that she and Dr. McAvoy, who looked to be in his mid 30s, had worked together in Ireland and "were like family. I convinced him to come to the Gulf."

Dr. McAvoy said he heard that Cecelia was having a problem with her hands, and said that "my specialty is dealing with hands. I do all kinds of plastic surgery but I trained to be a specialist with hand problems."

Cecelia showed him her left hand and said it did not hurt as much as it bothered her because bumps were forming on her palm and they sometimes interfered with her holding things. The doctor moved his fingers over her palm and pointed out how the three or four bumps were aligned almost one after the other.

"What you have is a thickening of the connective tissue under your skin. The nodules show up like a cord. You have them on the hand but they can extend to the fingers."

"Isn't there a name for this?" asked Dr. Jalilla, who said "I am trained as a psychiatrist, Cecelia, so this is a bit out of my area."

Dr. McAvoy said "it is a condition called Dupuytren's contracture—I will write it down, Cecelia—and in a worst-case scenario, your fingers would begin to contract or bend over. Then you would consider surgery because otherwise you could have problems with the functioning of the hand. But since it does not hurt you, we will let it go now but it is important that you exercise it all the time."

"Ben, she does exercise it a lot in her type of work," said Jalilla.

"No, I want her to do some special exercises. With a small rubber ball and some other things. I will get them for her."

Then he asked to see her right hand.

"Thank goodness that is okay," said Cecelia. "I am right-handed."

Dr. McAvoy used his thumb to go carefully over her right palm and said: "Feel this here. You are starting to get a small nodule. So we will keep watching both hands. You will be fine. I will check you again in three months. For right now, go back to work and I will give my wife your name so she can make a hair appointment."

As they left, Cecelia profusely thanked Jalilla for bringing her to Dr. McAvoy.

"He is not only a good doctor, but he is nice and he really is a handsome Irishman," said Cecelia.

"You should see his brother. Ben introduced us when his brother, Bill, stopped to visit at the hospital in Dublin where we were doing our residencies. I fell for Bill the minute I saw him."

"You dated an Irishman?" asked Cecelia.

"Well, yes, I guess you could say that. We spent a lot of time together and it was hard because of my Muslim faith and all that. My family has no idea. Ben and Mary, of course, know all about it and Mary, a lawyer—she is on our legal staff here now—thinks I should tell my relatives and take the consequences. Being a psychiatrist, I may wind up needing my own help."

"Gosh," said Cecelia, "Life is not quite so complicated in my country. I have one son there and his wife is Hindu. We are Catholic. He was 35 before he got married and I did not care what religion the girl was. She seems nice although I don't know her too well. I only get to The Philippines every two years."

"But what about children? What religion would they be?"

"My son said they will raise them in both faiths. Said it would be good for them. Of course, their first child is only 2. They have another on the way. I help them out financially when I can."

"Life is crazy," said Jalilla as she walked Cecelia out of the building and down the street so the beautician could grab a taxi. "I was happy in Ireland; I finished medical school there and spent several more years there in my residency and advanced training. I lived in an apartment alone, not in a villa with servants like here. I was ready to stay there and practice psychiatry but the family kept imploring me to come back to Abu Dhabi. You know, we own this hospital. That is why I am an administrator now. I have a part-time practice, though. I insisted on that. I am going to do this medical director bit for another few months until we get someone good on board. We had a disaster of an administrator from Cairo before and we are looking for a new director now. Then I will work fulltime in my psychiatry practice."

"Why don't you go back to Ireland?" asked Cecelia.

"Or why doesn't Bill come here? He is a doctor, too. An orthopedic surgeon. One of the best. One of the British royals just came to Dublin to have Bill operate on his knee. But Bill does not want to face my family. At least Ben and Mary are here so Bill might come over and visit them and then I could see him."

"You should tell your family and see what happens. Life is too short. And you are a psychiatrist. What would you advise someone in your position to do?"

"You are a smart woman, Cecelia. I will be at the salon on Thursday for a wash and blowout. I have to go to a wedding."

*   *   *

The preliminaries for the first Women's University public speaking contest were about to get underway. Teresa secured the judging services of two of her Communication Department colleagues, known as Dr. Paul and Dr. Gina to the students. Gina was happy to take on the role as she owed Teresa for several favors, including substituting for Gina, a Californian, when she took time off to give her visiting parents a tour of the UAE. Convincing the curmudgeonly Paul was a bit more difficult; he taught film criticism and said the girls did not have a suitable command of English for his classes so why would he listen to them speak in some contest? A bottle of a highly-rated Merlot from Teresa sealed the deal, though.

Sheikha Asma came into Dr. Teresa's office to say that the 18 competitors were ready for the prelims. Asma had given each of them a time when they were to appear before the judges; Dr. Teresa would be with her two colleagues but her vote on picking the 10 finalists would be made only if needed.

Asma also said she had judges for the finals scheduled for the following week.

"The academic VP—she is being supportive but I think she is really nervous about this—got three professors from the Dubai campus. She said that would be good because they don't know any of the girls in the competition. I am getting everything set up for that day, too, including gifts for all of the judges."

One by one the Women's University students presented their preliminary talks before Dr. Paul and Dr. Gina who had rating sheets in front of them as did Teresa in the event she was needed to break a tie or give input as requested. Asma also was invited to sit in and listen; Teresa considered that a precaution. If Asma, Student Council president and a member of the ruling family, thought a speech would create any kind of a fuss, she would be able to alert the judges. They agreed.

The first few speakers talked about how they thought the time had come to let women pick their husbands. Yet they admitted that the best way to find a spouse in the UAE is for parents to seek out a match since most girls are not allowed to socialize with men outside their families. One girl said she thought it was "ridiculous" that a man's female relatives were the ones to select his bride; she argued that relatives of a woman should be able to approach a man's family and ask if he might consider being a bridegroom.

Teresa believed that some of the speakers had strong ideas, but she did not think their oratorical skills were strong enough to merit a move into the finals. Perhaps she was being too critical, she thought. She was happy that these students had the fortitude to enter the contest.

One student detailed the exorbitant cost of her brother's wedding; he married a bride chosen by his family.

"She is a sweet girl from Ajman but she did not want to live here in Abu Dhabi," said the student speaker. "She had told her parents that but they insisted that she marry into our family. The marriage ended a year later but my brother still keeps in touch with her. She is getting married to a man she knows from her job in Dubai. I introduced my brother to my supervisor at my internship, and now they are engaged and go out to dinner all the time. They will get married after they spend time together. That is how it should be."

The girl who wore the niqab looked through the slits that revealed only her eyes and sort of stared at the judges. Teresa figured that is how these covered girls strengthen their communication; she thought it would be a good academic research topic although she had never taught a girl who wore the niqab in class. The student started off with these words: "I am covered because that is what my husband wants. And what he wants is the most important thing to me. I did not wear the niqab until I married my husband when I was 17. I never met him until our wedding. He said that his wife was to be like his mother and he handed me this covering. I have worn it from that day forward. Some women would consider it a burden to marry without knowing their spouses. I was happy that my parents married me to my distant cousin from Shahama. He does not want any other man to see my face. I am honored that he feels like that…..."

When the girl finished her talk and left the room, Paul asked Sheikha Asma if she ever wore the niqab.

"Once," she said, "when we were going through a mall to a cinema. I stumbled and fell. Cut my nose. My mother said I was not to try that again and so I wear the gishwa when I need to cover."

"The what?" asked Dr. Paul.

Asma pulled one out from her purse and put it on for a minute. The thin veil allows the wearer to see through it but it is hard for anyone to see the face of the woman sporting it.

Iman al Bader was next up in the preliminaries. She smiled as she entered the conference room and began by saying: "I am not pure."

Dr. Paul looked startled. In America, the term 'not pure' described a girl who had experienced a sexual relationship.

She continued: "Yes, I am the product of a mixed marriage. A Muslim Emirati father and an Irish-American Catholic mother. Thank goodness they met and married. Repeat: they met, got to know each other, and then married!"

Her talk focused on her argument that all women should be allowed to choose their spouses and know them ahead of time. Dr. Teresa thought Iman had done a credible job. She exhibited strong written and oral skills as did her sister, Mariam, who had been one of Teresa's students the year before.

A few speakers supported arranged marriages because they had faith in their parents to find them good Muslim husbands. One young woman said she did not care how good-looking the intended spouse was, "as long as he is kind. And I think my parents would choose a kind man." Another said she hoped her parents would find a young man who had a college degree as she did not want to marry "someone who does not understand what I have learned here or wants to stop me from a career." A few mentioned that they knew they had a right to say "No" to any marriage proposal but wondered how a woman can reject someone she never has met.

At least two speakers spoke strongly against the UAE's unofficial rule that girls must marry Emiratis while men were not limited to that and often sought foreign brides. "Who will be left for us to marry?" asked one girl as she rattled off the growing numbers of single, educated professional UAE women.

One speaker struggled with English and Teresa wondered what prompted her even to enter the competition.

Maitha arrived with her usual smile on her face. Teresa felt sorry for her, though, because Maitha truly had a problem with obesity. The professor also knew, though, that Maitha had earned A on every speech she had given in Teresa's class. Up to form, Maitha delivered a well-crafted speech centered on her belief that an arranged marriage can be detrimental to a girl's well-being. She cited statistics on divorce and its rising numbers in the UAE, and wondered why anyone, male or female, would want an arranged marriage. She also alluded to abuse, saying that she actually knew women who divorced soon after their honeymoons because they wound up wed to what she called "not-so-nice guys." Teresa thought that Maitha's delivery was top-notch, as usual, and was glad that Maitha did not mention her sister's divorce and subsequent move to Geneva. Who knows what reaction such a personal insertion into a talk might get when the auditorium was filled at the finals, and Maitha no doubt would move on to that level.

One of the final speakers in the preliminaries was a woman who looked older than the average collegian. Indeed she was, as her initial remarks indicated.

"I am 30 years old and have three children. I am divorced. Last week, my former husband took my oldest child, my son, away from me. He said he can do that because my son is 12 and they say that is when a boy can be sent to live with his father. I don't know the exact rules. Now my son calls and cries. He does not want to live with his stepmother and her kids. I am lucky to go to school now. The army sent me. I now work part-time and still get my pay. I have been a secretary at the army base since I finished high school and got married. My dream was to go to college but my parents said I had to marry this man. I won't give his name. He was 40. I was his third wife. All he wanted was the money from the Marriage Fund to marry an Emirati woman. Do you know what it is like to be a teenager and live with an older man already married two times? And you have to work because he has no education and not enough income to support his children? And some women think arranged marriages are fine?"

Teresa and the others were riveted as the student talked quickly to make the seven-limit minute. When she said at the end that "I wish I had been born a sheikha," Asma's eyes turned toward the floor. Then the speaker said, "But even they have to marry cousins they don't want to marry sometimes."

As the judges handed in their scoring sheets, Dr. Gina said she wanted to thank Teresa for this "eye-opening afternoon." Dr. Paul said he was amazed at some of the things he heard, and asked Asma if it were true that sheikhas must marry their cousins.

"Well, I don't think it is a rule but it seems to be expected. Cousins or members of families of rulers in the other emirates. I think it is going to change, though. Sheikhas are remaining single and some are arguing that they should be able to marry a Muslim from another country. I think things may get better..."

Teresa added the scores and said: "OK, nine girls have enough points to move ahead. But we have a tie among two girls for the last spot."

She said that one of the two had better presentation skills than the other and would be a better finals participant. Dr. Paul and Dr. Gina agreed.

It was Asma's job to notify those selected, including Iman, Maitha, the niqab wearer and the divorcee. First, Asma turned on her mobile phone as she left the conference room. There was a text from her aunt, Sheikha Mowza. It read: "Hassan coming to AD next week. Should be interesting."

Asma texted back: "Maybe he should come to the speaking competition."

*   *   *

The headmaster at Al Koba had received no objections from the sheik about internationalizing the student body. The board decided to inform the parents of the current students about the proposed changes before putting a formal announcement in ads in local papers. A number of parents called to object to the school's bid to move from an all-Emirati school to one that enrolled students of all nationalities.

The board members met to discuss the complaints.

"How many calls did you get from fathers of the students?" asked Nasser al Shari.

"Come to think of it, all the calls were from mothers," said the headmaster.

"Yes, because we deal every day in business with foreigners who live here and we would love to see their children come to Al Koba," said Nasser. "I have a few expats working for me whose children would be outstanding students. And I pay the tuition for them now at some other schools. I would rather the money go here."

Judith wanted to know which mothers complained. The headmaster was hesitant to give names, but Judith said, "This is a private school in a country that is not a democracy. The board can even see the students' grades if they want, let alone records of calls to the administration."

The headmaster took out a list. He had received four calls from women of students in the boys' high school.

"I got the impression that they did not want to have their sons lose their spots on the varsity teams to boys from other countries."

"Hey, my son Sultan is a second-year high schooler and he wants to start off next year," said Nasser. "But the coach cannot just hand him a place on the starting lineup because his father is on the board. Let him compete to be a starter. In fact, he will work harder if he knows he has competition from more boys."

Judith smiled, thinking how much she respected and liked Nasser. He and Tahnoun called each other "blood brothers."

"I know all those women who called," said Judith. "Helicopter parents."

"They own helicopters?" asked a board member, a lieutenant general in the UAE Army and an award-winning pilot.

"No, no," laughed Judith. "That is what you call parents who hover over their children. You know, like in a helicopter hovering over something. These parents are on top of everything a child does and they try to make sure that the kids are the best at everything. They complain a lot, too, if the children are not the best. They blame the school. Not the kids."

"I am not a helicopter parent," said the Army officer. "But if you ever want to tour the city in my personal helicopter, I am available."

They all chuckled.

Nasser said the headmaster had written a "wonderful" letter to Al Koba parents to explain the proposed changes.

"Most people I talked to were happy to know that we want the school to move forward and not lose any other nationals to schools with an international student body," said Nasser.

He moved to have the board send letters to the four women who had called and nicely explain that "their complaints had been discussed but that, because of overwhelming support to the contrary, the school would move forward with accepting non-Emirati students."

"Well-stated, Nasser," said Judith. "I second the motion."

After it passed with no objections, Nasser asked if the headmaster got any calls from mothers who thought the change would be good.

"I did get a few. The one who was most effusive in her remarks was a lady who just called yesterday and said she had two boys in the lower school and one in our kindergarten. She did not tell me the last names of the boys; of course, they would have their father's name. I forgot to ask I was so taken by her kind words. She said that it was important for youngsters to get to know those from other countries. She also said that her boys had cousins who were

American, or half-American, and they were all wonderful people. And she offered to help out with any event we have."

"Well, you got her name? Her maiden name?" asked Nasser.

"I wrote it in my notes. Ayesha al Baloud. That is her name."

Nasser about choked. He looked at Judith and said: "Khalid's wife?"

Judith stared at the headmaster.

"She and I are married to the Al Bader brothers. All I can say is: Put me on the committee she joins. I don't want to miss that."

As she and Nasser walked out together, he said "that was one interesting meeting. I am amazed every time I go to one."

"Holy cow," said Judith, "I cannot believe Ayesha called to say something positive and to volunteer to help out at Al Koba. I am still amazed that she came to the golf championship and helped Diab keep up with the scores. Something is going on."

"Maybe she will be a helicopter parent," said Nasser.

"In her case, that might be good," replied Judith. "At least she would pay attention to those lovely little sons of hers. Oh, gosh, I have to call Tahnoun about this one."

"Great. And tell him we are on for Avalon."

"What?" asked Judith.

"Oh, he did not tell you? Well, maybe you won't be so thrilled. We had lunch two days ago and Tahnoun said Sabeen and I should come to Avalon with the kids for a vacation this summer. I mentioned it to Sabeen and Mona and Sultan and they were all for it. Sultan was practically jumping for joy. He wants to play basketball with your boys there; they are like his big brothers, I think. Well, Sabeen said that she wanted to play golf—she loves her lessons—but no cookie baking this time. She also mentioned going to New York to shop for a few days but I pretended I did not hear that. She will bankrupt me at Saks."

"Great," said Judith. "It will be so much fun. It might be a bit crowded at our place, though."

"No, we went online and I called a real estate guy there in Avalon. Saw the photos for rentals on his website. He knows your family; I guess everybody does because you all have homes there. I rented a house for July. Down the street from yours. I am really thrilled. You know, I spent time at the Jersey shore with friends when I was at Penn."

Judith got into her car and hit the speed dial on her mobile.

"Iman," she said when her daughter answered. "The Al Sharis are coming to Avalon this summer."

"I know. Mona told me a little while ago. She is so excited. She should be here any minute."

"Where are you?"

"Believe it or not, Mariam and I are with Aunt Hessa at Dhabi Golf Club. She arranged to get us lessons there. And Mona is coming, too. She wants to learn. Maybe she will give up skiing."

"After all of my pleading, you are now taking up golf?" asked Judith of her daughter.

"Well, we are the nieces of the national champ. We will still play tennis, though, and ski when we can. We are becoming all-around athletes."

Before she closed down her phone, Iman said: "Mom, I forgot. Aunt Ayesha called and invited us to a family dinner next week, on Uncle Khalid's birthday. Of course, Aunt Hessa and Grandma Farah also were invited and Aunt Fatima, but she leaves tomorrow for Canada. Aunt Hessa told Grandma that maybe it is a plot to poison us all and apparently Grandma got a bit angry and said something about Aunt Ayesha going to the doctor. Bye, Momma."

Judith mulled the events of late as she drove to her home. If only she knew how to write a book. For years, she had been a bit of an anomaly as an American in Abu Dhabi, a Catholic woman with a spouse and children who were practicing Muslims but respectful of her religion. She had a businesswoman/mother-in-law who no longer wore a burqua and sported slacks and gym clothes under her abaya, and of late had taken up exercising, losing weight, and meeting new friends. She had an attractive sister-in-law who was a national sports champion and whose name was becoming a household word in golf circles. She had a relative, the wife of her brother-in-law, who had earned "nasty stripes" for her treatment of those she considered less worthy than herself and now all of a sudden was doing a quick about-face. She had a daughter who was earning a living in the business world and another one ready to join friends in an interesting enterprise. She had a son who had given up his favorite sport to concentrate on academics at her American alma mater and another one moving into the "star" ranks on his high school basketball team. To add to the interesting scenario, Judith had homes in Abu Dhabi and New Jersey, and a part-time career with Al Bader Enterprises.

It all made for a good piece of writing. But who would ever put this into words? Judith had overheard the American woman, Helen, the friend of Tahnoun's mother, Farah, say that she once had been a columnist. Maybe she would write something interesting about the changing Emirati families, especially how the lives of women were moving forward while they tried to maintain such traditions as wearing the abaya and shayla, and making sure that families spent much time together.

Just thinking about all of this overwhelmed Judith. She drove through the gates of her family's villa, walked in, and headed to the kitchen to make chocolate-chip cookies.

*　　*　　*

Rowena Pagan was back in Abu Dhabi. She returned with a pocketful of pictures of her son, John Michael, now recuperating at their small apartment in Manila and getting regular visits from his grandmothers and other relatives there. She felt comfortable in returning to the Emirates, although she did not relish her work week of more than 75 hours. Rowena had vowed to finish off her contract within six months and return for good to the Philippines, with the hope that she could land some sort of job in art education. From what she had seen and heard when she was in Manila, it would be a longshot.

All of her fellow employees at Your Nails were happy to have her back. Not only was she a warm-hearted person, but her artistic talents, often requested as part of a manicure, were considered the best in the UAE capital city. Just about every regular customer knew Rowena, even though they infrequently got to be her client as the shop assigned women to nail technicians as ones were available. There were exceptions, of course, for people like Ayesha al Baloud, who insisted on having Rowena or kicking up a fuss that the manager wanted to avoid.

On her second day back, Rowena saw Dr. Jalilla al Zabi walk in for her regular manicure/pedicure. This time, Rowena went to the manager and asked her to assign the doctor to her because "I want to thank her for what she did for me and John Michael."

Jalilla was just starting the nails process with Rowena when who should walk into the salon but Ayesha. Jalilla looked at Rowena, who rolled her eyes and said quietly: "And it was such a nice morning until this."

But then Ayesha waved at Jalilla, who smiled, waved back and said hello.

Rowena was puzzled.

"You know her?"

Just then Ayesha walked over and greeted Dr. Jalilla with a peck on her cheek before turning to Rowena and saying: "I think one of the other girls is in line for me at this time. I am sure they are all good. I hope you don't mind."

"I understand," said Rowena.

"Oh, and I brought these for you. Some prepaid phone cards so you can keep in touch with Manila."

Rowena was practically speechless as Ayesha put them down on the work station.

"Thanks," said Rowena with a bit of a rattle in her voice. She could see her cousins and the other nail technicians looking at her. They probably thought they were witnessing a bit of history.

After Ayesha returned to the waiting area, Rowena said to Jalilla: "She

101

thinks I mind if someone else handles her today? I am ecstatic. How did this happen? She gave me these cards? And she even kissed you. She seems so nice all of a sudden."

"She is nice," said Jalilla. "Just give her a chance."

"She must be on feel-good medicine or something," said Rowena.

Dr. Jalilla said nothing.

Then they heard Ayesha greet someone walking into Your Nails. It was Helen Walker.

"She was here the day I got the call, remember?" said Rowena to Jalilla. "She asked what she could do to help."

"I remember but I wonder how she knows Ayesha."

Then they heard Ayesha and Helen talk about the golf championship and all the fun they had watching Hessa al Bader win it and going on a bus with a lot of people.

Jalilla recalled to herself that Ayesha had told her what a wonderful time she had with the family at the national championship.

Just then Dr. Jalilla saw a text message come in on her mobile that was set in her lap. She saw that it was from Bill in Ireland.

"Just a minute, please," she said to Rowena, who was just about to start putting on the color polish. "I want to read this."

The message read: "Coming next week to Abu Dhabi. To visit Ben and Mary. And maybe to face the music."

Jalilla looked at Rowena and said: "I want a decoration on my thumbs."

"Like what?"

"Well," said Jalilla, "do you know how to draw four-leaf clovers? I need some Irish luck."

*   *   *

CHAPTER 10

Four nights before the Philadelphia "consultants" were due into the UAE, the Taste of The Emirates partners gathered at Iman's home to watch "Bakery Uno," the television show emanating from the shop by that name in South Philadelphia. While the local public station in Pennsylvania filmed the program, it was carried on many other local public stations in the U.S. and was gaining in popularity. The program, though, was not available in Abu Dhabi, even with the extensive satellite capabilities in the Al Bader home. Yet Iman was able to find it on the Internet that was hooked up to the mammoth television in her family's theatre-like TV room.

So Mona, Essa and Ali joined Iman, who served them popcorn, candy and lemonade, to watch a program that had aired within the previous week in America.

"Maybe I should have ordered a cake or something for us to eat," Iman laughingly said.

The show started with such views of Philadelphia as its famous museum, the historic Independence Hall, and the University of Pennsylvania, and then zeroed in to South Philly, home to the famous cheesesteak sandwiches and to Bakery Uno. Rosa and Connie Alberti, Italian-American sisters, owned the bakery and were the on-air stars of the reality show. They were funny and creative as they discussed the cake-baking feats that would highlight this particular show.

"I thought these ladies would be fat," said Alia. "You know, from eating cakes and Italian spaghetti."

To the contrary, the Alberti sisters were lean and blond, and sported gold necklaces even as they mixed the dough and narrated their work. They first showed a taped discussion with their two brothers about creating a special cake for their parents' 60th wedding anniversary. The men said, instead of toasting their parents with champagne, they wanted a large cake that looked like a champagne bottle. Then the viewers saw two young female bakers creating a four-foot-high cake that turned out to be extraordinary. The top of the "bottle" featured a small cake on its side as if it were the cork that had popped up.

"How did they do that?" asked Mona al Shari.

The Alberti sisters and few other staff members were working on an even fancier cake for the retirement party of a gentleman who owned the area's largest auto dealership. They were designing a sleek, silver sports car about the size of one that a child would drive around in. Rosa was shaping the wheels with rims that used chocolate-covered pretzel rods for the spokes. When her sister suggested that perhaps she might re-do them in white chocolate, Rosa said "it's a cake for god's sake, not a Mercedes like yours." Connie looked at the camera and remarked: "I always eat my words around here."

The girls in Abu Dhabi laughed out loud.

The program also showed the arrival of the edible sports car to a fancy hotel ballroom. The dealership employees, who had commissioned the cake, helped transport it in the back of one of their panel trucks. They kept two people sitting aside the car-cake so it would not move. When they arrived just as the party was kicking off, the guests went ballistic at the sight of this creation.

"Is it from Bakery Uno?" asked the honoree.

"Yes, sir," said one of his proud employees.

Essa turned to her Abu Dhabi pals and said: "It is obvious that people love those cakes!"

While the TV show basically was filmed in the expansive Bakery Uno kitchen, where the cakes were baked and fashioned into unusual offerings, shots of the retail operation were also included.

"Wow, they sell all kinds of baked goods in the front store," said Mona. "Will our place do that?"

"Depends," said Iman. "Americans are more into breakfast rolls and bagels and breads. And, in this case, some Italian pastries. Emiratis have a lot of baked goods made by our cooks at home. We may just limit our operation to cakes and cupcakes. We have to discuss all this."

"But will we be able to have a successful business if we do that?" asked Essa.

Iman said that the girls had to realize the difference between a business in Abu Dhabi and one in Philadelphia.

"It is called taxes. They pay income tax and business tax and property tax and have money taken out for Social Security and all kinds of things. You should hear my American relatives complain about that. We don't know what tax means here in the UAE. Of course, we don't know what a democracy really is, either, even though some selected people get to vote for the Federal National Council. And by the way, those baking women must be doing okay if they have a Mercedes. They cost more in Philadelphia than here. I know because I was with my mother last summer when she got one there. The car we keep in Avalon."

"But do you think these ladies make oodles of money from the show?" asked Mona.

"I doubt it," said Iman. "Public television stations do not have advertisements; they get donations and corporate sponsors sometimes and the government gives some funding. Bakery Uno probably does make some money from its contract with the stations but not like they would on a major network. The show, though, is making them famous and that is helping their business."

"Then why don't WE have a show?" said Essa.

"Which one of us has a decent enough speaking voice to be on a show?" asked Alia.

Mona looked at her and said: "Iman. Our hostess tonight. She is going to win that public speaking contest. Right, Iman? And we are all going to be there."

"Yes, you and all my relatives," said Iman.

"What are you going to say?" asked Mona.

"Well, I just gave the speech in the preliminaries and you are supposed to give the same one for the finals, I guess because they timed it and everything. Asma was there just to listen in case some girl said something that might not be appropriate and she said there was no problem with the talks. Anyway, I said in my speech that I was glad I was not pure. If my father had an arranged marriage, it would not have been to my mother and I would not be here today."

"You said that, Iman?" Essa asked.

"Well, sort of. I certainly do not favor arranged marriages; that is for sure. So I spoke about that."

"Iman, if it were not for arranged marriages, I would not be here," said Alia. "My parents met the day of the wedding. Of course, they got divorced three years later. My father had a girlfriend the whole time in Morocco. My grandfather still gets upset about the whole thing. Thank goodness he could set my mother up with her boutiques or we would be in trouble since my father took off to Morocco to live and has not done well there and Umy now has seven boutiques and one about to open in Kuwait City. But I am a pure Emirati from an arranged union. Nevertheless, frankly, I do not want to have anything to do with an arranged marriage."

"Me neither," said Mona. "I want to meet the guy and get to know him first. My father met my mother at my aunt's house in America. He later went to Syria and asked for her hand in marriage."

Essa was not sure that she would argue against arranged marriages.

"My parents had one and they are happy. And I did not mention this to you but my mother said that she had received a call from one of the Al Hashi women who said she wanted to visit us about a possible arrangement of marriage of me to her son. They are our second cousins on my mother's side."

"Did you say that was all right?" asked Mona. "Are they coming to your home?"

"I am thinking about it. It is a nice family and a wealthy one, too."

"Essa," said Alia. "You are from one of the wealthiest families in the Gulf. So marry for love, not money."

"Maybe I will use that phrase in my speech," said Iman as the others got up to leave her home.

*　　*　　*

Sheikha Mowza wondered if she should go to the first-ever meeting of the Emirates Women of Business. Female members of her family had shunned these associations over the years, but now several were beginning to become involved as their ownership of businesses increased. She posed the question as to whether she should attend the meeting to a young Emirati woman who worked at CASPER as an administrative assistant.

"Why not?" said Hamda. "The networking alone might be good for your business plus you would get to meet women outside of your family."

Hamda was right. The ruling family had become so expansive—Mowza's many-times-married great-grandfathers each had about 20 children and scores of descendants. Mowza did spend most of her time with relatives when she was in Abu Dhabi. She kept in touch by email with many classmates from the university in Al Ain but they were scattered in all seven emirates and overseas.

"You are one smart woman, Hamda. How are classes going?"

"Fine. I have a test tomorrow in statistics. Ugh."

"I hated statistics in grad school," said the sheikha. "But I am glad you are taking it at Women's University."

Hamda again expressed her thanks to Mowza for allowing her to spend three mornings a week at WU and still get her full pay at CASPER. Married at 17, Hamda had four children by the time she was 24. Like a large number of Emirati men, her husband had dropped out of high school and was struggling with a low-level government job. They lived in a small village, outside of the city, where government-built homes, all looking alike, were distributed at no cost to nationals. When Hamda, now 30, applied for the job, she said she had graduated first in her government high school class and later had learned English on her own. Mowza remembered thinking during the interview that she and Hamda were practically the same age and yet had such different lives. So she hired Hamda on a probationary contract to see if she could handle the work. Hamda turned out to be one of the most efficient employees at CASPER and one who could certainly move up once she got the degree.

"OK," said Mowza. "I will forward you the email about the businesswomen's meeting and can you call and ask if it is too late to sign up? It is tomorrow morning in Al Ghantoot."

"Will do," said Hamda, who called and made the arrangements.

"Oh," said Mowza when Hamda returned to tell her that was she was registered for the meeting. "I also have an email from my niece who is president of the student council at WU. She invited me to a public speaking competition there. I think it is on Thursday. The topic is about choosing a husband."

Hamda said she knew about it because "one of the other WU women with kids is in it. She was talking about it in class yesterday. My sociology professor told us we had to go to it but it is on a day when I am working here."

"No, go to it. You can go over to the university with me."

"Great," said Hamda. "And enjoy tomorrow's meeting."

The next morning, Sheikha Mowza headed with her driver to Ghantoot, about 45 minutes from the capital on the main road to Dubai. Mowza did not like the fact that her family insisted that she travel with a driver in the UAE; she preferred to drive herself as she often did in London. She had learned to drive at the large farm owned by her uncle outside of Abu Dhabi City; she and her cousins would just take a key to one of the many vehicles there and drive around the private premises. Mowza got her UAE license after taking a driving test when she was about 19, after her brothers interceded on her behalf with her parents, who did not think a woman needed to drive. It was her brother Ahmed who took her to the motor vehicle center, and when he introduced his sister to a Moroccan employee who would be with her for a test drive, the gentleman just nodded at the mention of their last name. So Mowza got behind the wheel and was told to drive forward about 30 yards and then backward the same length. That was it. She and Ahmed thought it was ridiculous, but years before had realized that their royal status gave them lots of privileges.

Mowza still had to travel with drivers in Abu Dhabi, though, but used her license as an entrée for one that allowed her to drive in England. Even there, where she kept a convertible, she often used drivers for security reasons.

As she neared the hotel where the meeting would take place, Mowza checked the emails on her fancy mobile. She had the usual score of Monday morning messages from London and New York since it was the start of the work week in the West. She saw that one email came from Hassan. She opened it to find a brief message that he would be arriving for the Energy Conference on Wednesday morning and would call her when he arrived.

Her mind was racing a bit as she headed to the table where she signed in for the meeting.

"Welcome, Sheikha," said a woman whose name tag indicated she was from a Dubai company.

"Please call me Mowza," she answered.

"Of course," the woman responded. "Here is our agenda. It is brief. We have close to 30 women registered, with most from Dubai. I think eight or nine are from Abu Dhabi. We got the largest conference room with a gigantic round table that all of us can be seated at. We will look like the UN or something. So we will begin with a discussion as to whether having this organization is a good idea, and then we can break into smaller groups to focus on ideas as to what we might accomplish and how. We should be finished by 1 o'clock and lunch will be available for anyone who wants it. I know some women have to get back to their jobs, though."

The meeting was led by the Dubai woman who had suggested it. Her name was Maha and she said she was an executive with her family's jewelry businesses. Mowza figured she was in her late 40s but, with all the plastic surgeons moving into the oil-wealthy countries in the past few years, it was hard to determine one's age. Maha explained that the role of women in Emirati businesses had virtually exploded and that she thought a networking association would help them all. She noted that indeed there was a businesswomen's organization already established in her emirate, but said "all the members are nationals. I think we need an organization that includes women from all nationalities. We have so many different countries represented in our companies now."

Her words got a big YES from several women who obviously were Westerners.

"I agree," said one. "I am from Scotland and I know that many women in businesses here would welcome this."

Mowza looked across the table to the other side. She thought she recognized a national woman wearing a shayla and abaya, but was too far away to see her name tag. Then the woman waved to her, so Mowza smiled back, still wondering who the person might be.

One woman, whose name appeared to be Sally or Sandy—Mowza could not make it out on her nametag—described a business group to which she belonged in London and said "it has opened up so many doors for me. I work for a hotel firm and I have met women who are executives in construction companies and some architects. We actually contracted with some of them after I introduced them to others in my firm. One woman had contacts in New York and we are using one of those companies to build a hotel there. So, for me, it has been great. I go back to work in London a lot and when I am there, I go to the meetings of that organization."

Mowza started jotting down notes on a pad in front of her. She wanted to meet that woman and get involved in the London group.

A few women asked about setting up workshops and inviting speakers to meetings. They all agreed that these would be an important part of the organizational approach.

A young woman who appeared to be an American said that some of the group's meetings should be strictly for networking, for members to talk to each other about business and to socialize.

Again, they all said that would be great.

One Emirati woman, whose shayla was dotted with pink crystals, asked about the name of the organization as stated on the email invitations.

"We agreed that we need others besides Emirati women and the name Emirates Women in Business sounds as if the members are all nationals."

Maha said she "just made that one up for the email and we are free to call it whatever we want. Maybe Businesswomen of the Emirates or whatever."

The woman who had waved to Mowza then raised her hand to speak and was called on.

"Jalilla," said Maha. "What do you think?"

Then it struck Mowza. She knew that person from Al Koba Academy Girls' School. Jalilla was a year or two ahead of her there. She was the only one with the name Jalilla at Al Koba at the time. That was why she waved—she had recognized Mowza.

Jalilla said she wondered about using a title that seemed to limit membership to women in business. She said that would appear to exclude professionals, like lawyers and doctors, who would be good additions to the group.

"For example," she said, "I was invited here, I suppose, because my name is listed in a family business. Right now I am an administrator at New Road Hospital in Abu Dhabi and I serve on the board of Al Zabi Enterprises that owns it. But in reality, I am a physician, a psychiatrist with a part-time and soon-to-be in fulltime practice when we hire a new medical director. Doctors and lawyers usually fall into the professional category and not necessarily the business one in the minds of many people. Architects and accountants, too,

I think. And I believe this organization should recruit women who are in the professions, too."

Mowza spoke up.

"I agree. We certainly want them in this group. In fact, Professional is a better word to describe us all as we are all professional women when you think about it. Let's just call ourselves the Professional Women's Association. Short and simple."

"And not have the word Emirates or UAE in the title?" asked Maha.

"No," said Mowza. "We might have chapters in the different cities and then we would have PWA Abu Dhabi or PWA Dubai. That would be fine, I think."

"You are so right, Sheikha Mowza," said Jalilla.

Some of the others looked at Mowza. They obviously had no idea that a member of the ruling family was part of the new group.

They voted unanimously to start the Professional Women's Association. Mowza offered to write a monthly newsletter for the group, knowing that Hamda would help her with that task.

When they divided up into small groups for discussion, Dr. Jalilla and Sheikha Mowza were assigned to the same one. For an hour, the women debated as to what type of workshops they would have and how new members could be solicited. Each group reported back to the entire assemblage before the meeting ended and then broke for lunch. Mowza asked Jalilla if she were going to stay and eat at the hotel before returning to Abu Dhabi and Jalilla said: "Probably. My car died this morning and I had to get a car service at the last minute. I have to call for the driver to come back and get me. That will take awhile."

"I have a driver," said Mowza. "Come with me. Maybe we can find a nice restaurant and have lunch alone. Talk about the Al Koba days."

"I know a great restaurant in the hotel down the road. Italian food," stated Jalilla.

"My kind of place," laughed Sheikha Mowza.

A few minutes later, they were sitting on the veranda overlooking The Gulf at another hotel in Ghantoot.

"I can never figure out why people stay out here at these hotels," said Jalilla. "I mean the water here is pretty and everything but Ghantoot is halfway between Abu Dhabi and Dubai and there is really nothing to do. Is there even a town here?"

"Maybe it is a secret place to meet or something," remarked Mowza.

As they lingered over their pasta dishes, they laughed about some of their Al Koba teachers and brought each up to date on their whereabouts in the intervening years. Jalilla said that she had gone to UAE University for two years and then transferred to Duke University in the United States.

"I was 20 when I graduated because I finished high school here at 16 and so I was the youngest in my class over there."

She entered medical school right away in Dublin and was 24 when she got her degree. Then she had to intern, do a residency and specialize for a few years in psychiatry, all the time in Dublin, where she also practiced for a short time before returning to the Emirates "within the last year. So I was really gone from here, except for holidays, from the time I was 18 until I was 31. My family was insistent that I come back."

Mowza described her journey that included two years at the London School of Economics and then her work in CASPER where she was a partner with her brother, Ahmed.

"And I spend a lot of time in London still today," said Mowza. "I work from there sometimes."

"You like London?" asked Jalilla.

"I love it. Of course, I guess there is a reason for that."

"And that would be what?" asked Jalilla.

"Well, I cannot really say."

"It must a man," said Jalilla.

"How would you know that?" asked Mowza.

"I spent a lot of time studying in my field. And I have seen Gulf women especially face problems because they cannot be with the men they love. It is in the literature, too."

"Gee, maybe I should be your patient. I am getting depressed about the whole thing, I think. And he is coming here for a conference."

Jalilla sort of gasped.

"So you think I need some help to deal with this?" asked Mowza in a half-serious tone.

"Well, I think we may be able to support each other in a doctor-patient confidential way. See, I am in love with an Irish doctor who, believe it or not, is coming here this week to see his brother who works at our hospital. He wants to face the music, as he says, and meet my family."

"Is he Muslim?

"Nope. He is Catholic."

"Geez," said Mowza, "you are worst shape than I am. Of course, Hassan might as well be a Christian because he is a foreigner and lacks royal blood."

They sat for another hour and complained about the restrictions that prevented them from having happy relationships and marrying foreigners.

"We should be able to choose our own spouses," said Jalilla.

Mowza concurred.

"And that is the topic for a public speaking competition I am going to at Women's University on Thursday. My niece is running it."

"Really?" said Jalilla. "We would have been expelled from Al Koba if we ever mentioned the idea of picking our own husbands. Let me know what they say."

*   *   *

CHAPTER 11

Because they had classes for most of the day, The TOTE Cakes girls could not go to the airport to greet the two women from South Philadelphia. Essa arranged for a greeting service to meet the Bakery Uno owners as they came off the plane and then clear them quickly through immigration. A car service then transported the bakery owners to a hotel owned by Essa's family. They all had agreed to meet in the evening at the hotel lobby and then head to a restaurant on the premises.

Iman arrived first. She looked around to face a sea of Emirati men decked out in their national dress with a few wearing the bisht, a wedding jacket worn over their long white dishdashas. That signaled that a men's wedding was about to begin at the hotel and the groom obviously was one of those wearing the brown shiny covering. Iman's father called these all-male gatherings "boring." The women's wedding no doubt was being held elsewhere in the city at the same time, or perhaps the following night.

Just then two smartly-dressed Western women came out of the elevator. Iman recognized them from the "Bakery Uno" show. She walked over and introduced herself to Rosa and Connie. They greeted her warmly as they looked at her abaya and shayla, both adorned with some subtle gold decorations. Iman explained that Emirati women cover their clothing with the abaya, and opened hers up to show she had dress slacks underneath. The shayla, she explained, covers a woman's hair, but not all of it, depending on the wearer. Iman's shayla came halfway up the top of her head and the visitors could see she had beautiful dark reddish locks.

Iman explained that wearing the abaya and shayla is an Emirati tradition, not a religious mandate.

"I don't wear the abaya and shayla when I am in America, but I do usually have a head scarf on and clothes that cover me because I am a Muslim. My mother and her family are Catholics, though, and occasionally I dress like they do. Modest clothing at all times, though."

"You come to America often?" asked Connie.

"Every summer to our home in Avalon, New Jersey."

"No kidding," said Rosa. "I have a home there. On 26th Street. And Connie has one across the bridge in Sea Isle City. Everybody in Philly goes to the Jersey shore. You should come to our Fourth of July party there. We take turns. It will be in Avalon this year."

"Did I hear Avalon mentioned?" asked Mona as she walked over to Iman and the consultants.

"This is my best friend, Mona al Shari," said Iman. "Our parents have been friends for years. And her family has rented for the month of July in Avalon."

Rosa and Connie were shocked.

"We come all the way here—oh, thanks for the first-class tickets—and we meet girls who want to start a specialty cake business and then we find out that they speak perfect English and go to Avalon."

Essa and Alia showed up a few minutes later and Iman complimented them for not being late.

"Time means nothing in the Emirates," said Iman to the two women. "But things change as business demands it."

During dinner, the girls outlined their ideas to start the cake business. Connie and Rosa loved the name Taste of the Emirates, and agreed that TOTE Cakes would be the way to go from a marketing and sales approach.

Connie and Rosa had brought spreadsheets that detailed some of the costs for their operation and said they would show them to the TOTE girls at a meeting they had planned for the next afternoon.

"We didn't think we should bring them to dinner," said Rosa.

It turned out that Bakery Uno had been in the Alberti family for decades; their immigrant father started it and they worked there as teenagers. Their frame home was a block away in South Philadelphia.

"Great place to grow up," said Connie. "Frankie Avalon, Fabian, you name them. All from our neighborhood in South Philly."

Iman said she had heard of those singers through her maternal grandmother.

"She died last year but she knew a lot about rock and roll. My friends here never heard of Frankie Avalon, believe me."

"Oh, right, I keep forgetting," said Connie. "We are in Abu Dhabi. I never heard of this place until your aunt came into the bakery and told us about your plans. "

"Well, I called your bakery before that," said Iman, "and talked to a woman who was not interested in me or Abu Dhabi."

"Gosh, that must have been someone in the office. Not us. Who told you about us, anyway?"

"Well," explained Iman. "I have a younger brother at UPenn. He graduated from St. Clement's Prep and…"

"My goodness," interrupted Connie. "Our sons went there, and our husbands, too. This is all so unbelievable. Was your family living there?"

"Long story. My brother Mohammed stayed at my grandparents' home in Ardmore and went to St. Clem's for two years. Anyway, first I called my American cousin who is interning in Boston at a station with food shows. The people there told her that there is a reality show about cakes in Philadelphia. I called my brother at Penn; he does not watch food shows, he said emphatically, but he found out from his girlfriend—well, I am not sure it is his girlfriend—that her mother watches your show and that you made a hockey rink cake for a wedding of someone in her family."

"Meg made it with some help of two interns who are big hockey guys at their schools," said Connie. "They later made one of a baseball field and it won a prize at the Bake-Down in Atlantic City."

Rosa then said she wanted the girls to realize that they have to set up an office as part of the business.

"Our dad never had one. He just made all of these tasty desserts and handled everything in cash. If people could not pay, he would tell them he would put it on their bill. But he never kept records. He never got repaid by many of them. He just knew how much money came in from customers and what went out for the mortgage, supplies and other bills. Our mother learned English —our parents were from Sicily—just to figure out what taxes were owed."

"Where do you have the office?" asked Alia.

"Upstairs over the bakery," said Rosa. "Our father had two apartments there that he rented out. When we bought the business and the building from our parents, we made one into an office and the other is still an apartment. We can use it when we want. We both live in the suburbs—in Wayne. Last week my husband and I went to a concert at Symphony Hall and then to a late dinner so we stayed at the apartment overnight."

Alia pressed her: "How is the office set up?"

Rosa said the bakery employs a fulltime office manager who is also a bookkeeper, and a part-timer. Interns from local colleges also are a big part of the overall operation, she said, not only in the kitchen but in the office.

"In the office we have three computers—one for the manager, one for the part-timer and a third that anyone can use to send email or check things on the Internet. We have the usual office stuff—copy machine and Fax and phones. We have two phone numbers—one to the office and one to the bake shop. They both connect by extension to the kitchen. And we use our cell phones, too."

"Not like we do here," laughed Iman. "This country, according to one of my professors, has about 108 mobiles—that is what we call cell phones—for every 100 citizens. We are over-mobiled."

Rosa noted that Bakery Uno has a contract, too, with a certified public accountant who takes care of the work related to taxes. And, Rosa said, she and Connie were considering contracting with a payroll firm to handle the salary checks.

"One of our nieces works in sales for the payroll company and she has been talking to us about that. Right now the office manager cuts the checks."

"How many employees?" asked Alia.

"Between 15 and 20 usually. Depends on the time of the year. We add staff over the holidays. My father was known for his fruitcakes and we have kept up the tradition, although both of us despise them. But we sell hundreds of them at Christmas to people who love fruitcake."

Alia wanted to know more about the business side but Iman reminded them that this was to be a social gathering to welcome the women to the UAE capital city. Business would be the main agenda for the meeting scheduled the next afternoon, after the girls finished their respective college classes for the day.

The next morning, Connie and Rosa were treated to a tour of the city courtesy of Iman's mother. Judith had volunteered to handle that chore as she loved to take Americans, especially those from her beloved Philadelphia area, around Abu Dhabi. While she normally would have driven her own car for the tour, she engaged the family driver so she would not have to bother with parking and thus could concentrate on providing a bit of informal narration for the around-the-city trip. She also had booked lunch at a restaurant on the Corniche.

"Is there anything of interest you want to see?" she asked Rosa and Connie as she met them outside the hotel. "Something you have heard about?"

Connie mentioned the large mosque that had taken years to complete and wanted to know if Catholics could go there.

"Yes, "said Judith. "I was raised a Catholic, by the way, although I was not married in my parish church. The pastor refused when he found out I was marrying a Muslim. So I got married in the church in Devon and a Jesuit, a friend of the family, officiated. And you are welcome to our mosque here."

Rosa said her husband's nephew works with the State Department and told her not to miss seeing the U.S. Embassy.

"Every American should see that," laughed Judith. "Let's drive by there now."

They entered into what Judith called the Embassy Area.

"Since we are in the capital, we have lots of embassies. They are all over Abu Dhabi and then this section of the city was designated maybe eight or nine years ago for new embassy buildings. Well, we Americans had a run-down embassy over on 11th Street and so the U.S. built this, um, whatever."

The car passed typical embassy buildings, all surrounded by sandy desert terrain.

"What is that monstrosity?" asked Connie as she stared at a mammoth structure.

"That would be your tax dollars at work," answered Judith.

Rosa said it looked like a whale. Connie said that the small windows resembled those on a cruise liner. Judith said she heard that some famous architect built the U. S. Embassy to resemble the desert.

"Some people call it the American fortress," she stated.

"I want to take a picture of that," said Rosa but Judith pointed to a sign on the street that said "No Photos in This Area." She said she had been inside a number of times over the years for embassy events and to renew passports.

"It is a typical building inside, but the exterior is so out of place with the other embassies. I really think it was built this way for security purposes."

They drove to the mosque and took a short tour that allowed the Americans to see what was promoted as the largest one-piece carpet in the world. Judith explained that, to complete it, the UAE rulers reportedly brought in the carpet makers from Iran and somewhere else to finish it on site.

Judith took them next to the gold souk for a quick look around at the many shops. She said the building was a far cry from the old souk area that had closed several years earlier after a big fire destroyed most of the structures.

"It was block after block of little shops, some just kiosks made out of a tent material. I loved to go there and haggle over prices for all kinds of goods. My brother Joe came to visit us once and spent literally two hours negotiating over the price of a watch. He could not speak Arabic and the guy selling the watches could not speak English. Joe had to call my husband to come down and interpret, and my brother said he saved hundreds of dollars from the price in the states."

Connie asked about carpet dealers and Judith said she would make sure that they got the address of her favorite one.

They headed to the Corniche and Judith asked the driver to let them out two blocks from the site of the restaurant where they would have lunch so the bakers from South Philly could walk along the promenade.

"The water is beautiful," said Rosa.

"This body of water is the famous Persian Gulf," said Judith. "You know, from the two Persian Gulf wars. But here we call it the Arabian Gulf. In fact, all of the Arab countries along the water call it that. A controversy since the 1960s, I believe, but I am not sure."

The Corniche amazed the sisters; they both mentioned its beauty as they walked along the tiled pathway with its fountains, benches and plantings. They passed Westerners jogging slowly in the heat and saw a number of women, dressed in abayas and shaylas, walking along.

"Holy cow," said Judith. "Look who it is."

Farah and Amna came over to them and both greeted Judith with the typical two-cheek buss.

"Connie and Rosa, I would like you to meet my mother-in-law, Farah, and her dear friend, Amna."

Judith explained to the Emirati women that the Americans owned a bakery in Philadelphia and were in Abu Dhabi to help "the girls" with the cake business they were considering.

"We know all about that," said Farah. "One is my granddaughter Iman and another is Amna's grandchild, Mona. We both gave them the initial money the needed so they did not have to bother our sons about it."

Connie remembered that both of those girls said they would be in Avalon in the summer and mentioned that to Farah and Amna.

"We both own homes down there," said Connie. "We were talking about getting together for a Fourth of July party."

Amna said her son, Nasser, and his family had invited her to go with them to Avalon and she was considering it as long as Farah went at the time to visit Judith and her family.

"I am counting on that," said Farah. "I am planning to go to the exercise class in the morning there."

Rosa laughed.

"I go there when I am in Avalon."

"Well, it will be fun," said Farah. "It was so nice meeting you, Connie and Rosa. What are your last names?"

"Well, we go by our maiden names, Alberti, in the bakery business. But our last name is Haley. We are married to brothers."

As they entered the restaurant, Judith said she went to St. Rose Academy with a Joan Haley.

"Any relation?"

"Sure is," said Connie. "She is our sister-in-law. This is such a small world."

During the lunch, they talked all about their Philadelphia roots and their Avalon connection. Later, Judith dropped the Alberti women at the building where the girls were planning to house their business. The four girls were there, having arrived together from the WU campus for the meeting. They first sat in a conference room and the TOTE girls asked many questions of the consultants.

"What do we need in terms of supplies?" asked Alia.

Connie and Rosa took out a list they had brought with them.

"It depends. Are you girls going to stick to cakes and cupcakes or are you going to sell other baked goods in the retail shop?"

"We probably would make more money if we added pies and all kinds of things but we want to focus first on the cake business. And, we want you to know, that our tax liabilities are nothing compared to the U.S."

As she perused the spreadsheet she had with her, Connie said: "Well, this whole column here refers to taxes. We have to take a lot of money out of our employees' paychecks to cover health care costs and federal pension money. And income taxes, of course. You are telling me that there are no income taxes here?"

"Not yet," said Iman.

Connie pointed out a column that showed expenses including a mortgage on the bakery building in South Philadelphia.

"We took out a mortgage to pay our parents for the business and then paid that off. Now we have another mortgage because we put on an addition to the back of the kitchen last year."

"Why didn't you pay for that in cash if you were making money?" asked Essa.

"Well, we could have come up with the money," said Connie, "but our accountant advised us to take a mortgage for tax purposes. I don't understand it all but our cousin, who is a lawyer, agreed. You are going to rent, correct? Don't tell me that all of the rents are free here, too."

"My father owns this building," explained Essa, "and we will be on the first floor that was designed for retail shops. We will take the space of a few of them and build the bakery. And we will pay rent. We agreed to that. We will go down to show you the space in a little while."

A man who looked South Asian came into the room with tea and cookies. Connie wondered where he came from. Essa said he was on the staff for the building and always available to bring tea or coffee to meetings in the conference rooms.

"This city is more amazing by the minute," said Connie.

The women were not forthcoming about exactly how much money they made; Iman earlier had said that it would be wrong for the girls to ask. But Connie and Rosa did lay out the data related to their purchases of supplies.

The bakery bought what amounted to tons of flour and sugar and butter over the course of a year.

"We have a big bill for ricotta cheese, too," said Rosa "or the rigoat, as my father would say. "We sell more cannolis than any bakery in Pennsylvania."

"Cannolis? What the hell are they?" asked Alia.

The women looked surprised that a Muslim girl would speak in that type of language, but Rosa explained how they bake shells and fill them with a cheese mixture and sometimes candied citrus peels or pistachios.

"I love cannolis," said Iman. "We get them at Ann's Bakery in Avalon."

"You go to Ann's, too?" said Connie. "We go there all the time when we are at the shore. Guess what? They are OUR cannolis. We bring them down in coolers in our cars on the weekends and they sell out by Monday at Ann's. We have been doing that for years. We make little money off them, though. It really is just to provide cannolis for people who love to have them as they walk around town or take a break from the beach."

"Wow," said Iman. "And my mother used to work at Ann's Bakery."

"Judith worked at Ann's? She didn't mention that when we were with her today. This is getting crazier by the minute."

The girls learned that creating specialty cakes took a lot of fondant that either could be made at the bakery or purchased in rolled-out form. It was the smooth icing that covered the fancy cakes and could be cut easily into varied shapes.

"Here are our specs on prices for that and everything we need for fillings," said Connie. "You will also need a lot of equipment, not just the ovens and large refrigerators but things like piping cones and edible decorations for cakes. We can supply you with all of the addresses for companies that sell these things. And we have a list of other things, like uniforms. Everyone at Bakery Uno wears the same white jacket, like chefs wear. That makes us more professional, we think, but we do have a big laundry bill because we send everything out to be washed and cleaned. Those costs are on this sheet that you can have."

"Well, we have maids who can do that," said Essa as her friends said: "No."

"Our staffs at home are not getting involved," said Alia.

"You have staffs at your homes?" asked Connie.

"It is quite a bit different from Philly, believe me," said Iman. "My grandparents always had a cleaning woman come in every week to their house in Ardmore, and we do the same thing at our shore house. In Abu Dhabi, just about everyone we know in our circle of friends has a fulltime maid or two, a cook, a nanny, a man who is the driver and gardener. People like that. They are from overseas and the price is right, as my mom would say."

Connie uttered a remark about wanting to move to the UAE, as she opened her briefcase and took out a book filled with photos of cakes that had been created at Bakery Uno. The designs were "off the top," as Mona said, mimicking Dr. Teresa and one of her phrases.

One cake was designed with a marzipan figure wearing a bright costume with large feathers emanating from the back.

"We made it for one of the Mummers' organizations," said Rosa. "Philadelphia has the famous Mummer's Day parade on New Year's and all the groups dance up the street with these costumes on. It is great. This cake was for one of the parties some group had afterwards. Carrie made most of it with help from Jimmy. He is my son and he works in the business. Handles advertising in addition to actually helping with the cakes. He went to Villanova in business and worked all the way through college with us. Connie has a son who works with us now. We have no daughters, only sons. Carrie is Jimmy's wife. She works part-time because they have two children who are 6 and 7 now. They live in downtown Philadelphia. Her sister, Meg, works with us fulltime and she is great. Has a degree in art and also went to a culinary school to specialize in pastry making. She does a lot of the designs on a computer before the cakes are made. We pay her a top salary."

"I was at the New Year's parade one year when we were in America for Christmas with my grandmother," said Iman. "It was cold but fun. We were doing the Mummers' Strut to the music."

One by one, the girls raved about the varied cakes displayed in the photos. They paid special attention to the names of the Bakery Uno staffers identified as those having worked on the well-crafted creations. The baker named Meg appeared to be involved in designing and making many of the award-winning cakes.

"OK," said Alia, continually assuming her business mindset in this undertaking. "We have the money to buy the equipment, set up the space we need, and hire people. But we are not going to be involved as much as owners as you are in Philadelphia. We will have other careers and this is our side business, an investment, something we want to do. We will be checking on everything but we need to hire a really good person who also can bake cakes and train people here to create these cakes."

"Will you hire other staffers from your country?" asked Connie.

"If you mean will be employing nationals, that would be nice but most Emiratis work in management or business and are in white-collar jobs. I think that is the term," said Alia. "We need one or two top cake bakers from the U.S. because that is where these businesses are successful, and then hire and train Filipinos or Sri Lankans or some people from other Arab countries. Right now, can you two think of anyone who is really good who will come here from America and help us run the bakery? We will pay a good salary and provide housing."

"You provide housing?" said a startled Rosa.

"Sure. Our companies do that for people in white-collar jobs," said Alia. "Like our professors at Women's University. They all get apartments with at least two bedrooms. And, oh, if the people have children, we will pay for them to go to private school."

"Maybe at Al Koba Academy," said Mona. "Where we all went to school. It is just for nationals but next year will be open to all nationalities. My father is on the board, and Iman's mother, too. That will be a real change for Al Koba but it is needed."

After two hours of discussion, the group took an elevator to the first-floor premises and the future Taste Of The Emirates space.

Connie and Rosa took out folded rulers they had brought with them, and did some measuring of the room.

"This looks like an adequate space to build a retail area and the kitchen," said Connie. "And you have on-street parking, it looks like. We have a problem with that because our bakery neighborhood has lots of houses with no garages and the people keep their cars in the street. We managed to get two spaces in front just to use for customers and we rent a garage a block away for our two trucks. That is something you will need—delivery trucks. We keep our own cars in the driveway at our parents' home down the street. Most of our employees take a train or bus to work."

Alia said her business plan included two panel trucks and that her uncle could order them from his Mercedes dealership.

A young woman walked into the large, empty space and said: "I am looking for Essa."

"Right here," said Essa as she extended her hand. "You must be Eileen. Any trouble finding this place?"

"No, I took a car service. The driver will wait."

"We loved your wedding photo," said Iman, explaining to the Alberti sisters the story of the Leaning Tower of Pisa cake.

"We've had problems like that," laughed Connie. "Rosa, remember the tower we made for the wedding cake for those two air controllers? Jimmy was delivering it; he was in college then and working part-time to learn the business. The darn control tower cake fell just as he brought it into the hotel about an hour before the wedding."

"What did you do?" asked Alia.

"Well, we went into crisis mode. From the start we set that up. You should know about that. We make an extra cake every weekend and store it in the frig. Usually it is four tiers with little or no decoration. Then, if we have a disaster, we have a back-up. Otherwise, we sell it at a bargain price. With the tower fiasco, Jimmy told the family that another cake would arrive, not one with an airport control tower that took a few days to make, but a beautiful cake nevertheless. And we would not charge for either cake. Back at the bakery, after Jimmy called, we took out the crisis cake, as we call it, and decorated it. In fact, the florist is across the street and we got fresh roses to put on it. The bride's family said it was nicer than the tower cake. Because we did that—and we lost $2,000 on the deal—the bride's friends and family told everyone about it and we got a lot more business. It is important to remember that customers come first and they are great PR people for us."

"Interesting," mumbled Alia as she wrote that down.

Eileen, as the Philadelphians learned, was an American architect who worked out of a Dubai firm. She had been requested by the TOTE team members to come to Abu Dhabi and take a look at the space and discuss how it might be designed in concert with what the American consultants recommended. Eileen asked a lot of questions of Connie and Rosa, who said they used a Philadelphia architectural firm, Clarion-Williams Associates, when they redesigned the bakery.

"One of my friends interned at that firm one summer," said Eileen. "I bet they can send your design by attachment if you give them permission."

Connie took out her mobile and sent an email to her contact at Clarion-Willams.

For the next hour or so, all of the discussion centered on creating the Taste of the Emirates business. Then everyone left, including Connie and Rosa, who said they would have an early dinner at the hotel and then lounge for awhile at the pool while writing down anything they can think might help the young Emirati entrepreneurs.

*   *   *

Ayesha al Baloud said goodbye to her driver and walked into New Road Medical Center, a private hospital. She passed the emergency room section and noticed many foreigners waiting to be treated. Ayesha thought to herself how lucky they were to be able to afford private care, as she was.

She checked in with the secretary in the office suite for the psychiatrists. Only two names were listed. One appeared to be an American name and the other was Jalilla al Zabi, M.D. As Dr. Jalilla had said, the problem was clear: the UAE's fledgling health system had never concentrated on psychologists or psychiatrists.

As she sat down to wait, the secretary said to her: "Madame, Dr. Jalilla is on her way down from her administrative office and says she is stopping to grab a drink at the café. She wants to know if you want one."

"Great," said Ayeshsa. "A diet Coke if they have one."

A few minutes later, Ayesha sat at the end of the couch in Jalilla's medical office. Once again, she thanked Jalilla for "coming over and talking to me that afternoon."

Ayesha was referring to the day when she bolted out of Your Nails because Rowena could not complete the eyebrow-threading services after getting a phone call that her son had been injured in Manila. Ayesha angrily left and sat outside on a bench after calling her driver, who could not return for at least 30 minutes because he had gone to pick up the Al Bader boys at school. She had been sitting there a good 10 minutes when another Emirati client emerged from Your Nails and saw her. She came over to Ayesha.

"I am Jalilla al Zabi and you are married to an Al Bader, correct?"

"How do you know?" said a somber Ayesha.

"One day when I was getting my nails done they called out your name and I knew that my brother had gone to school overseas with an Al Baloud from Dubai. I asked him if his friend has a sister and he said that he did and she lived in Abu Dhabi and was married to Khalid al Bader."

Jalilla asked if she could sit down and Ayesha reluctantly agreed.

"You seem to get upset easily," said Jalilla.

"Sometimes I get nervous and upset. I just want to stay in bed."

"You have children?

"Three boys. A year apart. 7, 6 and 5."

Jalilla was beginning to revert to her psychiatric mindset. She thought maybe Ayesha could use her help but she could not be forthright in saying that. So she took out her business card and said: "I have had patients who feel as you do. If you ever need to talk, call me."

That night, Ayesha showed the card to Khalid. It was he who made the phone call and brought Ayesha to see Dr. Jalilla. After a lengthy session in which the couple described how difficult it was for Ayesha after giving birth three times in what amounted to 24 months, Jalilla said she wondered if Ayesha had suffered post-partum depression and it had evolved into something with similar symptoms. Khaild and Ayesha both seemed relieved after Jalilla said she could help. She later gave Ayesha some blood tests to rule out some potential ailments, and gave her a prescription to help mitigate the funk that Ayesha seemed to be in. Dr. Jalilla scheduled Ayesha for weekly appointments to check on her progress.

Khalid later told his mother, Farah, that he could see Ayesha smile the first time they left the doctor's office.

"She did not even have the medicine yet and she was happy because she knew this doctor would help her and she knew that I was supporting her. Just being with that doctor changed Ayesha's outlook on life."

From Day One, as she called it, Ayesha became more outgoing and pleasant. Lourdes and Angela could not believe it when "the queen" came down to help them make breakfast for the boys; they had never seen her get up at that time of the morning. And when Ayesha went outside to kick around a football with her sons and Joseph, Angela was convinced that "she must be on something."

Indeed she was. Her personality was changing or, as Khalid said to his mother, "changing back to the way she was when we got married. And I think I owe a great deal to Dr. Jalilla for seeking out Ayesha and putting her on medication. It is working."

Now, as Ayesha sat in the psychiatrist's office, she lamented about the years she had wasted with rather unpredictable behavior.

"Now I have started to enjoy life. I had so much fun at the women's golf tournament. I so enjoyed keeping score for the groups with Diab, Khalid's nephew, while my boys were driving in carts with their older cousins."

Dr. Jalilla said she had recalled seeing Ayesha's picture on the front page of the paper with all of the friends and relatives surrounding Hessa after she won the event.

"Even my mother Nama was in the picture. She came over from Jumeriah. She was rooting bigtime for Hessa."

They spent the appointment hour in talking about Ayesha and her changed moods. Ayesha said she had taken the doctor's advice to become more productive and more caring.

"I am spending lots of time with the boys and trying to help people. I want to do more for the girls at Yours Nail. I heard you paid for Rowena to go home."

"Ironically," said Jalilla. "I am setting up what I am calling a fund or foundation to pay for medical costs for foreign women who don't have health coverage. I had Rowena's aunt here the other day and paid for her to see a specialist."

"Do you have people who will help with the foundation and pay for these costs?" asked Ayesha.

"So far, only me. I just got the idea recently when Rowena's aunt, who cuts my hair at a salon, told me she had a problem but was avoiding doctors because of the cost. So I just blurted out that I was starting a foundation and she would be the first to use its funds, but really I am the foundation."

"Can I help?" asked Ayesha. "I would be happy to pay with the Al Baloud and Al Bader money!"

"Well, you can be my first board member. Just come up with a name for this foundation."

"Will do, Dr. Jalilla. See you next week unless we run into each other getting pedicures."

*　　*　　*

Hassan Hadad came through immigration and out to the baggage claim at the Abu Dhabi Airport. He got into a cab and headed to the hotel that was serving as headquarters for those attending the Energy Conference. He had told Sheikha Mowza he would be arriving shortly after noon but did not give her details about the exact time or flight. It was quite clear to her that he was a bit ill at ease about spending time with her in a country where she was a royal. Yet to ignore the fact that they were in the same city would be a bit crazy from either's perspective.

Hassan asked if there were many palaces in the city and the taxi driver said he would drive by some of them for the passenger—for an extra 20 dirhams. They veered off the main road and into a section of the city that housed a number of palaces. The driver was saying "Sheik So-and-So lives there" as he pointed out the many palaces.

"They all have walls around them for security, huh?" asked Hassan.

"Yes," said the driver. "But not only the palaces. Look at all the villas that have walls around them. Security? Maybe. But maybe to keep the sand from flying in. You know, Abu Dhabi City is an island, like Manhattan, and you have to go over the bridges to get to the other parts of the emirate. We also have many embassies here because this is the capital of the UAE. The Americans always want to see their embassy. It is crazy-looking. The British Embassy is up near the Corniche. Older but pretty nice."

Hassan had been keeping in touch with Mowza mostly by email and by texting. He had heard that often phone lines were tapped into the palaces; Mowza herself said that might be true. But today, after checking in at the hotel, he took out Mowza's business card and dialed her office. A woman named Hamda answered and he asked for Mowza.

"She is in a meeting at the moment, sir. Can you leave your name, please."

"Hassan Hadad from Ridings Energy Investments. I am here for the Energy Conference and wanted to speak to her."

He gave her his number at the hotel and then picked up a copy of the English language newspaper that was left on a coffee table. He read about a sheikh who had purchased a rugby team and another who was head of the Army. They were all Mowza's relatives, he surmised. He felt a bit out of his element.

A half-hour later, the phone rang. It was Mowza and she was greeting him on his arrival "to my hometown."

"I think you mean your country as it looks as if your family owns it."

Mowza laughed and told Hassan to take a cab to her offices and she would introduce him to Sheik Ahmed, her brother and partner.

"Does he know about us?" asked Hassan.

"Yes, and he wants to meet you. In fact, we want to know about energy investments."

Not long thereafter, Hassan walked into the plush offices of CASPER in a sleek silver tower. Mowza came to greet him and held out her hand. She introduced "Mr. Hadad" to Hamda and then walked down the hall with him to her brother's offices. She said nothing along the way, but simply smiled at him.

Sheik Ahmed stood up as soon as they entered the room and walked up to Hassan.

"So nice to meet you. My sister told me all about you. Right, sis?"

In his engaging way, Ahmed made Hassan feel at home. The sheik asked about potential energy-related investments and also about contacts he may have in New York.

"We are going to invest in a big development there and want someone to be on top of it so we will open an office. I know your firm is not in the real estate investment game but you might know someone from your time living in New York."

"I do, Ahmed, as a matter of fact. I had a close friend from the U.S. who went to the London School of Economics with me—you both went there, too, so that is a bit of a coincidence. He works for a big development firm and is ready to make a move. Plus he knows others in the field."

"Can we meet him through videoconferencing?" asked Ahmed.

"Sure. I can contact him about that and let you know."

"Now," said Ahmed. "Let's talk about you and my sister."

"Oh no," said Hassan. "What did she say about me?"

"I said you were a great Muslim guy with a great family," said Mowza.

Ahmed said that the ruling family mostly looked askance at its women dating men at all. They were expected just to wind up marrying some cousins they hardly knew.

"And you, Ahmed," said Hassan. "You are expected to marry a cousin?"

"Yes, sort of, but we as men have more freedom. Sheiks often marry women from some of the top families in the UAE. Of course, if I marry a foreigner, the sheikhas will probably say they hope my second wife is a cousin."

"Ahmed," pleaded Mowza, "tell Hassan what you think about him and me."

"Hassan, I told Mowza that I will support her no matter what. She is my little sister and my business partner and I am the reason she has a driver's license."

"Ha, ha," said Mowza.

Hassan asked if he should meet their family.

Ahmed said, "No. Not now. I think you should wait until the summer when our parents are in London and then tell them what is going on. You can deal with it better there."

"I agree," said Sheikha Mowza. "In Abu Dhabi, we have to watch it with all the potential gossip."

Ahmed then suggested that Hassan and Mowza join him and his girlfriend, Noor, for dinner that night.

"How are we going to get away with that?" asked Mowza.

"I will say I am driving you to a business meeting and Hassan, I will arrange a car service for you. Noor will come from Dubai with a driver."

Mowza said: "And where would we be meeting for dinner, my dear brother?"

"Ghantoot. A restaurant in Ghantoot."

*   *   *

CHAPTER 12

Sheikha Asma, in her own words, was "going loco."

"Where are the flowers?" she asked someone on the other end of her mobile phone conversation. "They were to be here 30 minutes ago. No, not the palace. I said Women's University. Second-floor auditorium."

Asma got off the phone and turned to Dr. Teresa: "So I order the flowers for the stage from our regular florist and I give my name and tell them where to deliver the flowers and they don't listen and send them to the palace. Not our home, mind you, the BIG palace where the Cabinet meets. But the florist is going to retrieve them and get them here."

"Did you ask them to send the bill?" asked Mona al Shari who was helping Asma set up for the public speaking event. "Remember, we have the sponsorship from my father."

"Oh, I just told them to charge it to my father's account," said Asma.

Dr. Teresa laughed. Where else would two students spend their parents' money without any qualms, she wondered. And these girls were two of the nicest young women she had taught. Money had not corrupted them at all.

The professor checked off the programs that Asma had printed off.

"Who drew the cover?" asked Dr. Teresa.

"My sister Rahma," said Sheikha Asma. "It is nice to have a younger sister who is an art major. Of course, I had to drag her away from 'Oprah' to do it. And later she came into my closet and took my new skinny jeans to wear. But she did the cover art and that is what counts."

Dr. Teresa asked about the food for the reception following the public speaking competition.

"That food is on its way. I had the palace staff make it all," said Asma.

"What?" said Mona. "I thought Al Shari Inc. was paying for it and you would order it."

"Oh, it is easier this way," said Asma. "The program has a big ad for your father's company and it says he is the sponsor. I spent a lot of his money on the crystal vases. Your father will be here to give out the cash awards, right?"

"Yes, he is coming. I think my mother, too. And my grandmother Amna is coming with Iman's grandmother."

Dr. Teresa said Iman had told her that her parents were coming and some other relatives.

"My favorite and youngest aunt, Sheikha Mowza, is coming, too," said Asma. "She thinks the topic is great."

"Oh, sure," said Mona. "As if a sheikha could ever choose a husband. Maybe after you run out of male cousins."

"Things will change, Mona. Things will change."

"Too bad we Muslims cannot bet bigtime on that, Asma," said Mona. "I would put a thousand dirhams on that one."

The judges arrived from Dubai and introduced themselves. Dr. Teresa explained how they would score the competition. Each judge would be given a sheet that ranked speakers on a point system for such things as good content, presentation style, articulation, etc. The points would be added for the 10 speakers and the top three would receive cash awards and the usual crystal vases.

"Ever see so many crystal vases in your home countries?" asked Teresa.

The three Dubai professors laughed.

"You will all be getting them for helping out," said Asma, "including you, Dr. Teresa."

Maitha walked in, wearing a beaded abaya and shayla flowing over her heavy body.

"My mother is here and I hope she listens to what I say today. But then, she hardly knows English. I wish my sister were here from Geneva to hear me speak."

The other competitors were starting to arrive and most wore heavy makeup and dark lipstick. Teresa marveled at how much time her students spent on making their faces look pretty. But then, their faces were all that most people saw of these girls. And the perfume—you could smell the Arabian oud a mile away.

People were flocking into the auditorium.

Tahnoun and Judith arrived, with Diab, who told Dr. Teresa, "I am here to support my sister. I am here to support my sister." He apparently had been warned not to express his reluctance at being dragged from the basketball court outside his family's villa to attend an event in which his older sister would participate.

Teresa said: "You really are a hoot, Diab."

"A hoot? Is that another one of your American phrases, Dr. Teresa?" asked Mona.

"I know what it means," said Diab. "When I went to school for a year in Pennsylvania, all my buddies said I was a hoot because I was funny. I think it was my Arab accent."

Nasser al Shari shook hands with Tahnoun al Bader and said "I hope I get to give some of my cash to your daughter today."

Tahnoun said he was just happy that Iman was competing as "girls need to be public speakers."

Farah and Amna arrived and waved as they headed to seats near the front. Their American friend, Helen Walker, was with them and Teresa still wondered what type of writer she had been and why she no longer pursued the craft.

Essa and Alia of the TOTE group arrived.

"Look whom we brought," said Essa. "Our consultants."

"Good luck, Iman," said Connie.

"Break a leg," added Rosa.

A puzzled Sheikha Asma looked at Dr. Teresa, who smiled and said: "It doesn't mean that literally. It means do well. They want Iman to do well. Soon you all will know every American phrase."

Hessa was next to show up and said: "Let's go for another family victory today, Iman," who replied to her golf-champ aunt, "I don't need any pressure. I am nervous already. Where are all these relatives coming from?"

Right behind Hessa came Iman's uncle, Khalid, and his wife, Ayesha. Hessa looked a bit puzzled, but greeted the couple warmly and then sat down with them behind Farah and the others.

The guys from the flower shop got off the elevator; they were practically running toward the stage. One said to Sheikha Asma: "Sorry about the mixup."

She wanted to know if they had trouble retrieving the flowers from the palace where they were taken in error.

"Well," said the one guy, "let's just say they tried to stop us. Some guard thought we were stealing the flowers from the palace."

"Stealing flowers from the palace?"

The words came from the mouth of a smiling Sheikha Mowza, who had arrived with her assistant, Hamda.

"Is that you underneath the gishwa?" she said to her niece, Sheikha Asma.

"Yes. Following the family rules."

"Take it off," said Mowza. "You must have a lot to do today and you don't need that."

"OK, if someone from the older generation, even though you are young, says so, then I will gladly agree."

She removed the face veil and kissed her aunt.

Mowza introduced her assistant, Hamda—"she goes to WU"—and said they both were eager to hear the speeches.

"I love the topic, as you know," Mowza said just as Asma noticed her uncle, Ahmed, walking in.

"Uncle Ahmed is really coming?"

"Yes," said Mowza. "He knows you are in charge of this and he is interested in the topic, too."

"And who is with him?' asked Asma.

Mowza did not answer.

"No, could it be…?"

"Yes, it is," said Mowza, and then she whispered to her niece: "Hassan and I had dinner in Ghantoot last night with Ahmed and Noor, the one from Jordan. She is gorgeous, smart, and very nice."

While her brother and Hassan headed to a back row and Hamda sat down with some of her WU classmates, Sheikha Mowza sat with Sheikha Asma and her professor, Dr. Teresa Wilson, in the front row.

Mona al Shari had offered to give the introductory remarks and present each speaker in turn, so she walked to the lectern.

"Good afternoon and welcome to the first Public Speaking Competition finals at Women's University. My name is Mona al Shari and I want to thank the sponsor for the event, Al Shari Incorporated."

Everybody laughed and the competition got underway.

Teresa took notes throughout the speeches, and thanked herself for doing so as she later penned her monthly email newsletter:

This marked the first time that Women's University has had a formal speaking competition and I actually was the one who suggested it but the students handled the whole thing. Sheikha Asma, who is from the ruling family, agreed to run the competition in her role as Student Council president. I have mentioned her before in these communiqués; she is sweet and smart as a whip. She went to the Academic VP and got the okay for this. I doubt if I would have been able to do that because of the topic.

We decided to have students give talks on "Choosing Your Spouse." Now this is one big problem here in the UAE. Since time immemorial, families pick spouses. The mothers of young men go to weddings and look for future brides among the guests for their sons. If they find a likely candidate, they go to the girl's home and see if her family agrees. The young woman can say NO if she wants. Weddings to Emirati women have become so expensive, though, that the men, whose families foot the bill, are marrying foreigners. No one is happy about that as the government wants to keep the national bloodlines going, and the UAE actually gives money to an Emirati man who marries a national woman. But the money is not really enough to make it all worthwhile.

To add to the problems: Emirati women are expected to marry national men. And obviously they are not too available as the men are marrying outsiders. Besides, the women are finishing college at rapid rates but not the men and the women say they want educated spouses. So it would make sense for the country, I think, to allow, even encourage women, to marry Muslims from other countries. Of course, I keep my two cents out of this discussion.

Ten girls competed in the finals; it was an interesting mix of students. One wore the niqab so we could only see her eyes; she said she was happy to marry her cousin and abide by his demands that she wear the veil. You could not hear everything she said with her mouth covered, but she made her point—and most every student I know disagrees. One or two other speakers supported arranged marriage but most decried the idea of it. Iman al Bader—she is the niece of the national golf champion that I wrote about in the last newsletter—said her parents met at the University of Pennsylvania and, though her mom is American, the marriage has been fine. She said she cannot even fathom the idea of an arranged marriage. When she finished, she got a standing ovation from her relatives and their friends in the audience. One girl, Maitha, whom I will describe as "big" but I am being nice about that, had stats about divorces from arranged marriages and said "it is cruel to marry us off to men we don't know. Just ask my sister." She didn't explain but I know that her sister had a bad time with an arranged marriage. Maitha, who really is quite well-spoken, got a big round of applause from the audience.

Every one of the speakers made a point and overall they were very good, I thought, although I was not a judge but just an observer. We got the judges from our Dubai campus.

The final speaker was a 30-year-old WU student and mother. She blasted the UAE system for allowing her to lose her 12-year-old son to his father in a divorce. (That apparently is what happens here. I don't know if it is written in stone, though). I had heard this student talk in the preliminaries and knew that she would say that her spouse was 40 when, as a teenager, she was married off to him in an arranged union and that she was his third wife. But then she veered from the original speech. All of a sudden she looked down at the first row, where I was seated with Sheikha Asma and her aunt, and started criticizing the sheikhas. She said it was the women of the ruling family who are to blame for the plight of UAE females. "You marry your cousins. All arranged marriages. So the rest of us are supposed to go do likewise. If it is good enough for the sheikha, it is good enough for the rest of us; that is what my family said to me and I was a teenager.

Why don't the sheikhas wise up and marry for love? We would all be better off because we could do the same."

When this speaker sat down, the place was silent. No one applauded—for a LONG minute. I think people were embarrassed because of the presence of members of the ruling family. Then Asma's aunt, Sheikha Mowza, who was seated right next to me, stood up and clapped. Sheikha Asma did likewise. I saw Asma's uncle, Sheik Ahmed, whom I had met before the event, stand up and applaud loudly as did some Western man with him. Others in the audience then stood up and clapped—I think they were following the lead of the royals. Sheikha Mowza then sat down and said to me: "She is so right. We should marry for love." I was astounded. In this country, you do not insult the members of the ruling family and here they were saluting criticism aimed at them.

That speaker took third place—I think her pouty facial expression probably hurt her cause. Second place went to Iman al Bader; her relatives gave her a noisy reception when she walked to the stage to get an envelope from Mona's father. Her funny younger brother, Diab, stood on a chair and yelled "Go Sis."

First place? Maitha, who had mentioned her sister's disastrous marriage. Maitha's mother stood up and clapped loudly. Maitha said later that she was happy her mom does not speak English as she "would not have been thrilled about what I said if she knew what I said."

At the reception afterward, I saw Sheikha Mowza talking to her brother and his friend. Then she came over to me when I was speaking to the academic VP and said: "I hope you have more of these events. They can be really valuable for things that we need to address in the UAE. And if you need a sponsor, my company, CASPER, is ready to help." The administrator seemed relieved.

And at a party later at Iman's home—well, that is a story for another day.

Well, I am off to the beach club for a few hours in the Arabian sun. It will not be long until I am lounging on the beach at Spring Lake. And for those of you who inquired as to whether I am coming back to Abu Dhabi after my two-year contract expires in June, the answer is YES. I re-upped for two years here. But I look forward to two months at the Jersey shore!

*   *   *

Farah walked across the street to the home of Khalid and Ayesha. She thought about how seldom she had done this over the past several years, as she and Hessa tried to avoid being thrown into Ayesha's questionable behavioral path. Today Farah was arriving with cupcakes that she had made with the cook for the young Al Bader boys. Farah thought it was time to become more acclimated to her own large kitchen. Besides, she had learned how to make the icing into creative toppings courtesy of some experts.

It had all happened a week earlier after her granddaughter Iman's second-place finish in the speaking competition. Farah had asked her relatives and friends to come over for a late lunch at her home. The cook and maid were on alert because Farah figured that, even if Iman did not fare well in the event, they still could get together. Among those she invited were Connie and Rosa, the two Philadelphia women who were in Abu Dhabi as consultants for the bakery endeavor for which Farah had put up some money.

Helen Walker, who also came to Farah's home, started talking non-stop to Connie and Rosa; Helen wanted to know all about the bakery business and how these women earned an invitation to the UAE. Farah thought Helen sounded like a seasoned reporter as she asked the questions.

Connie and Rosa were amazed at the size of Farah's kitchen, and said it was much larger than those in their respective suburban homes. Connie said "we could do some serious baking here."

"Except my grandmother does not have all those baking dishes you need for regular cakes," said Iman, "but she has lots of ones for cupcakes because we used to have the cooks bake enough for all of Al Koba Academy where we went."

"And where I go," said her brother Diab. "The boys' school. Forget cupcakes. I would be laughed right out of my class. I would be a hero if I brought Big Macs for everyone, though."

Farah and Iman showed the bakers the storage room where all of the baking needs were stored. The shelves were lined with bags of sugar and flour and everything one would need to bake. Cupcake tins by the dozens were stacked along one shelf.

"If you want to make some cupcakes, go ahead," said Farah.

She was half-kidding, but the Alberti sisters looked at Iman who said to them: "Lunch is over and my uncles and the boys are leaving. I think it would be fun if the women want to do it."

Thus began one of the most endearing days in Farah's household. Instead of aprons, the women put on old abayas that Hessa found upstairs in a trunk. The Alberti sisters and Helen were laughing uproariously at the sight of themselves. Then Dr. Teresa came in, a late arrival because she had stayed behind to make sure everything was cleaned up at the university.

"And this would be what?" she asked. "Make your own lunch?"

"No," said Hessa as she threw an abaya at the professor. "We are making cupcakes."

"For what reason?" asked Teresa.

"For fun," said Iman.

Mariam then appeared. Iman's older sister had to return to her marketing job after the speaking competition and then drove over to her grandmother's villa after work. She had no idea what was going on. Here were several

American women and her grandmother and her sister and her Aunts Hessa and Ayesha and her mother, Judith, all wearing abayas in her grandmother's kitchen. Mariam started snapping photos. She joined in after removing her own expensive abaya that featured extensive silver trim.

"I am not wasting a good abaya on whatever we are doing," said Mariam, who grabbed one of the old abayas. "Were these Grandma's from the old days?"

"Probably," said Iman. "I wish Mona and her mother and grandmother were still here. They would enjoy this. They went to see Mona's brother, Sultan, play in a tennis match."

Mariam said, "I can send them some pictures."

The Albertis started mixing the ingredients together in a big bowl. They had removed a number of lemons from the large refrigerator and asked Farah's cook if she had a "zester." The cook said she had never heard of one. Ayesha said she thought there was one in her kitchen across the street, and made a call.

"Lourdes, our cook, is on her way with it now," said Ayesha.

In less than two minutes, Lourdes appeared and they all took turns zesting some lemon rind into the batter.

"A special ingredient for these cupcakes," said Connie.

Then the women put the mix into sprayed cupcake molds. Into the large ovens went the tins. As the cupcakes baked, Connie and Rosa started directing their "pupils," as they called them, in creating icing. They checked the storage area and found some ingredients but could not find any "sparkles" or citron fruit or things that could be used to top the icing.

"Is there any food coloring?" asked Rosa.

"I have all of those things across the street," said Lourdes. "I love to bake. My mother works in a bakery in Manila."

So, she and Rosa went over to Ayesha's villa and gathered a lot of supplies for the icing. Rosa returned and said: "You all have the most beautiful homes."

During a coffee break in between baking and decorating, Teresa sat down in the women's majlis with Hessa. A minute later, Helen walked out of the nearby bathroom and said: "Hessa, can you explain to me about the toilets in there?"

Hessa smiled.

"Oh, of course. It can be a bit shocking. In addition to the modern toilet, my mother insisted that the bathroom there—it is used by lots of guests—also have the old type of toilet that we used even when I was young. With an opening in the floor and a chain to pull for flushing. She said she wanted people to realize how things had changed. Actually, there are still lots of them in Abu Dhabi in the shops behind the main streets. But you know, Helen, my mother and Amna and those their age did not have any plumbing when they were young. They seldom talk about that but I think the Gulf and the desert were bathrooms then."

"Wow, such interesting things I am learning here," said Helen.

Teresa, Hessa and Helen talked about plans to play golf together.

"Well, I can play golf but I think I would have a problem learning how to bake," said Hessa. "I never had to step foot in the kitchen, really. I keep thinking how different my life is from my mother's upbringing. She lived in a barasti and was married as a kid. I am single, have a career, and now have that golf title. Of course, my family has given up on trying to get me married off. Not at this age."

"How old are you, Hessa?" said Helen.

"37."

"My daughter would be that exact age if she were alive."

Teresa and Hessa said nothing.

After Helen rejoined the kitchen group, Hessa quietly asked Teresa: "Should we have asked about how her daughter died? Maybe as an infant. I did not know what to say."

Dr. Teresa thought for a moment.

"You know, Hessa, she was a journalist. Her husband told me that on the bus to the golf tournament. I keep thinking I know the byline of Helen Walker."

"Maybe we could check one of the search engines later," said Hessa as Teresa nodded her head.

Then it was back to the kitchen revelry as the Albertis and their pupils mixed varied colors of icing. The women made all kinds of designs over the icing, using edible beads and colored sugars from Lourdes' cache in Ayesha's home.

"This is so much fun for us," said Rosa. "Being in the Middle East and wearing these abayas with some of the national women."

"Believe me, it is not the usual undertaking," said Hessa. "We do have fun but remember, we stop to pray several times a day."

"Me, too," said Rosa. "I keep the rosary in my pocket when I work and say a decade of it each time I have a break."

"She does the praying for me," said Connie. "I am not quite that religious."

Then Rosa had a thought.

"Does anyone here have a video camera?"

"I do," said Iman. "I have a small flip one for my film class at WU. It is in my car."

"Well, if we tape some of our baking here, we can put it on our TV show in Philadelphia. It is a reality show after all, and we are really here in Abu Dhabi. It would be a great part of our upcoming program. Sorry we are leaving tomorrow. We have so enjoyed this experience. And Avalon is next!"

That had been such a great afternoon, Farah thought as she walked a week later into Ayesha and Khalid's home. The Al Bader boys had just returned from school and they jumped all over their grandmother when they saw her. She handed them the cupcakes and they ran with Farah into the kitchen where their nanny distributed one to each of them.

Ayesha came downstairs when she heard the commotion. She was dressed in jeans and a tee-shirt.

"What do you think of my new hairdo?" she asked her mother-in-law as she kissed each of her sons who then bolted for the yard where they could devour the cupcakes while kicking the ball around.

"I love the length. It falls so nicely on your shoulders. It is respectful and modern, I guess."

"The trendsetter—that is what Dr. Jalilla calls it. She is my doctor and she got her hair cut recently this way. So I liked it and I went to her beautician, Cecelia, at the hotel salon. Dr. Jalilla went to Cecelia after seeing how she had cut the hair of one of the sheikhas. Cecelia is 60 or 61—Jalilla told me that—and she is really good. The other beauticians stand and watch her as she works sometimes."

"Well, I guess she will be getting a lot of business because I really think it becoming. Of course, I am a bit old for that haircut, and a bit too gray."

"No, you are not. My mother is coming here tomorrow from Dubai to get her hair cut. She saw mine yesterday when I went to meet her and my aunt for lunch at the new restaurant on the creek in Dubai."

"Great. Bring her over to see me. I love your mom. And I want to tell you how much we enjoyed being here for Khalid's birthday dinner. It is so good, Ayesha, to see you having fun."

"Well, that dinner was enjoyable but the baking day was the most fun I have had in years," said Ayesha. "I wound up with a pink abaya from the icing. Of course, it was not my abaya. Good thing you save the old ones."

"Yes," said Farah. "For history's sake. We wore mostly all-black abayas until everyone started decorating them—like the cupcakes. The maid had to wash all the abayas twice after we finished doing those cupcakes."

Farah wanted to know more about Dr. Jalilla.

"She is an Al Zabi, right?"

"Yes," said Ayesha, "and I met her at the nails salon. She is a good psychiatrist but not practicing fulltime yet because she is in administration right now at the medical center that her family owns. She was away for years in the U.S. and mostly in Ireland and now she is back. She is 31. My age."

"She has helped you out?"

"Yes, she identified some sort of extension of post-partum depression that I had —she is not exactly sure—but she gave me medicine and she counsels me and I feel terrific and Khalid seems so happy, too. She even invited me to be a board member of a new foundation she is starting to provide free care for foreigners without health insurance, and for some other things they need."

"Really?"

"In fact, she got the idea when the beautician Cecelia said she was having a problem with her hands and had not gone to a doctor because she had no insurance. Dr. Jalilla brought her to New Road Medical Center and to some specialist from Ireland who is there. Jalilla paid for it through what she called her foundation although she did not really have one yet. Then she found out from Cecelia that one of the maintenance guys at the hospital is a former teacher from the Philippines and his school closed there and now he is working in this job. That is sad. But he loves to read, like Cecelia who gets books through Dr. Teresa. This guy, I think his name is Frank, has no such access to a lot of books—you know, it cost 400 dirhams to join the national library—so Jalilla wants to start buying and providing some books for people like him. You know a lot of them have college degrees—did you know that? By the way, you know how Jalilla met Cecelia? Jalilla was getting her nails done one day at Yours Nail where Cecelia's niece, Rowena, works. She has an art degree and could not get a teaching job at home. Well, Cecelia came to the nail salon that day after she got word that Rowena's young son had fallen in Manila and needed surgery. Cecelia said she would try to get the money together to fly the niece home. Dr. Jalilla overheard that and made all the arrangements and flew Rowena home first class. And then she got her a doctor there for the surgery. I think she paid for that, too. She is really a good person as well as a good doctor."

Farah was fascinated as Ayesha told her about the need for a foundation.

"Can I contribute to this foundation? What is its name?"

"I am sure Jalilla would be happy to get your donation or help. As for the name—she asked me to pick a name for it. You know what I did? I asked Lourdes and Angela if they had any ideas. After all, a lot of the people we will be helping are also Filipinos. Thank goodness we cover health costs for our household staffs; they all appreciate that. Well, Angela and Lourdes told me the next day that there was a St. Gemma who was poor and helped the poor, too. Her real name was Gemma Galgani. They suggested we call it the Gemma Foundation, not just because of the saint but because they liked the name Gemma. It is like a gem, maybe a diamond or something. They said we are 'gems' for organizing this. I told Jalilla and she said the last name Galgani sounded Arabic although I think it is Italian. Jalilla spent years in a Catholic country so naming it after a saint was fine with her and she liked the idea that Lourdes and Angela made the suggestion. We will just say it is a nice name if anyone asks. So we are going to set it up and maybe do a lot of things for the Filipinos and others."

"I will be happy to send a donation as soon as you set it up."

"Maybe you can join the board, too," said Ayesha.

"No, I think one from a family is enough on a board. But maybe my friend Amna will be interested. She is always looking for something to do, and she certainly can part with some of that Al Shari money she inherited from her husband."

The boys came in from the yard to get some lemonade just as Khalid walked in. He was on his way from one meeting to another and stopped for a quick visit. He sat down to join his mother and wife as the boys hugged him and took off again to the yard.

"I had coffee this morning with Tahnoun and Nasser al Shari at the Corniche Café across from our offices. They were planning their golf matches in New Jersey. Tahnoun's father-in-law, Jack Shanley, is setting up a lot of things for them at a golf club somewhere near there. Tahnoun really has fun with that guy. Apparently Mr. Shanley had a hemorrhoid operation recently and Tahnoun went online and ordered a tailbone cushion for him as a joke and had them write a note that it was for the golf cart. His father-in-law sent an email and said the dog enjoyed his new bed. That is funny."

"I like all the Shanleys," said Farah. "Of course, we all miss Judith's mother, Anne. I am definitely going to Avalon with Tahnoun and Judith, and Hessa will be there most of the time, too. And with the Al Sharis renting there, it will be like Abu Dhabi East. Or is it West?"

Khalid turned to his wife.

"Would you be interested in going to New Jersey?"

"Us? The family? The boys, too?"

"Tahnoun said the boys would love the beach and they have a morning camp for young kids right near there."

"Well, I was thinking London again this summer but this sounds like more fun. Would Judith and Tahnoun mind if we show up there, too?"

"He is the one who suggested it. Nasser then showed me photos on his mobile camera of places we can rent. He showed me the house he is renting and it is nice. Okay, they might not be Abu Dhabi villas but I saw one with four bedrooms and three baths and we could get it."

"Would we bring the nanny?"

"That is one big NO. Tahnoun and Nasser agreed that we Arabs need not flaunt our household staff around the Jersey shore. There is such a thing in America called babysitters. We will hire them if we need them. Frankly, I think it is time that the two of us spent nanny time with the boys. Of course, when I am not playing golf."

"And can I go to New York for a day or two?"

"Sure. I will watch the boys. And I will get that list of babysitters!"

As Khalid left to his next meeting, Ayesha turned to Farah and said: "Can you believe all of this is happening?"

She could not.

*   *   *

CHAPTER 13

Dr. Bill McAvoy strolled into the offices of his brother, Ben, at New Road Medical Center. Bill had arrived the night before and was picked up by his sister-in-law, Mary, at the airport. On the way to her Abu Dhabi apartment, Mary kept questioning her brother-in-law about how he was going to deal with Jalilla and her family. He said he did not know but hoped that Ben and Mary could get him and his girlfriend together at their home.

"You have to understand this society. We don't really understand it yet because we are newbies in Abu Dhabi. But I must tell you that Ben sees Jalilla only at work and I have met her for coffee a few times at the mall cafes. I don't think she really socializes with men at all in this place except relatives, I guess."

"Yes, she said that is all different here," said Bill. "In Dublin, we could go out and have dinner. She often wore a head scarf but it was no big deal getting together. Or she would make me dinner at her apartment—or mostly order in, as she admits she never really had to cook. But here—I am the Irish Catholic. She can't hang out with a Catholic guy."

"From what I can see," said Mary, "it does not matter what religion you are. The national girls who work at the hospital as administrative assistants in the legal department with me or as PR staffers tell me that they cannot really socialize with any men, even Muslims, until they are married. One girl in my office is getting married next month and she started talking to her future spouse on the phone and everyone got excited that she even did that. Last week he showed up one day at our office and she put on a veil and ran to our coffee room. She was happy to see he was handsome, though, and thought it was kind of cute that he would break the rules and come to see her. I get the impression that things are loosening up a bit as women go to work, but I don't know. Jalilla probably has to follow some rules, but yet she has been out of the country for so long and this must be difficult for her…"

Jalilla knew Bill had arrived in the UAE and phoned him at his brother's apartment. They decided to meet the next day at the hospital with Bill using the ruse that he was visiting his brother and wanted to see the operation of the hospital, too. So the brothers drove to the hospital together and Ben took his sibling into Jalilla's private office. They followed the same routine the next day, with Bill also taking time to go through the facility and take notes as if he were checking out the hospital as a potential new hire. He and Jalilla, though, did not know how to handle their personal situation.

Jalilla was keeping in touch with Sheikha Mowza about Bill's visit. Mowza had told Jalilla that, through her brother Ahmed, she had seen Hassan a few times when he was in the city for the Energy Conference and they had agreed not to tell her parents about the relationship until the family was in London during the summer. She also said that Hassan had just informed her that his company was considering transferring him back to New York as the office was expanding there, and he was trying to ward that off, at least for awhile.

"Maybe I should go to New York," laughed Jalilla as she spoke by phone to the sheikha one morning before Bill was due to arrive at her office.

"No, we need a good psychiatrist in the UAE; we do not have enough of them," said Mowza. "You need to live here. And if that means you want to marry Bill and have him come here, then introduce him to your family."

"You think I should do that?" asked Jalilla. "When?"

"While he is here. Jalilla, you have spent years overseas and your parents should realize that things are different now."

"I am not as worried about my parents, Mowza, as I am about my older brothers."

"Damnation," said Sheikha Mowza. "Oops. I better not say that outside of London. But this whole bit about older brothers making decisions about their sisters and deciding what they can do is ridiculous. For crying out loud, we have fathers—and mothers. Thank God Ahmed supports me. He would never let my other brothers have a say in my life. Hey, I have an idea. Why not tell Bill to come over to CASPER offices tomorrow to meet Ahmed and me. Then you come over from work. We can have lunch brought in. That would be delightful."

"Great," said "Jalilla. "Is 1:30 a good time?"

"See you then," said Mowza.

The next afternoon, at the appointed time, Jalilla walked into the impressive offices of Sheikha Mowza.

"Oh, there she is, my fellow charter member of the Professional Women's Association," said Mowza. "My assistant, Hamda, is sending out emails right now for articles for the first newsletter—remember I said I would handle those."

"You are a gem for doing that, and for having Bill and me for lunch."

At that moment, in walked Dr. William McAvoy, and Jailla introduced him to Sheikha Mowza.

"I thought you were kidding about how good looking this guy is," said Mowza, as Bill laughed and said "you don't seem like a royal to me."

"You know many royals?" smiled Mowza.

"Only the ones I've operated on. And they could be demanding."

From his office, in walked Sheik Ahmed. Actually, he was limping a bit.

"This is my brother and partner, Ahmed," said Mowza. "Is it the knee again?"

"Yes," said Ahmed as he greeted Dr. Bill and Jalilla al Zabi. "I don't know what is happening but it started to hurt again last night when I was playing tennis with my usual group. I think one of your brothers or cousins is in our group, Jalilla. Salem al Zabi. We have eight guys and we take turns playing each other."

"Salem is one of my older brothers," said Jalilla.

"We went to Al Koba together in the dark ages," said Ahmed.

"You old guy, Ahmed," said his sister. "Hitting 35 one of these days."

"I saw that nearly two years ago," said Bill. "Same time I finished paying off my medical school education."

The food arrived from a nearby restaurant.

"I know you like Italian, Jalilla," said Mowza. "Hope you do, too, Bill."

As they were eating on a table in the conference room, Ahmed explained to Bill how the UAE was set up.

"Up until 1971, Abu Dhabi was the largest of several emirates in this area. Each emirate, like today, had a ruling family. Together the emirates were known as the Trucial States and were British protectorates. The British decided to leave the area and the rulers of the emirates got together and formed a country in 1971 and called it the United Arab Emirates. So we have federal laws but the individual emirates also have their own regulations. The rulers of the seven emirates elect a president from among their group. The UAE has an advisory body, called the Federal National Council, with members from all emirates. The rulers have been very generous to the UAE citizens, giving out free homes and land for businesses. We are trying hard to maintain traditions but it is difficult in the 21st century as most of us are educated and many of us have traveled and studied or worked abroad. And we are a technologically-savvy country, and that makes life interesting, too."

"I know that my brother Ben and his wife are finding it a great place to live," said Bill.

Ahmed acknowledged that he knew from Mowza that their lunch guests were in a relationship.

"We are in the same boat," said Ahmed. "Mowza loves this great guy who was here at a conference last week. I plan to marry a girl from Jordan and do not care what my family says. That is the good part of having this business. Mowza and I do not have to rely on the largesse of the ruling family like some of our relatives might. So if the family disowns us because of our choice of spouses, we will not starve to death."

Ahmed also said he agreed with his sister that Bill should meet Jalilla's family.

"She thinks her brothers will raise a big fuss," said Mowza to Ahmed.

"Well, if Salem does, I will have a few words with him. That's the one good thing about being a sheik. As we say, they shake at the words of a sheik!"

When a limping Ahmed got up to get some more iced tea, Bill asked who was treating him for his bad knee.

"Well, no one really. We usually go to doctors in London or the U.S. if we need treatment or surgery. I don't know what is wrong but one of my friends told me last night that he bet I had torn a meni-something."

"A torn meniscus in the knee? Probably that is what it is. I wish I could help you. You know, I am an orthopedic surgeon."

"You are?" said Ahmed.

"And he has operated on members of the royal family from England," said Jalilla proudly. "And how many prime ministers?"

"Two," said Bill.

"Could you check out my knee here?" asked Ahmed.

Jalilla said she could help set that up at New Road Medical Center.

"We own it, as you know and I am the medical director right now. We have one orthopedic guy on staff but only part-time as we share him with the U.S. Hospital in Dubai. But we have all the equipment for X-rays, MRIs, whatever. Bill, I can get you visiting privileges. As Ben's brother, of course. No one realizes that you are a close friend of mine from Ireland."

After Bill and Jalilla left, Ahmed said he liked meeting Bill and wondered "if he really is a top-notch doctor. Let's look him up on the Web."

Mowza hit a search engine button on her laptop and put in the words Dr. William McAvoy. The first link was headlined: McAvoy Named One of Top Ten Orthopedic Surgeons in Europe.

"I am heading to New Road tomorrow morning," said Ahmed. "This knee is bothering me."

* * *

Dr. Teresa was sitting with her colleagues in the department chairman's office and they were discussing some of the offerings for the upcoming fall. One Women's University faculty member wanted to consider adding a class in print journalism.

"How can we teach journalism in a country that does not have a free press?" asked Dr. Paul. "If you say something against the government, you get shut down. We are all from countries where a free press is an integral part of our being."

The chairman said he thought that it would be good to teach Journalistic Writing, so that students would know how to secure information, write it up and edit the copy.

"There are many stories they can write up and lots of features and profiles. We can beef up the university newspaper that is just a little newsletter at this point. We will just watch what is published…"

"I support the idea," said Teresa. "I took a few journalism classes in undergraduate school. And it really helped me when I was writing papers for my master's and my doctorate."

They all agreed it would be a good class. But who would teach it? They figured an adjunct might have to be brought aboard.

"I know an American woman here who has a background in newspaper work. For many papers, she told me. I don't know the specifics and have no idea if she ever taught. I could ask her."

"What is her name?" asked Dr. Paul.

"Helen Walker."

"The columnist?"

"I understand she was a newspaperwoman but she gave up writing awhile ago," answered Teresa.

"Yes," said Paul. "After writing the column about her daughter. She won several awards for that last column and refused to accept any of them."

"What was the column about?" asked the department chairman. "She wrote what about her daughter?"

"About losing her daughter."

"How did it happen?" asked Teresa.

"9-11. Her daughter worked in the Twin Towers. And in that final column, Helen Walker blasted the terrorists and their homelands. It is an unbelievable piece of writing."

Teresa practically cried as she left to return to her office. Her mobile was ringing. It was Hessa al Bader, calling about getting together for golf with Judith and Helen Walker.

"Oh my god, Hessa, remember we said we were going to search online to see about Helen after she said she had a daughter who would be your age."

"I forgot about it," said the golf champion.

"I was just at a meeting and a colleague said Helen's daughter died on 9-11. And Helen wrote her last column about it. I am going to look it up online now."

"Oh, no. I will check on my computer, too, and get back to you, Teresa. Wait until my mother hears this."

It was easy to find Helen's column on the Internet. Teresa began to wonder why she had not read the piece or read about it. Maybe it was because she could not face reading a paper for weeks after the attacks. She had been playing in her women's golf league near Spring Lake that beautiful Tuesday in September and never heard about the attack until a few hours after it had happened. Her husband, Ray, drove down from his Jersey City offices; he could not get near Manhattan, where they lived most of the year in an upper West Side apartment, as the city was blocked off. She remembers heading that night with her husband to a restaurant near their shore home and lots of people were there, and no one was saying anything. Teresa and Ray stayed in Spring Lake for a week before returning to their Manhattan residence. She spent most of that time watching television reports and packing goods at a Spring Lake church to help the victims' families.

Hessa called back.

"Teresa, did you find it? I did and I cannot believe what she wrote."

Indeed, Teresa had read it and her reaction had been the same. What was Helen doing in Abu Dhabi after writing that?

The column attracted a reader's attention from the start:

Let me introduce you to two of the worst countries in the world: Saudi Arabia and the United Arab Emirates. Home to the vicious terrorists whose creative attacks on New York last week took the life of my only daughter, Carrie. Home to people who have no idea about the meaning of a free press and whose women kowtow to the rules of their older brothers or their spouses. Home to outrageous oil wealth that cannot stop the insidious disease known as terrorism. Home to a religion that calls for peace yet harbors a radical conservatism that infects the world.

The rest of the column not only took the Muslim countries to task, but also described Helen's "beautiful" daughter, a stock broker in her late 20s, and how Carrie's death had affected a family and a Long Island town. The words were powerful and mind-grabbing.

"Hessa," said Teresa. "I don't know what to say."

"Well, as I recall, two of those terrorists came from the northern Emirates. We were horrified. Many of our families got our young men out of the U.S.

where they were studying. It was awful. I don't know what to say to Helen. I cannot believe she would come to live here."

"Hessa, let's just play golf and not mention it. Maybe you should tell your mother about the column. Read it to her. Maybe she and her friend, Amna, will mention it to Helen. But I am not sure they should, either."

"Ok," said Hessa. "Meet us at Dhabi Golf Club on Saturday at 7 a.m."

"What? That early?" said Teresa.

"The hot months are almost upon us, dear Professor. We have to play before the hottest part of the day. And, of course, we will have lunch after we play."

*　　*　　*

Mohammed al Bader was outside shooting hoops with his younger brother, Diab. Judith smiled as she watched her sons tussle over every rebound and laugh as they did so. It was so good to see them together. Mo had arrived home two hours earlier, just two days after his exams ended at Penn. She almost did not recognize him with his pony-tailed hair and closely-shaved beard.

"You guys want some lemonade?" yelled Judith to her sons as they took a break from the searing May sun and came into the air-conditioned villa.

"How about a beer?" asked Mohammed.

She laughed, hoping that her son was not scrapping his Muslim heritage and heading for alcohol, especially at his age. They settled for their cook's special ice tea, made with some spices that she kept secret.

"Diab, how is the Al Koba team looking like for next year?" asked Mo.

"We are losing our guards to graduation, so who knows?"

Mohammed said Al Koba better watch out for the American Academy because he knew a guy who probably would be attending there next year.

"I play pickup ball in the gym with his brother and this kid came down from Connecticut one weekend and played with us. The kid is good! Already a starter at some high school. Turns out their old man is coming to work in Abu Dhabi with a bank, and this guy, who is 15, I think, will be living here with the family. I assume he will go to the American Academy."

"Get him to Al Koba."

"Well," said Mo, "he is not exactly a national. Try Greek-American."

Their mother interrupted.

"Diab is right. Our board voted to take all nationalities starting in the fall."

"Really? I will send a text to my buddy, his brother. And if the kid goes to your school, you might be off the starting roster, bro."

"Funny, "said Diab. "Bring the Greek-American on! This Emirati-American can handle it!"

Their Aunt Hessa walked in through the front door and said: "Where is my favorite nephew of all those in America?"

"I am here," said Mohammed as he bowed to his aunt and said, "Oh, champion! I am sorry I missed seeing your win."

She hugged him, pulled on his long hair, and said: "Dean's List?"

"Maybe," said Mohammed. "If Grandma Anne is up there praying for me."

"Well, your other grandmother here prays five times a day and I am sure she thinks it is Dean's List for you. If she knew what the Dean's List was. Judith, do you remember when I made the Dean's List in college and told her? She wanted to visit the dean in Al Ain to see what trouble I was in."

Another car pulled in through the gates just as the Al Bader brothers were about to return to their basketball game.

"Is that I MAN?" asked Mohammed.

He was pronouncing his sister's name as they had heard Americans do so often. Many times his parents would explain that their daughter's name is pronounced like E Mahn, and that she was named after one of Tahnoun's ancestors.

"They should have named you Betty or something," laughed Mohammed as he and his sister high-fived each other and he said: "Want to join your brothers for a bit of basketball?"

"No way. Too hot. And what is the ponytail bit?" said Iman as she headed into the cool kitchen and sat down with her mother and aunt.

"I just saw Dr. Teresa at WU and she said she is going to play golf with you two and the American woman, Helen, the one who is Gramma's friend," said Iman.

"Did Teresa say anything about Helen Walker to you?" asked Hessa.

"No," said her niece. "I saw Dr. Teresa in the parking lot and we spoke for about 10 seconds."

"Hessa, what about Helen?" asked Judith.

"Well, you should hear this. OK, when we were making the cupcakes that day at our home and took a break, Helen told us that her daughter would be the same age as me if she were alive. Teresa and I did not know what to say and we all went back to the cupcake fun. Teresa had said that Helen's name was familiar and we talked about checking her name out later on the Web. But we both forgot. Then just yesterday I called Teresa about playing golf and she had just come from a Women's University meeting where—I don't know how but Helen Walker's name came up—one of the professors said that Helen was the journalist who quit after writing a column about her daughter's death in the Twin Towers on 9-11. Helen got all kinds of awards for the column and refused them all, according to this colleague of Teresa's. So Teresa, who was stunned, had just heard all that when I called so we got off the phone and both went to our computers. You should read what Helen wrote. She called the UAE pretty bad things, and Saudi Arabia, too, of course. You can look it up yourselves."

"Oh my goodness," said Iman. "Did you tell Gramma Farah?"

"No. I don't know if I should. I mean she really likes Helen. And you know, Iman, well, maybe not, because you were in grade school then, but did you know our family donated 1 million dirhams to the 9-11 Fund? Your grandmother insisted on that."

"She went to Mass with us adults here in Abu Dhabi on September 12," said Judith. "Every American of every religion in the city was at church to pray for the victims. We all found out about the special Mass through emails and phone calls. And believe me, you also saw a lot of people in national dress at church that day. Even some of the sheikhs and sheikhas. The Archbishop said it was the most non-denominational service he had ever seen. There were Muslims and Hindus and lots of people from other Christian churches in the city. The archbishop and the Episcopal pastor both spoke and said that they knew Islam was a peaceful religion. But I know many Muslims, including Tahnoun, were embarrassed and outraged at the same time."

"Oh," said Hessa. "I was there and I will never forget when at the end of the service they sang—what was it, Judith?"

"God Bless America. And everyone in the church was in tears."

Judith mumbled something about "this Helen situation. I will check it out on the Internet. And Hessa, don't say anything to your mom unless we think about it some more."

Mariam was next to arrive home, after what she called "a busy day" at the marketing firm. She was happy, though, that at a meeting in the morning, the head of the company encouraged those without master's degrees to attend graduate school. The company even offered to pay the tuition.

"I decided I am going to apply to schools in America."

"No way. Don't come to UPenn; you will drive me crazy if we are both there," said Mohammed as he and Diab came into the villa to greet their oldest sibling.

"It is too late to apply for the fall," said Judith.

"Not really," said Mariam. "Some schools have rolling admissions. And I already took the Graduate Record Exams last year and can use the scores. I am thinking Penn or maybe NYU. Definitely a big city. No middle of the country for me."

They sat around for the next hour until Tahnoun arrived home and said he had booked dinner reservations at a new fish restaurant on the beach outside of the city.

"Made reservations for eight people. You and your mother are coming, too, I hope," he said to his sister-in-law.

"Well, if you are buying, we will be there," said Hessa, who added: "I hope we go to some good fish restaurants when we all get to Avalon."

* * *

Dr. William McAvoy switched from his casual togs into appropriate surgical garb as he prepared to walk into the well-equipped operating room at New Road Medical Center. He was in a good mood as he thought about the events of the past two days.

After determining that indeed Sheik Ahmed had a meniscus tear in the left knee, the visiting orthopedic surgeon made arrangements for arthroscopic surgery at New Road.

In the interim, Ahmed said he would accompany Bill to Jalilla's home to meet her parents. It proved to be a scene out of a book as Jalilla introduced her mother and father to her "doctor friend from Ireland, Bill McAvoy, and his friend, Sheik Ahmed." She did not mention that the pair had never met until that very week.

The parents, whose English language skills were far from the level of the next generation, were honored to have a member of the ruling family in their home. When Jalilla said Bill had come to ask if he might marry her, the confused parents thought she was going to wed Sheik Ahmed and reacted happily. Bill was at a loss for words but Ahmed explained it perfectly, saying that he was not the groom-to-be but that "your daughter wants to marry this man, Dr. William McAvoy, one of the finest surgeons in all of Europe. I would be happy to have him marry a sheikha from my family, but he has chosen your daughter with whom he worked in Ireland."

Before the parents could say anything, Bill took out a large diamond ring that he had purchased earlier that day in the company of Ahmed, who did the negotiating for the price and laughed as he left the upscale jewelry store because "they gave me the royal discount." Bill presented the ring to his intended as her mother said: "Oh, it is beautiful." The father asked Bill if he were a good Muslim, and the doctor said "Not yet. If I convert, I will be a good one." Jalilla and Sheik Ahmed tried to keep from chuckling. When the parents aired their concern that Jalilla would be leaving the UAE again, Bill surprised them all by saying: "My brother works at your medical center. He is a fine plastic surgeon. He is my only brother and I would like to work at the same place as he does. If I can get a job here, I will take it."

Jalilla's father responded: "I own it. I made my money in trading but I own that hospital although I don't run it. Jalilla, you can hire him, can't you?"

"Yes, Baba, after we are married. And I am sure he wants a big salary."

As Ahmed and Bill walked out of the spacious villa, Jalilla's brother Salem was arriving. He was surprised to see his tennis friend, Sheik Ahmed, coming out of the Al Zabi home.

"Hi. What are you doing here?" he asked.

"Marriage proposal."

"You and my sister?"

"No, she is going to marry this guy, Dr. Bill McAvoy from Ireland."

Salem looked a bit ashen.

"Dr. McAvoy came from Ireland to operate on my knee tomorrow. He knows your sister from there. She is one lucky young woman to marry a famous orthopedic surgeon."

The following day, as the operation was to get underway, Bill assured Ahmed that it would take less than an hour and that he could go home later in the afternoon after spending some time in the recovery room. With brother Ben assisting him, Bill handled the surgery with ease.

He was looking forward to working and living in Abu Dhabi.

*　　*　　*

The academic year was nearing the end at Women's University.

Sheikha Asma sat with Iman and Mona in the university cafeteria. They had been together in school, first at Al Koba and then at WU, for more than 15 years and they were lamenting the end of their journey together.

"I hate it to be over," said Asma. "I feel so free when I am here with you guys. I hate to lose this happy feeling. We have to vow to keep in touch."

"I only wish you could have joined us in the cake business," said Iman.

"You really are going to do it?" said Asma.

"Yes," said Mona. "But it will be our side business. We all agreed we can pursue other careers or studies but we hope to learn how to manage the business. Actually, we plan to hire a fulltime manager but right now we are still debating who will be the chief cake baker. Our consultants in Philadelphia, two women with a TV baking show, are handling that for us."

"When will you open?" asked Asma.

"We are aiming for October," said Mona. "The rented space will be put together this summer and we have a great young American architect who designed it. We have all of the legal papers signed and my sister Mariam's company will help with marketing. Alia is our business whiz. She is not travelling this summer so she will be overseeing a lot of the stuff. And Essa might be around most of the time. She said she is going to get married soon. I think she is too young."

Asma laughed.

"Our mothers would have considered themselves spinsters if they were not married by about 20 or 21, and our grandmothers by 15 or 16. But now you look foolish if you don't finish college or graduate school first."

"What are you going to do next year, Asma?" asked Iman. "You cannot sit around at the palace and do nothing."

"Well, as usual I will spend the summer in London and then head back here to Abu Dhabi. Then I might go to graduate school. Perhaps next January. If my aunt has any say in it, I will go overseas to school."

"Your aunt who came to the speaking competition?"

"Yes, Mowza. My youngest aunt. She is great. Oh, and she has a friend starting a foundation—the Gemma Foundation—and Mowza suggested to her that I be a board member. I could make contact with young people to help. It is to provide assistance to foreigners who need health care and other things. I have to find out the specifics."

"My Aunt Ayesha is helping to start that," said Iman. "My grandmother already pledged some money for it."

Dr. Teresa was walking across the university plaza with Helen Walker and the girls yelled to her to join them. She said she would be right back, after she walked Helen to the parking lot. When she returned, Iman asked what her grandmother's friend was doing at WU.

"She is going to teach a journalism class here in the fall; she came to meet the faculty and dean. She was an adjunct at a university in Long Island awhile ago. And she has a master's from Columbia Journalism and years in the newspaper business. Too bad you will not be around here next year to take her class."

"Did she ever mention the column she wrote about her daughter who died in the Twin Towers?" asked Iman.

"Who told you that?" asked Dr. Teresa.

"My aunt and then my grandmother. Mona, your grandmother told you, right?"

"Yes. Helen told them about it last week. She really said she wrote some awful things about our country. Now she said she is happy here. Oh, and our grandmothers had us look up Helen's column on the computers and read it off to them. They lost children, too, so they know how it feels, although 9-11 was simply horrible."

"Remind me to tell Hessa that her mother already knows the story," said Teresa.

Asma's mobile phone rang. It was her dear aunt, Sheikha Mowza.

"You are where, Mowza? You flew from London to where? Ireland? And Uncle Ahmed is with you? And Hassan? Whose wedding? Yours? Who? Jalilla al Zabi? From Abu Dhabi? The one starting the foundation? And you want to know if I want a handmade Irish woolen sweater? OK."

"My aunt is at a wedding in Dublin," said Asma as she closed her mobile. "What is that all about?"

"I know," said Iman. "My aunt is there, too. The one I mentioned, Ayesha al Baloud. My Uncle Khalid's wife. The bride is Jalilla al Zabi, a doctor, and she is marrying an Irish surgeon who will come here and work. He already has done some surgery here, on your uncle, I think, Asma. The doctors wanted a small, mixed wedding in the place where they met. Ireland. Ayesha, as I said, is on the board of the bride's new foundation. I think she said the bride's parents were going over, too. About time things changed. My parents were ahead of the curve getting married in Philly and my grandmother coming to it."

"Hey, I could use an Irish sweater for skiing," said Mona. "Call your Aunt Mowza back and see what you can do."

"Forget it," said Asma. "I am not supporting the sport that put you on crutches."

"It was not the sport. It was an obese Australian."

Teresa laughed along with the girls and thought how glad she was to have known them and how sad it was that they were about to separate to some degree after years of being together in school. She showed them the airplane ticket she had picked up earlier in the day at a travel agency.

"I am flying home on Friday for more than two months. Home to Spring Lake."

"What about New York? I thought you lived there," said Asma.

"I did. I rented an apartment there for ages, starting right out of my MBA program when I took a banking job in Manhattan. I got married when I was in my late 30s. My husband worked and lived in Jersey City, across the river in New Jersey. He owned an insurance business with agencies around the Northeast U.S. I still own it but have people running it for me. We lived in my apartment in Manhattan but, right after we married, we bought a summer home at the shore in a town called Spring Lake, New Jersey. Actually, we lived there a lot of the time. We joined a golf club there and that sport is my love. I quit working in my late 40s and went back to graduate school in New Jersey at Rutgers University so I either took the train there from Manhattan or drove from our summer place. I was just finishing my doctorate when Ray died suddenly. Doctors thought it was an aneurysm. It was a shock because he was 55 and in good health, or so we thought. I taught part-time for two years at NYU after that and then a colleague told me about WU and Abu Dhabi. I thought it might be a good change for me. So, before I came here, I gave up the New York apartment. Spring Lake is my home now. When I am not there, my niece Abby—well, she is Ray's niece, really, and she lives in New York—spends lot of weekends there with her friends. It is right across from the beach and I also have a pool, so they enjoy having a free place to stay. Abby probably will stay with me there all summer. She did last summer. We had a lot of fun."

"How far did you say you were from Avalon?" asked Iman.

"Maybe an hour or so north on the Garden State Parkway."

"Mona and I will come and visit you one day in July when she is there. I am leaving with my family next week."

"I would love having you visit me. I have six bedrooms, God knows why. But we always had lots of visitors in the summer. Maybe we can go up to New York because we can take the train from Spring Lake. Hessa will be coming up to Spring Lake from Avalon on July 15 for the Member-Guest at our club. I cannot wait until she wears the hijab on the course. And I can say my guest is a national champion. All my friends will love talking to her. I send a monthly email newsletter to lots of people and everyone knows about the UAE. I wrote about the golf championship tournament and about our cupcake making. I get many, many emails reacting to my newsletter. My friends all want to take a vacation here. I think I should have a women's golf trip here next year."

"And we will have golf hats made with TOTE Cakes written on them," smiled Mona.

"Hey, that gives me an idea," said Iman. "Let's get tee shirts made with Taste of the Emirates on them. We can wear them on the Avalon beach. Of course, we will have to get some long-sleeved ones to make everyone happy."

"Speaking of the beach, that is where I am headed this minute," said Teresa. "To the beach club. I will sit and read a novel and have dinner at the pool bar."

"With a glass of wine?" asked Mona with a snicker.

"No, not there," said Teresa. "I am driving and I abide by the no-tolerance drink-and-drive laws in your country. But I have my liquor license with me—thank you, UAE, for allowing non-Muslims to get these—and I'll pick up some good wine on my way back to my apartment. I never drink alone so I will call a few of the other professors who live in my building and we will enjoy celebrating the last week of school."

*　　*　　*

CHAPTER 14

Judith was running around and checking with the maid to make sure everything was packed for the annual trip to Avalon. The flight was leaving in less than 10 hours.

The family members really did not take much but clothes. The New Jersey house had everything, including extra sets of golf clubs. She was just happy that Mariam's firm, like many UAE companies, gave employees extensive vacation time and their oldest child could make the trip with them, although she probably would return to Abu Dhabi ahead of the rest of the Al Baders who would stay through the end of August.

The girls wanted to bring their laptops and Judith was arguing that it would not be necessary as there was a computer in Avalon and another at her father's summer home down the street. Iman said that she wanted to use the laptop on the plane.

"Why?" asked Judith. "How about reading a book or watching TV or a movie? The plane has a monitor for each person and plenty of selections."

It took awhile but Judith won out, after reminding her daughters that they would be bringing a carry-on bag for their abayas. When the girls were younger, they wore regular clothes all the time, usually skirts as was the accepted dress at the time. Once they reached puberty, Emirati girls would start wearing abayas over their clothes and shaylas over part of their hair. But the nationals seldom wore abayas when they travelled to other countries. They would wear the national garb as they boarded the plane and then, midway through the trip, remove the coverings and put them in a carry-on bag. When in a foreign country, the girls would wear modest clothing that covered their arms and legs—jeans and long tee-shirts were the choice of late—and colorful head scarves that showed that they indeed were of the Muslim faith.

"It was a lot easier when you all were younger," said Judith as her four children pretty much ignored what she said.

Diab kept asking about clothes for basketball camp. He had received an email from the man who coached his team at St. Clement's when Diab played there as a freshman. The coach thought Diab might be interested in going to a one-week sleep-away camp in Massachusetts with some of his friends who were now on St. Clem's varsity. Diab was excited because he knew that college coaches came to see players there and Diab was going to have to consider U.S. college choices as soon as he started senior year in the fall at Al Koba.

"You are not going to that camp until August," said his mother. "We can buy whatever you need in the U.S. I want us to travel as lightly as we can."

"Are we flying first-class?" said Mohammed.

"Business class. All we could get for tomorrow. Every American is leaving now for the summer, it seems. If you want first-class, you will have to wait and come over with your grandmother and Aunt Hessa in two weeks. June 29. They got first-class tickets. Actually, I should have put you all in coach. It would do you all some good."

"With the Bangladeshis?" said Diab. "Forget it."

Judith looked at the four of them. They were spoiled, she admitted to herself, with servants and private schools and fancy cars. At least she had made sure they were a bit different from their Abu Dhabi friends whose maids and nannies would go along with their families on trips to fancy hotels in Europe or the Gold Coast in Australia. In Avalon, Judith had no fulltime help; a cleaning service came in weekly to vacuum and dust, and to change the sheets. Judith insisted that her children make their own beds every morning and help her cook some meals. Most times, Tahnoun would grill steaks or chicken on the grill, or they would walk to the small business area and eat at a restaurant. But if she did decide to make a pasta dish or a meatloaf, she would have the children working alongside her. Tahnoun thought it was funny but he would never let one of the children make an excuse to avoid work.

"Can I check two bags on the plane?" asked Mariam.

"Probably," said her mother. "But I said one bag each was enough."

Diab started taunting his sister.

"Your makeup bag, right? The national girls love their makeup."

"Knock it off, D. How many bottles of that perfume are you bringing? You can smell the Arab man a block away."

Tahnoun walked into the house as his offspring continued to argue.

"Did you get a van or something for us to get from Newark Liberty Airport to Avalon?" he asked his wife.

"My father made the arrangements from a Philadelphia service. He rented a small shuttle bus, I think. Anyway, I have the information with the tickets."

"Don't forget the passports," said Tahnoun.

"As if those fancy diplomatic ones count," said Mohammed. "Maybe at the airport here, but I get pulled out of line all the time in other places because I am an Arab guy from the UAE. I guess they think I am a terrorist."

"With that ponytail and beard, you look like one," said Iman.

"Use your American passport, Mohammed," said his mother. "And think about a haircut. I cannot believe you look like that at your parents' alma mater."

With the time change, they were at their lovely Avalon home early the next afternoon and Tahnoun headed right to the supermarket for steaks to grill, and the children went to the beach. It was a weekend and scores of people were enjoying the sun and surf. The first people they saw, though, were their grandfather, Jack Shanley, and some other relatives.

The Al Baders were happy to be back in Avalon.

*   *   *

The Fourth of July party hosted by Rosa's family was in full swing at her home a block from the Avalon beach. Her Italian-American relatives had come out in force as had the Irish-American Haleys from her husband Mike's side. They were all delighted to see the Abu Dhabi contingent because Rosa and Connie had not stopped talking about their consulting trip to the UAE. Mike Haley, who with his brother Hugh owned a large Philadelphia-based contracting firm, had welcomed Tahnoun and Judy with a big "Hey, I saw you with your family on the beach in past years. Sorry I never went over and said hello."

"Well, some people stay away from the Arabs," laughed Tahnoun as Judith said "Stop it, Tahnoun. Mike, I have been coming here since I was a kid. I am a Shanley from Ardmore. Your sister was in my class at St. Rose."

"The Shanleys. Of course. I hope the other Shanleys are coming over today. We have enough hot dogs and hamburgers and chicken and ribs and lasagna for the town."

Everyone mingled and ate a bit.

"This is the pre-beachtime food. Come back later for the good stuff," said Mike Haley.

So the group headed to an Avalon beach, the one nearest the Haley home and a block south of the houses where the Shanleys and Al Sharis and Al Baders were staying. The beach was crowded for the holiday but Mike and Rosa and their sons had staked out a large area where they put up umbrellas and placed chairs and towels around on the sand. Farah and Amna, both wearing light pants, matching long cotton shirts and colorful silk head scarves, sat in a circle with Judith, Sabeen, Connie, Ayesha, Rosa and other women from the party.

"Are you not hot with those head scarves?" asked Connie.

"Are you kidding? This is cool compared to the desert where we grew up. And we wore heavier clothing and burquas, too, for years."

"It is part of who we are," said Ayesha. "And it is no problem. Notice my nieces and their friend Mona and my sister-in-law, Hessa. They took off their scarves and put on baseball caps with their hair pulled up under. Better for their volleyball game. I would play too, but I am keeping an eye on my boys, who love making sand castles with other kids they met here yesterday."

The beach volleyball game was in full swing. The Alberti-Haley group had challenged the Abu Dhabians, who included Hessa, Mariam, Iman, Tahnoun, Khalid, Mohammed, Diab, and the Al Sharis—Mona, Sultan and their father, Nasser. The 10 of them took turns coming in and out on the nine-person team that faced Connie and Rosa's husbands and their relatives, male and female, on the other side of the net. The winner would take on a bunch of the Shanley cousins and friends, who were standing by and waiting.

Farah was enjoying watching her family having such fun.

"You know, it is so nice to see them all together. I think restricting our young women from socializing with men is a bit crazy. The girls are out of college. And I think they are better volleyball players than the boys."

"I heard that," said Jack Shanley as he walked by. "Don't tell my grandsons. Your grandsons, Farah."

"We heard Tahnoun sent you a nice pillow," said Farah. "And you gave it to the dog for a bed?"

"I bet it was your idea," said Jack as the encircled women laughed heartily.

They were all watching the volleyball match when they saw the Abu Dhabi team go into a huddle.

"Must be getting a strategy. They need it. They lost the first game out of three," said Jack.

The strategy was evidenced in minutes. The Emiratis had decided to rattle the Haleys' team by speaking in loud Arabic. Nasser al Shari was the odd man out at the time, and from the sidelines he acted like some sort of a coach, screaming Arabic directions to the players as they would yell out Arabic phrases while hitting the ball across the net. It was all in fun and the opponents were laughing about it.

"What is Arabic for LOSERS?" yelled a smiling Mike Haley as he jumped high to hit the ball across the net. Up went blockers Diab and Mohammed, just as they often jumped on the basketball court, and together smacked the oncoming ball hard. It veered off the makeshift sand court and onto the tattooed back of a young man sitting with his buddies on the beach. As the Al Bader boys walked over to retrieve the ball and apologize, the young guy and his four friends started yelling at them: "You damn Arabs. Who the hell do the bunch of you think you are? Go back to where you came from. Al Qaeda land. We don't need any more terrorists in New Jersey. Get off our beaches. Remember 9-11."

Mohammed started toward the guys before Mike Haley and Nasser al Shari grabbed him.

"No, let it go," said Nasser, who later said he faced the same type of "ignorance" when he was a student at Penn.

A large crowd of beachgoers began to swell around the volleyball net. A few people were on their cell phones, apparently calling the beach patrol or the town's police headquarters. The volleyball players just stood silently. Farah and Amna and the other women got up and walked over. With fire in her eyes, Judith looked as if she were about to say something when her father came into the middle of the crowd and faced the young men who had made the remarks.

"Now listen to me, you ignoramuses. My name is Jack Shanley and I have owned a home here for 35 years. This is my daughter and she owns a home here. And these two young men who came over to get the ball—they are my grandsons. Some of you from the Philadelphia suburbs know them from St. Clement's Prep. Mohammed here holds the scoring record there. These other people are their friends and relatives from Abu Dhabi in the United Arab Emirates. People there gave lots—I mean lots of money to the 9-11 Fund. And when Katrina hit New Orleans, this country quietly presented a check for $100 million to our ambassador in Abu Dhabi. By the way, you ever heard of any Al Qaeda group in the UAE? I don't think so. And these people right here, with the exception of my daughter, are Muslims. They come from a peaceful religion. Oh, there are some crazy fundamentalists in their religion, just as there are crazy Christians who blow up federal buildings. Don't you dare call these Muslims damn Arabs and accuse them of being terrorists. It is you who have displayed your true stripes—or tattoos, as it appears. You need to get out of this town quickly. I notice you all have day badges so you do not rent or own here, as these players do. Take a hike—now—or I personally will use the resources of my law firm to have you charged with making what many consider to be racist remarks."

As Jack Shanley finished speaking and turned around to walk slowly toward the water's edge, the crowd burst into applause. A few men ran over to pat Jack on the back, and other people came to the Abu Dhabi team members and shook their hands and welcomed them to the beach. Some women picked up their beach chairs and joined Farah, Amna and the others in a widening circle.

"You bullies get the hell out of here," said Mike Haley as a beach patrol staffer arrived with a local policeman and escorted the five young men off the beach.

The volleyball game resumed with more than 200 people watching and clapping. Many of them were putting together teams to get in on the action and wait their turns to play.

By the end of the day, 10 teams had formed and Tahnoun and Mike Haley had agreed to co-sponsor a volleyball tourney the following weekend.

"We will have tee-shirts made this week for everyone," Mike told the crowd. "The Al Bader/Haley Beach Volleyball Tournament. Sign up here!"

*   *   *

Hessa Al Bader rented a car in Avalon and headed north in the late afternoon to Spring Lake. She so looked forward to staying overnight with Dr. Teresa and playing in the Member-Guest tournament at the golf club. Hessa was enjoying New Jersey golf; she and Judith had played a number of times at a club near Avalon while her brothers played often with Nasser al Shari. Jack Shanley joined them a few times, as did Mike Haley or his brother, Hugh.

Following the GPS on the rental vehicle, Hessa turned onto the street that ran along the ocean in Spring Lake. She checked the addresses until she came upon the one for Teresa's home. A wide front porch wrapped around the large white home and scores of hydrangea plants formed the perimeter of the house. Hessa loved those colorful bushes that dotted so many Jersey shore properties.

Teresa was sitting on the porch with another woman who turned out to be her niece-by-marriage, Abby Wilson. They spoke for a bit before Teresa headed inside to make dinner.

"I have heard so much about you, Hessa," said Abby. "My aunt cannot stop talking about Abu Dhabi and her students and friends."

"You have to come and visit," said Hessa.

"I was there a few months ago. Saw the mosque and the fancy hotels and, of course, my best memory of all: going to Women's University graduation. What a show. And the diamonds on the graduates. Wow."

"I was there, too," said Hessa. "My niece Mariam graduated although she was out of school for almost a year. My mother, Farah, was having a fit. The sheikhas came in late and then that crazy light show."

"And passing the food. I had never seen anything like it," said Abby.

"It was a shock to me, too. When I finished UAE University, it was much more reserved. And I did not get 20,000 dirhams for making the Dean's List like Mariam did."

Hessa then asked Abby if she resided in Spring Lake.

"As we say in the U.S., I bum off Aunt Teresa, especially during the summer. A lot of singles my age rent here in groups in the summer, and I used to do that. Now I just stay here several days a week and take the train to work in Manhattan where I am a lawyer, and where I own a small condo, by the way. I seldom use it in the summer. But I have a new boyfriend in New York so I guess I will be spending more time there. Who knows?"

"Well, I am single and 37 and there is no way I could rent my own place unless I were living overseas," said Hessa. "That is the way it is with our culture. I just cannot wait to retire and maybe go somewhere and learn to be a golf instructor."

Teresa walked out from the kitchen.

"I heard that, Hessa. You are decades from retiring."

"No I am not. A woman who works for the government, and I am at a government bank, can retire after 15 years if she is married and 25 years if she is single."

"That is discrimination," said Abby. "You women could use my law firm."

"So how long before you are there 25 years?" asked Teresa.

"Ten. I came when I was 22 so I have 15 years in."

"So," snickered Abby, "find a husband and you can retire now."

"Exactly, and I have done so but my family is yet to be told."

"Who?" asked Teresa.

"Tariq al Shamhi. You met him at the championship. He works with me."

"Oh, he is handsome. Isn't he married? His daughter was at your mother's home after the golf championship. Or are you going to be a second wife?"

"Second wife, yes. But not two at the same time. His wife died last year. He does have a 14-year-old daughter—I have known Latifa since she was little— and he made sure it was okay with her. He asked me to marry him right before I left for Avalon. I was playing golf in a foursome with him and we were literally driving in a cart on the course when he said we should get married. I thought he was kidding, but I was excited because he is dear person. And so handsome! He repeated his proposal the next day at work. On his knees in my office. He has called me on my mobile phone every day for two weeks in Avalon and wants to talk to my mother and brothers. I finally told him to call Tahnoun; they play golf together all the time in the UAE. I gave him Tahnoun's mobile number yesterday but I don't think Tariq has called yet. Guess I will know soon."

The three women ate much of the chicken casserole and spinach salad that

Teresa had made and then took a stroll on the Spring Lake boardwalk. They sat together on a bench and looked out over the dark Atlantic.

"It is so peaceful here," said Hessa. "Even more peaceful than in Abu Dhabi where islands made from reclaimed land are blocking much of the view of the Gulf from the Corniche."

"This peaceful atmosphere makes me tired," said Teresa. "Let's hit the hay. We want to win the Member-Guest."

They failed to take first place the next day despite Hessa's good round. The handicap tournament did not give her any advantage but she loved every minute of playing on the well-manicured course and of meeting the other women golfers. Hessa proved to be a big hit as she wore her hijab with a baseball cap on top. She took the laurels for longest drive, a shot that was close to 225 yards down the middle. At the luncheon following the golf, Hessa—now wearing a colorful scarf on her head— was asked to speak briefly about the UAE and the other players were mesmerized as she described her country.

"You can fly directly from New York so come over and play golf with me," she said.

As she drove back to Avalon, Hessa thought about how things were changing in life, especially in her own. She walked into Tahnoun and Judith's home, where she and her mother were staying, and was greeted with the following words from her brother: "Tariq al Shamhi called."

He hesitated and looked at his mother, and then back at his younger sister.

"And, Hessa, we could not be happier."

*   *   *

Jalilla was back in Abu Dhabi after her honeymoon in Europe, and the summer heat was getting to her.

"It is like an oven here," she said in a phone conversation to Ayesha in Avalon. "The air conditioning went off for some reason at our apartment building last night so Bill and I went to my parents' home to stay. They are in Geneva for the summer. And guess what? Air conditioning was off there, too. We finally got the idea to go to the medical center where we have back-up generators in case the air conditioning fails. We slept on couches in our offices."

"Too bad you are not here in Avalon in America," said Ayesha. "It is hot but cool at night and we go to the beach every day. My boys love it. And so do I."

"As your doctor, I am thrilled," said Jalilla.

She then revealed her real reason for calling.

"Ayesha, would you be the executive director of the Gemma Foundation?"

"Me?"

"I know you got your degree in business, right?" she asked of Ayesha.

"Yes, but I only worked, if you could call it that, for a brief time with the family businesses in Dubai, and then I got married, so I don't have any experience running an organization."

"You can do it. You will have an administrative assistant and we will get volunteers. Ayesha, you know a lot of people who can support us financially and you would be a good spokesperson for Gemma."

"If you think I can do it, then yes is the answer," said Ayesha. "And I know I can get some more good board members. I know my mother-in-law's friend, Amna, already says she would be happy to be on the board. And by the way, we will need a logo so do you have any ideas who can design that?"

"Oh, I already got someone to do that."

"Who?" asked Ayesha.

"Rowena."

"Rowena from Your Nails?"

"She has an art degree and she worked up some great logos from which we can choose when you get back. She was thrilled to do it after the help she got to return to Manila when her son was injured."

"Well, we should pay her for this work."

"She would not take any money. But I realized how bright she is as we discussed aspects of our goals for the organization. She is a tech whiz, too. So I hired her. She is your new administrative assistant. Isn't that a turn of events, as they say? You and Rowena...it is almost funny."

"Oh, I think we will work together quite well. And on a slow day, she can do my nails."

"No way," said Jalilla.

"I am joking," said Ayesha. "But we have to get her an apartment, right? Let's make sure it is big enough for her aunt to live with her, too."

"I am ahead of you, Ayesha. I got an apartment large enough for Rowena's family, if they want to move to Abu Dhabi. Her salary will be high enough to pass the standards for bringing families here. Her Aunt Cecelia will be living with her now, and I am thinking—just thinking—about investing in a small beauty parlor specializing in haircuts for women. Cecelia would manage it and I could get an apartment for her, too."

"You are so great, Doctor Jalilla. And we have to think about possibly establishing a private library with lots of books available for foreign workers."

"I agree, "said Jalilla. "And Ayesha, by the way, how are you and all the Abu Dhabi group doing on your vacations in New Jersey?"

"Jalilla, you would never believe how much fun we are having. Everyone is into beach volleyball and golf, of course. Even Tahnoun's daughters, Mariam and Iman, are taking up golf, along with Mona al Shari and her mother, Sabeen. I should do it when we get back to the Emirates. My mother-in-law, Farah, and her friend, Amna, walk every day on the beach. They wear light warm-up clothes and colorful scarves on their heads. There is an aerobics class some mornings on the boardwalk and they started going to it, and they became friendly right away with some of the American women in their 50s and 60s. One day last week, Farah and Amna brought a head scarf for everyone in the class and they all wore them that day. You should see the photos. Oh, and another thing. You know my sister-in-law, Hessa al Bader?"

"The golf champion?" said Jalilla.

"Well, she announced last week that she is getting married when we go back to Abu Dhabi. To a guy who works with her. Tariq al Shamhi. He is a widower. They plan on a small wedding. Signing the papers and then dinner or something. I am not sure."

"When do you return to Abu Dhabi?" asked Jalilla.

"In a week. On July 31st. Judith and Tahnoun and their family will be here until the end of the summer, though. As usual."

"Call me when you get back, Ayesha."

"Will do. I cannot wait to get started with the Gemma Foundation."

*   *   *

In an email to her friends Iman al Bader and Mona al Shari, Sheikha Asma described her summer in London as "pretty much uneventful." She and her sister, Rahma, were taking an art history class at a museum and spending weekends at a family-owned country estate where they had a choice of many horses to ride "and many young cousins to bother." The sisters ventured as often as possible to Harrod's, just a stone's throw from their London apartment, and, as expected, had run into several friends from Women's University.

"And, by the way," wrote Asma at the end of the communiqué, "I think we will be coming to New York next week."

Mona read the email at her family's rented house and walked a block to the Al Baders' summer home where Mohammed was cooking breakfast as his parents and his aunt, Hessa, applauded his every move.

"One flapjack in the air," he would say as he flipped a pancake.

"You cook, Mo?" said Mona. "I am impressed."

"Wait till you taste the omelets," said Mohammed. "Of course, I cook.

My Ardmore education. My grandmother spent a lot of time with me in the kitchen when she was ill. I loved cooking with her. Now I have to teach Aunt Hessa so she can cook for her new husband."

"I am writing everything down," said Hessa. "I just hope Tariq's cook can read it."

They all laughed just as Iman came running into the kitchen from her upstairs bedroom.

"Heard your voice, Mona. Did you read Asma's email?"

"That is why I came over. Let's call her in London and find out when she will be in New York so we might be able to meet her."

"Oh sure," said Mohammed. "Just call London. No big deal as long as our parents pay the phone bill."

"Hey, bro, we will have our own business soon and we will be rolling in the dough," said Iman as she dialed Asma's number.

"That's funny," said her father. "In the bakery."

Sheikha Asma could hear the noise in the background as she answered the phone in her London penthouse.

"Sounds like a party over there in America," she said.

"Actually," said Iman, "we are just watching the culinary endeavors of my brother, who is making breakfast for the family and Mona, who just popped in. But it has been one fun party here in Avalon. We are on a beach volleyball team and we ride rented bikes all over and have dinners together with some American friends. Even play golf. We love it here, as usual. So what is up with your New York trip?"

Asma explained that her aunt, Sheikha Mowza, had broken the news about her relationship with Hassan to the family. At first, Asma's grandparents were "less than enthused" that their youngest child wanted to marry someone outside of the royal fold, but Asma said they "came around" after her uncle, Ahmed, spoke to them.

"Mowza was going to marry him anyway. She has a good business and does not need the family or its money, and Uncle Ahmed told my grandparents that. So I think they realized it is good to support Mowza. Then they met Hassan and his parents, and everyone gets along. Oh, it turns out he has two handsome younger brothers! The wedding is in late Septmeber, but not a big, splashy affair in Abu Dhabi. A family wedding in London. Possibly men and women together. I am not sure. That would be a first for us."

"Great," said Iman. "But what about New York?"

"Well," said Asma. "Hassan has been reassigned for two years to New York starting in a couple of months, I think. So Mowza wants to come to New York to find an apartment for them and also to help set up an office for her company, CASPER, that is involved in some big development there. She will work out of that office. So Mowza asked my mother to go to New York with her to search for an apartment, and Rahma and I said we wanted to go, too, so we are all flying there on Monday. Staying at The Plaza for a week or more."

Iman told her that she and Mona, as well as Mariam, their mothers and their grandmothers and aunts were all heading to New York on Tuesday for a few days and would be at a hotel on Central Park South.

"And Dr. Teresa will be in New York, too, staying at her niece's apartment. By the way, Dr. Teresa has a beautiful home in Spring Lake, New Jersey. Mona and I and our moms went there yesterday to visit her. It is so pretty, and right across from the beautiful Atlantic."

"I miss Dr. Teresa," said Asma. "I would love to see her and all of you in New York."

"Want to go to Ground Zero with us?"

"Are you going there?"

"Well," said Iman, "our active grandmothers who, by the way, are right now at outdoor aerobics class or maybe having coffee at Ann's Bakery, are going to meet their friend, Helen Walker, in New York on Wednesday. You know, the one Dr. Teresa told us about—who wrote about her daughter's death on 9-11 and who is going to teach at Women's University in September. She is going to take us all to the site of the Twin Towers."

"Put us down for that," said Asma. "My mother was devastated about 9-11. I remember that she went to the Catholic church for a service in Abu Dhabi. I know she would like to see Ground Zero."

"OK. I will get the details. Can't wait to see you in Manhattan, Asma. Just make sure you stay away from Saks."

"No way," said the sheikha. "I already packed my credit card."

"The one with SHK for sheikha after your name on it?" asked Iman.

"That is the one."

*   *   *

CHAPTER 15

According to Mohammed, the Abu Dhabi women would be traveling to New York in style.

"You rented a party bus?" he asked his grandmother when the vehicle showed up in front of his family's summer home in Avalon.

"Your father made the arrangements for that," said Farah as she looked to Tahnoun for an explanation.

"Too many women for a limousine, Umy," he said to his mother. "You, Judith, Mariam, Iman, Mona, Sabeen, Ayesha, Hessa and Auntie Amna. And this guy will be your driver for the days you are in Manhattan. And there are more women in New York, right?"

"Right," said Farah. "Helen and the sheikhas, I guess."

"And Dr. Teresa," said Iman.

So off went the Avalon female contingent, spread all over the 30-passenger bus replete with a refrigerator filled with refreshments. Not long into the trip up the Parkway, Mona led the singing of a Women's University ditty with a chorus of "WU, oh WU, We are the girls of WU." Then she, Mariam and Iman would recite silly verses such as "We wear colorful watches, from purple to lime. But why do we bother? We're never on time!"

"Sheikha Asma made that one up," laughed Iman. "She had a few expensive watches, and still was always late, especially in high school. She got better in college, though, after Dr. Teresa threatened to lock the doors right at the time class started. Everybody got better. Now we actually look at our watches."

As they approached the Lincoln Tunnel, Judith broke into a rendition of "McNamara's Band." She said she and her college friends sang it every year as they drove from Philadelphia to New York for St. Patrick's Day weekend.

"Was that a fun time?" asked Mariam of her mother.

"What I remember of it," laughed Judith. "We had a lot of green beer."

"And you made us become Muslims so we cannot drink," said a smirking Mariam.

"Exactly. I knew what I was doing. I promised your father and Gram Farah you would be Muslims. And your grandmother said she would have no objection to my not converting to Islam."

"That is right," said Farah. "And it has worked out well. But I think these days things have changed so I don't know what I would say if someone in the family married a Catholic. Probably let it up to them about the kids' religion."

Ayesha spoke up: "Dr. Jalilla al Zabi just married a Catholic in Ireland and her family flew over for the wedding. I was there and some of the members of the ruling family, too, including Sheikha Mowza, whom we will see in New York. Jalilla and Bill are living in Abu Dhabi. He is not changing religions, as far as I know, but I have no idea what will happen when they have children."

"Life is different; that is for sure," said Amna. "So different from when we were little, Farah, and living in palm shelters with nothing, really. All we worried about was surviving in the heat. We drank camel's milk and ate camel meat and rode on camels. And today young people don't even understand how important those animals were to us."

The party bus headed north in the city until the sight of Central Park enthralled the riders.

"We are going to walk there, Amna," said Farah. "Hope you brought those sneakers."

The hotel doorman looked a bit surprised as he directed two bellhops to remove the women's luggage from the small bus. The group looked unusual—Judith with her bright red hair flowing in the breeze, and Sabeen with her jet black hair pulled back with a barrette, and the others wearing head scarves of various colors. They were chatting in Arabic and English, and he could discern their desire to know how far Bergdorf's was from the hotel.

"A few minutes that way," he pointed, as they all smiled.

They settled into three suites, each with three bedrooms, so basically each person had her own room. Minutes after unpacking their bags, Iman and Mona wanted to head out for a shopping adventure.

"Bergdorf's and then Saks," said Iman. "You coming with us, Mariam?"

"No, I have an appointment at NYU. Mom is coming with me."

"You are serious about applying there?" asked Iman.

"I did already, but I never heard anything. I want to see what's up."

Mona looked at her mobile and saw a text message from Sheikha Asma.

"She is at Saks now. About to look for purses."

"She has a million of them already," said Iman. "Let's go rescue her from the purse sellers."

Later, when the Avalon group got together for dinner at the hotel restaurant, Iman described the scene at Saks as Sheikha Asma negotiated the purchase of a "ridiculously overpriced" purse.

"Her sister, Rahma, and her aunt, Mowza, were with her and they even told her she was crazy to pay $1,000 for a purse. Asma kept telling us she was not going to pay the price on the sales tag but was going to bargain with the saleslady. Sheikha Mowza said you don't do that at Saks, and reminded Asma that this was not Abu Dhabi and the family credit card was not going to work magic for her like in the Emirates.

"The price was going to be as it said on the tag. Well, Asma refused to pay the full price and walked away from the counter. We were all amazed as Asma is a purse person and she had not bought anything. But—and this is the best part—we walked down the street and there was a guy selling purses on a cart. Knock-offs, I think they are called. One looked just like the purse Asma wanted to buy at Saks. So she bought one from the street guy. He wanted $15 and she bargained him down to $10. She told us she knew she could get a bargain in New York. Is that not funny?"

"Imagine Sheikha Asma with a $10 purse," said Mona. "I took her picture with my phone camera and sent it to her by email."

"Let's see it," said her grandmother, Amna.

"No, I erased it. Remember, we are not supposed to take photos of the sheikhas."

Just then they heard a familiar voice. Into the dining room came Fatima, Farah's daughter who lived in Toronto.

"Surprise, surprise. I just flew in to be with you all in New York."

They all got up and greeted her.

"Oh, we are out of bedrooms in the suites," said her mother. "So you can stay with Hessa in her room."

"Good. Now that you are getting married, Hessa, I can give you some advice."

"If it has anything to do with cooking, forget it, Fatima."

*   *   *

Helen Walker drove into the city from her Long Island home to meet her friends Farah and Amna and the others at their hotel. Dr. Teresa already had arrived after walking from her niece's Upper West Side apartment. They all boarded the rented bus and proceeded to The Plaza to pick up the sheikhas: Asma, Rahma, their mother Lubna, and their aunt Mowza.

As the bus maneuvered through Manhattan traffic on its way south in the city, Helen stood in the aisle near the front, much like a tour guide, and described her recollection of Sept. 11, 2001.

"I was on the golf course with friends. It was a beautiful day. You may not believe this, but we had no idea about the attacks. No one came out on the course to tell us about it. When we finished our round, people were speaking in hushed tones and we learned about the planes hitting the Towers. I guess they did not know my daughter worked there for an investment firm or they would have come out to the course and informed me about what happened. I used a phone in the golf shop to check my messages on my home phone and there was a message from my daughter that a plane had hit the other Twin Tower—not the one where she worked. She said they had been told—I don't know who told them—to stay where they were. I kept the message if you ever want to hear it. If I had answered that phone at home, I would have told her to get out of the building. But she stayed, I guess, and her tower was hit. Well, I did not know what to do. My husband and two sons were working at law firms in New York, and I was told that no phone calls were getting in or out of Manhattan. By the time I got home from the club—and it was after noon at this point—many friends and neighbors were arriving, all wanting to know about Carrie and my family. I had no idea where my husband and sons were although they did not work downtown so I prayed they were okay. As for my daughter, I knew it might be bad news. As it developed, my husband and sons got together and started a search right away but could not get near the site. They got through to me late at night finally and by the next day I got into New York—the police in my town took me in—and my husband and I and our sons stayed there three days and carried pictures of her. I knew from the start, though, that she was gone."

Helen stopped and said nothing for a minute. Farah stood up and put her arm around her.

"We know how difficult it must have been," said Farah, looking around to see all of the women with tears in their eyes.

"You know," continued Helen, "they never found her body or any part of her so we had a memorial Mass a week after the attacks and more than 1,000 people showed up, from her high school and college and MBA program and every relative and friend or neighbor we ever had. Many of them were outside because the church could not accommodate the crowd. And the newspaper I worked for wanted me to write a column when I could but I did not want to do it. All I wanted to do was find my only daughter. It was a few days after the Mass before I finally sat down and wrote that column that caused a bit of a sensation and got a lot of awards that I did not want. Unfortunately, I took your country to task as well as Saudi Arabia and maybe I should not have done so."

"Well," said Sheikha Mowza, "Asma sent me the column and I read it. Unfortunately one or two Emiratis were involved and apparently some of the terrorists' money came through Dubai. So I could see why you would write that stuff. But then you came to the UAE after all…"

"When my husband, Kirk, told me his law firm wanted him to go to Abu Dhabi, I could not believe it," said Helen. "But Kirk said we should fly over and see the place for ourselves, so we came for a week last fall and I really liked it. So I said I would move there, but told Kirk that if I later had any qualms about it, I would head back home. But right away I made friends with other Americans and then I met these two," she said as she pointed to Farah and Amna. "We have so much fun together and I got to meet you, Hessa, and play golf with you and Judith and others, and I love Abu Dhabi and look forward to going back in September and teaching a class at Women's University."

As they continued down Broadway, Dr. Teresa asked Helen if she ever would resume her newspaper writing.

"I am considering it," said Helen. "I could write columns from the UAE about cultural tourism and development and women's lives and all kinds of things. But I don't know."

"How about writing about taking Emirati women to Ground Zero?" asked Iman.

"Mm," said Helen. "That is an interesting idea, Iman. Interesting…"

Two weeks later, Helen's return to journalism was heralded in many major newspapers. Her syndicated column, *Walker Writes,* reappeared for the first time since 2001 and started out with these words:

When last you heard from the pen of Helen Walker, I was suffering miserably from the loss of my only daughter, Carrie, a victim of the 9-11 attacks. As my swan song to my journalism career, I wrote what I termed my final column about 10 days later. In it, I roundly criticized Saudi Arabia and the United Arab Emirates as breeding grounds for terrorism and noted that I never would step foot in those Middle Eastern countries.

Fast forward to the present…guess where my husband and I live? In Abu Dhabi, the federal capital of the UAE. When my husband's law firm assigned him there, I initially expressed my reluctance to accompany him for the three-year stint. But I decided to take my chances and see what it was like.

In a nutshell, I love Abu Dhabi, where I have made friends not only with other expatriates but with some marvelous national women. Two weeks ago, a group of these Emirati women, including members of the ruling family, were in Manhattan and I accompanied them to Ground Zero…

The column detailed the visit of the women and how they stood, looked down at what had been the foundation of the two large towers, held hands, and prayed for Carrie Walker. A few Emirati women mentioned how surprised they were at the lack of progress in constructing a memorial on the site, noting that the UAE would have built one within a year or so after such a tragedy. They took a lot of photos and Helen expected the sheikhas to step away from a group shot taken with Iman's camera by a man walking by. But Sheikha Mowza said the time had come for the women in her family to be more visible, and she moved into the picture, followed seconds later by her nieces and their mother. The picture appeared in promos for Helen's returning column and even made the front page of a UAE English-language newspaper that had contracted to carry *Walker Writes*.

The women also walked over to the nearby Church of St. Peter, and Helen explained that the church had been a staging ground for relief efforts and that many rescue workers slept in the pews in the days following the attacks. She said she often came to this church because it was where her daughter attended Mass frequently.

Asked by the Emirati women as to why candles are in a church, Helen explained that lighting candles is a form of prayer. With that, they all began lighting candles in memory of Carrie Walker. The young women—Iman, Mona, Mariam, Sheikha Asma, and Sheikha Rahma—even got on their knees and bent over in the typical way that Muslims pray. Helen told readers that she was astonished, but honored, at the way her Abu Dhabi friends reacted so sensitively to the 9-11 tragedy.

After the women returned to the bus, Helen announced that she was treating them for lunch at a midtown club to which she and her husband belonged.

"Let's enjoy ourselves now," she said.

In a private room at the club, they chatted amiably about how life was transpiring for all of them.

Mariam happily announced that she would not be returning to Abu Dhabi at the end of the summer, and was moving into the NYU graduate dorms.

"I am going to study communications. Like you, Dr. Teresa. And international relations, too."

"And I hope you spend some holiday breaks in Toronto with your relatives," said Fatima. "We would love that. Mohammed came up from Philadelphia during spring break this year. We had such a nice time although I threatened to cut his hair."

"You should have done it," said Judith.

Iman's pleas to stay in New York and get "a job or internship" fell on deaf ears with her mother.

"No," said Judith, "you need to go back to Abu Dhabi and get that cake business going and work in a job like Mariam did for the past year. Maybe next year you can go to graduate school here, Iman. Actually, if you come here next year, and Diab starts college in a year in the U. S., all my children will be in America. I am not sure I can face that empty nest in Abu Dhabi."

"All right," said a reluctant Iman. "I will head back to the UAE with you, Momma, at the end of the summer. Did I tell you that Meg, the really good cake person from Bakery Uno, is moving over to Abu Dhabi to head our operation? She is bringing another young woman baker, too. They are leaving Philadelphia in about 10 days. We got a big apartment for them on 30th Street so they can walk to TOTE. Alia says the kitchen and retail store are about finished. One of our first TOTE cakes probably will be for Essa's wedding."

"Yes, it should be in the shape of one big question mark," said Mona, "meaning why are you getting married right out of school?"

Iman laughed and added: "And she is marrying a relative. Maybe we should have a family tree cake."

"Do Tariq and I get a unique cake?" asked Hessa.

"Sure. How about a famous hole on some golf course?" asked Iman.

"Fine. From St. Andrew's in Scotland. We are going there on our honeymoon."

"How about MY cake?" asked Sheikha Mowza. "Will you deliver it to London?"

"Probably could do that," said Mona, "if we are open by then AND if one of your family's jets is heading there and will transport the cake."

"Well, I would like a cake with Casper the Friendly Ghost on it," said Mowza.

Sheikha Lubna asked her younger sister why she would want a ghost on her wedding cake.

"For CASPER, our company," Sheikha Mowza answered.

"Are you telling me that my sister and brother named their real estate investment firm after a cartoon?"

"Yep," said Mowza. "And dear older sister Lubna, please note that Ahmed and I want your lovely daughter Asma to work for us in Abu Dhabi. We need her. She is bright and can learn the business easily. I want her to join the new Professional Women's Association and help with the newsletter since I am off to Manhattan for a few years."

"It is okay with me," said Sheikha Lubna. "I am beginning to see how important it is for women to work on a daily basis, even those of us in the ruling family. I have been thinking about starting a small school to teach languages. I am sick of wasting my own education."

"If you are going to teach Arabic, count me in," said Dr. Teresa.

"Speaking of schools, I am on the board of Al Koba Academy and we are moving to an international student body," said Judith. "We are going to have at least 40 new students in the fall."

"Right, including the Greek-American kid who is going to give Diab a run for his money on the basketball team," said Iman. "Diab is really getting set to take on everyone at that basketball camp."

"My son Sultan is going to camp, too," said Sabeen. "Diab talked him into it since Sultan is on the Al Koba varsity, too. So I am going to stay with my relatives in North Jersey while Sultan is at the camp and then the two of us will fly home together. Mona and Nasser are leaving later this week for Abu Dhabi."

"With me," said Amna, "although I just might buy a place in Avalon one of these days."

Ayesha said she would be back "in hot Abu Dhabi within the week and I am looking forward to it. I am going to be the executive director of the Gemma Foundation and we are going to do a lot to help foreigners pay for health services and other things. What we plan to do from a marketing perspective, and I want to thank you, Mariam, for this idea, is to set up various funds named after donors or those designated by donors. For example, the Farah al Matari Fund, established by my dear mother-in-law who is right here, will provide money for annual mammograms for women who lack insurance."

"Could my daughters and I establish a fund?" asked Sheikha Lubna.

"Sure," said Ayesha. "Please do."

"I would like it to pay for overseas travel for specialized health care for foreigners who need it."

"And," Ayesha said, "what should we name it?"

"It will be named the Carrie Walker Fund, if that is okay with you, Helen."

They all clapped in unison.

All of the women were raving about the food at Helen's club, especially the flounder en papilotte.

"They should do this with hammour," said Judith. "Of course, I think that so-called Gulf fish is just the same white fish as this but with a different name."

"I order hammour all the time in Abu Dhabi because it is supposed to be a Gulf fish but you are right—they all taste the same," said Helen. "It sounds more Middle Eastern when it is called hammour."

"Do you like harees?" asked Sheikha Lubna.

"What is it?" Helen asked.

"Plan on an Iftar dinner at the palace during Ramadan and we will show you."

"I don't like harees," said Sheikha Rahma. "I go for the great desserts."

"You are going to be the death of me," said her mother.

Mowza then surveyed the other women about what to do relative to her housing options in New York.

"Hassan and I want a furnished apartment. I am not going to spend weeks getting furniture. Anyway, I like two places I saw with a realtor. One is an apartment up around 75th or 76th near Central Park West with a view of the park, and the other is off Fifth Avenue not far from Rock Center. My offices are at the corner of 46th and Fifth and Hassan will be on 54th near Sixth. So the Fifth Avenue place would be a good location, but I love Central Park."

They all voted for the Central Park locale and told her to take a cab to the office.

As they exited the club, Helen said to Sheikha Mowza: "This club has a lot of young members, including my sons and their wives. With lots of activities. So if you and Hassan want to join, let me know."

"They would let Arabs in?" Mowza asked laughingly.

"Absolutely," responded Helen. "They already have some of the UN staffers from the Middle East. Although I don't know about people who name their companies after friendly ghosts. I would keep that quiet."

They were all smiling as they headed uptown in the party bus.

*   *   *

CHAPTER 16

Farah Abdullah al Matari stood on the balcony of her Abu Dhabi villa and looked across the street at the home of her son, Khalid Al Bader, and his wife, Ayesha. Farah watched as her grandsons raced out of the villa and jumped into a SUV driven by their mother. As she had been doing of late, Ayesha would drop the children off at Al Koba Academy on her way to her offices at the Gemma Foundation.

A car pulled up and out got Hessa, who lived three blocks away. She had just dropped off her stepdaughter, Latifa, at Al Koba, and was stopping by to help set up her mother's villa for a morning meeting of the Americans in Abu Dhabi. Helen Walker had asked Farah and Amna to speak at one of the group's meetings about how their lives had changed over the decades in a country that went from a harsh desert area to a thriving megalopolis. Farah and Amna initially expressed their reluctance; Amna said she was not a public speaker. After talking to their granddaughters, Iman and Mona, though, the women changed their minds. Through contacts at a national historical society, the girls secured photos of the town from the 50s and 60s and added a number of pictures of their grandmothers in gym classes, in Avalon, and in Manhattan. They helped their grandmothers to create a computer presentation featuring the photos. Farah would handle the speaking duties, and Amna would be available to answer any post-talk questions from the American women.

Farah offered to host the meeting of about 50 women at her villa. She worked with the cooks and maids to set up rows of folding chairs, a projector and screen in her large foyer, and also assisted in preparing brunch for the visitors. She even ordered a TOTE cake that featured a replica of a palm frond dwelling in which she had lived as a young woman.

As the guests started filing out of cars and taxis, Farah looked down from the balcony and thought about her life.

In six decades, she had faced extreme poverty and had married when she was far too young. She had suffered the loss of a child and the embarrassment of having her spouse take on another wife.

She also had become a successful businesswoman, a fun grandmother, a traveler, a philanthropist and, in her granddaughter Iman's words, a "gym rat."

Farah's life had changed radically.

She no longer was watching and waiting. Or being waited on all the time.

Farah loved her active life, and she was about to give a talk on that exact subject.

GLOSSARY

Abaya: Long, black robe that Emirati women wear over their regular clothing

Agal (egal): cord fastened around the gutra to keep it in place

Barasti: Huts made from palm fronds

Burqa: Gold mask that covers part of the face of an Emirati woman

Corniche: waterfront promenade that usually runs alongside a main road.

Dirham: Unit of currency; worth about 27 cents in U.S. money

Dishdasha: a long (usually white) robe traditionally worn by men in the Middle East

Emirate: a territory under the jurisdiction of a ruling family. The United Arab Emirates includes seven individual emirates that together make up the country formed in 1971.

Ghaf: tree that provides shade from the sweltering desert sun

Gutra: Typical headdress worn by Emirati men

Hammour: In the Middle East, the name usually given to the fish known as grouper

Harees: Arabic dish made of wheat, meat (or chicken) and salt; the wheat is crushed to make it soft, like a porridge.

Henna: a plant from which dyes are used to decorate the hands and arms of brides and other women

Hijab: Head covering worn by many Arab women; it tightly covers the hair but the face is left uncovered

Iftar: Evening meal when Muslims break their fast during Ramadan

Ramadan: Islamic month of fasting from dawn until sunset.

Shayla: Large rectangular, lightweight, head covering worn by Emirati women

Sheik (sheikha): member of a ruling family in the UAE

Um: Mother. The word is placed in front of the name of the woman's oldest son for identification. Example: Um Abdullah would be a woman whose oldest son is Abdullah.

ABOUT THE AUTHOR

Tina Rodgers Lesher is a professor of journalism in the Department of Communication at William Paterson University of New Jersey, where she three times has been selected as a winner of the Students' First Award, given annually to professors who inspire students. She previously served as coordinator of the university's journalism/PR major and chairman of the Department of Communication.

An award-winning journalist, she twice served as a president of the New Jersey Press Women and was selected as a Communicator of Achievement in that organization. She has been the recipient of fellowships from the Knight Foundation and the American Press Institute.

In addition to writing chapters of several academic books, she is the author of "Club '43," a nonfiction work about women in Westfield, N.J., where she resides.

Lesher was a 2006-07 Fulbright Scholar to the United Arab Emirates and has been selected as a 2010-2012 Fulbright Ambassador.

A Dunmore, Pa., native, she is a graduate of Wheeling Jesuit University and the University of Missouri School of Journalism, and holds a doctorate in English Education from Rutgers University.

She and her husband, John, a Manhattan real estate development executive, have three grown children.